Also by DAVID KLASS

Whirlwind
Firestorm
Home of the Braves
You Don't Know Me
Screen Test
Danger Zone
California Blue

TIMELOCK

THE CARETAKER TRILOGY: BOOK 3

TIMELOCK

DAVID KLASS

FRANCES FOSTER BOOKS Farrar Straus Giroux New York

Copyright © 2009 by David Klass
All rights reserved
Distributed in Canada by Douglas & McIntyre Ltd.
Printed in the United States of America
Designed by Robbin Gourley
First edition, 2009
1   3   5   7   9   10   8   6   4   2

www.fsgkidsbooks.com

Library of Congress Cataloging-in-Publication Data
Klass, David.
  Timelock / David Klass.
    p.   cm.   —   (Caretaker trilogy ; bk. 3)
  Summary: Jack discovers that the only way to protect the Earth from
ecological disaster at the hands of the Dark Army is to lock time, and he must
choose between staying in the present or returning to the future world from
which he came.
  ISBN-13: 978-0-374-32309-7
  ISBN-10: 0-374-32309-7
  [1. Time travel—Fiction.   2. Global warming—Fiction.   3. Ecology—
Fiction.   4. Interpersonal relations—Fiction.   5. Science fiction.]   I. Title.
II. Title: Time lock.

PZ7.K67813 Ti 2009
[Fic]—dc22

2008023280

For Orlando

TIMELOCK

PART ONE

Manhattan. Seven-thirty in the evening. Indian summer. No way it should be this warm in late September, but I'm sweating in my T-shirt as I run through the gloaming and feel the cold prickle on the back of my neck. Someone is watching me. Now. Here. Close by.

Had enough sentence fragments yet? My English teacher said they were a weakness of mine. But that was more than a year ago, when I was a senior at Hadley High School, leading a relatively normal life.

I'm not in Hadley anymore, and I can never go back. Too much has happened to me since then. Firestorm adventure to save the oceans, over. Whirlwind trip to the Amazon, completed. I'm a year older. I hope a bit wiser. But I still like sentence fragments. They generate pace. If you want speed, stick around, my friend. If you enjoy weird, don't budge from that chair.

I feel that prickle again. Glance around quickly. Gangly guy in spandex checking his fancy stopwatch for lap time. Cute chick with red hair bopping along the wrong way, listening to her music, making all the other runners veer around her. Family of four jogging in pairs, mother-son, father-daughter. Everyone looks a bit strange.

This is Manhattan, after all. Hundreds of people in the park on a warm autumn evening doing their funky big-city things and surreptitiously checking each other out.

That's why I'm here. I came to the Big Apple because it

seemed like a good place to lose myself and start over. Shed a skin. Jump into the bubbling stew. Melting pot supreme.

Got a job working construction. See a lot of P.J. who's a freshman at Barnard College. There are days when I work fifteen hours and no one gives me a second look, and I almost believe that it's possible for me to live a relatively normal life.

And then there are the moments like this when I know I'm kidding myself.

I do a three-sixty, looking for telltale signs. No tall cyborgs. No bat creatures. No one dodges my gaze.

Could be a false alarm. Maybe I'm paranoid. Except that deep down I know it's real. Can't spitball who's watching me, but I'm positive they're out there.

I have only two choices, neither of them particularly appealing. I can wait for them to make their move. Or I can try to run away.

I pick up the pace as darkness settles over the reservoir. Outside the park, the lights of Central Park West and Fifth Avenue blink on. An urban constellation frames an oasis of dark, rippling water. I've seen the world a bit. Swum deep under the oceans to a virgin sea mount. Found the hidden valley of the Amazon. A beautiful evening in Manhattan is still a pretty spectacular thing.

I'm running fast now. Passing people. Arms pumping. No one can keep up with me. But they don't have to.

Whoever's watching me may be stationary, following my laps from a bench. Or maybe they're ensconced high up in an apartment overlooking the park, like the Gorm who lured me to her penthouse lair, watching me through a window with nightscopes. Or it could be a kid, or a mechanical bird, or even a shapeshifting squirrel.

I first felt the prickle one week ago, at P.J.'s dinner party. I admit I was nervous anyway.

Nice of her to invite me, but I didn't fit in. P.J.'s new friends. The college set. A dozen Columbia and Barnard freshmen. Giggling about a charming anthropology professor with endless eccentric anecdotes and complaining about an arduous chem lab. Comparing reading lists and writing assignments. Trying out new words, new hairstyles, and post–high school personas on each other.

One goofy guy not in college. Didn't even finish high school. Nice to meet you, Jack. What do you do? Oh, really, you work construction? How do you know P.J.? High school friend? Well, nice talking to you.

We're eating in the garden of a Greek restaurant downtown. I'm trying to pretend that I don't mind being completely ignored. Go ahead and converse. Posture. Pontificate. I'll just concentrate on this plate of kabobs.

I listen politely as I unskewer lamb chunks with my hands, calloused from heavy work. The physics phenom sitting next to me keeps stealing glances at my missing pinky. Want to know how I lost that one, Einstein? A fiend named Dargon cut it off on a trawler, while his thugs held me down. But don't mind me. Go on making fun of your linear algebra teaching assistant's stutter. I'm riveted.

P.J. isn't fooled. She's watching me. I give her a nonchalant grin and she smiles back. Okay, prep school lacrosse star. Tell her about your family's spread in the Hamptons. She'll listen and nod, but I'm the one who will be walking her home tonight. I'm the one who will be riding up in the elevator with her, to her dorm room. I'm the one who will follow her into the common room, past her three roommates, to her tiny bedroom filled with books.

And guess what? You may have the hip clothes and the preppy cool and the million-dollar summerhouse, but I'm the one who will put my arms around her and kiss her on her soft warm lips, and tell her I love her.

Except that she definitely seems interested in that place in Bridgehampton. And the lacrosse player is smart enough not to go after her too aggressively, but rather he makes it a group thing.

Somehow a party starts to get planned there, a big bash with costumes and a live band. And I don't think I'm on the guest list.

I excuse myself and head to the bathroom. Twenty other tables in the garden. Glasses clinking. Silverware clanking. And that's when I feel it.

On the back of my neck. The tactile equivalent of someone raking his fingernails across a blackboard. It makes me squirm and wheel around.

All I see are couples sipping wine and spooning lemon chicken soup by candlelight. There are a few large groups digging into platters of stuffed grape leaves and devouring baby lamb chops as they banter back and forth.

I burst inside and check out the bar, the waiters, and the kitchen staff. They're all busy with plates and trays and glasses. "The bathroom's down there, sir," a waiter explains, misinterpreting my distress.

Seconds later I'm in the bathroom splashing cold water on my face and trying to calm down. Because this is the nightmare I live with. That they'll find me again. Hunt me down. Rip off the bandage and open the scar.

And now it's happened.

I knew it instantly, at that dinner party, standing in the courtyard of the Greek restaurant. Sure, I tried to convince myself that it had just been a chill breeze on the back of my neck. But as I looked at myself in the bathroom mirror, I knew they had found me and it was starting all over again.

I knew it with even more certainty two days later at the construction site, hard hat on and tool belt in place, stepping out on a high girder. Couldn't afford to shiver up there, but I felt the cold prickle again. All of Manhattan below. Dozens of office buildings. Anyone could be watching me.

So now, in Central Park, it isn't a complete surprise. But this is strike three. No use pretending anymore. I go into full sprint for the last hundred yards, and as I fly along, arms pumping, I force myself to face the bitter truth. Have to act quickly. Take time off my job. Go out of town for a while. Maybe get myself a weapon. And most difficult of all, I must tell P.J.

She's so happy at Barnard, living a normal life again. She never told her parents what happened after she disappeared from Hadley. She feigned amnesia. They brought her to psychologists and specialists, and finally they just gave up and were glad she came back to them.

Now she's starting to enjoy life again. Making new friends. Taking classes. Excelling in art. Touring galleries. Going home on weekends to see her folks.

At the same time, I've noticed she's stopped talking to me about our Amazon experiences. If I bring it up, she'll nod and mumble a few words. But she herself never mentions it. She's put the whole thing behind her. Wiped the slate clean.

She won't enjoy hearing that it's not over. That it may never be over. But I have no choice. Because the Dark Army kidnapped her once. They may try again. She's a player in this now. If they've found me, they probably also know that she's here, so she has to be on her guard.

I finish my ten miles and leave the park, breathing hard. Normally, I would enjoy this feeling after a good run, my blood pumping, my wet shirt sticking to my chest and back as the evening wind blows. But the prospect of telling P.J. fills me with dread. I can imagine the look in her eyes when she hears it. Don't, Jack. Please stop now.

But there's no choice. No delay possible. I have to tell her. Tonight. At nine o'clock, when she comes home from the library. If I don't warn her and something happens, I'll never forgive myself.

So instead of heading to my own tiny room, I jog to Broadway and head uptown toward Barnard.

Broadway, eight in the evening.

Not the bohemian Broadway of Soho or the Village, or the touristy, glitzy Broadway of Times Square and the Theater District. This is the authentic Broadway for me, where New York starts to feel ethnic again.

I hear hip-hop. Smell pizza. Signs start popping up in Spanish. There's a curry joint. A Korean grocery. The White Lotus Karate Academy with a class going on inside. I peer through the window. Manhattanites of all different sizes and races learning to kick and punch. I bet Eko could show them a few tricks.

I haven't heard from the Ninja Babe since she jumped out a window in the Amazon in pursuit of a spider who was really the Dark Lord. Gisco hasn't dropped me a postcard, either. I wonder if he returned Mudinho to his village.

Just thinking about such things as I walk up Broadway makes me realize how wacky my life is. All around me is a pulsing city crammed with an endless variety of people returning home from school and work. They've come here from the ends of the earth, and have wildly different lives and sets of problems to worry about, but at least they're all playing in the same ballpark of reality.

None of them are plagued by memories of dark masterminds from a thousand years hence who shape-shift into tarantulas and scuttle off into the rain forest. None of them miss wizards or telepathic dogs or beautiful ninja babes, who have probably all returned to their now-pristine future world.

I walk faster, attempting to leave the memories and the doubts behind. But the most upsetting question of all continues to tug at me: Isn't that mysterious far future world really my world, since I was born into it, and both my parents still live there?

No, I tell myself. Don't walk down that path. It leads straight to madness. I've crawled out of the rabbit hole. It's time to draw a line. I am Jack Danielson now, construction worker. Public library user. Young man about town. On the way to see my lady-love.

But deep down I know it's not over. That's why they were watching me at the restaurant, at the construction site, and tonight at the reservoir. And that's why I need to warn P.J., even if she freaks.

I'm more than halfway to Barnard. Starting to freak a bit myself. Because I know that whatever words I use to tell her, however gently I break the news, I'm going to scare the daylights out of her. Worse than that. I'm going to widen the gulf between us. She'll once again associate me with a nightmare she's trying hard to forget.

Eventually, in her effort to construct a normal life, she'll reach for something safe and traditional. End up with the lacrosse player. Can I really blame her?

I pound my fist into my hand so hard it makes a smacking sound. People glance over at me. Yes, damn it, I can blame her. We love each other. Love is supposed to conquer all. Even the weird stuff. But what can I do?

Four blocks from P.J.'s dorm, I get the idea. It pops into my head out of the dark sky. Don't show up with bad news *and* empty-handed, dummy. Bring her something to sweeten the mood a bit. What do all girls love? Flowers.

Now I'm not a candy and flowers kind of a guy. My presents to P.J. usually run more along the lines of a new book that I've enjoyed, or a CD she can listen to while I give her a back rub.

Come to think of it, I don't even think P.J. likes candy. But she does like flowers.

And here's a nice corner flower store—the Gotham Garden. Surprisingly, it's still open and ready for business. There's a display of orchids outside. A sign in the window promises: "Bouquets made to order. Let our flowers touch the heart of your special one."

Yes, please touch her. Just what I need.

I push the door open and head inside.

Flower displays floor to ceiling. Roses. Tulips. Lilies. Irises. Dozens of vibrant blooms that I can't identify, but then I'm no flower expert.

Two young shop workers are performing menial tasks. A bored girl with a pierced nose sorts ferns. A big guy in a Giants cap sweeps up fallen leaves.

"Excuse me," I say, "but I need some help."

"Stanley!" the fern sorter calls. Then she tilts back her head, opens her mouth wide, and bellows: "STANLEY. CUSTOMER."

A pudgy middle-aged man hurries out of the flower-cooler room, wiping his hands on a towel. His bald head gleams under the lights and his eyeglasses are crooked. He looks me over quickly, taking in my shorts and sweaty T-shirt, perhaps wondering if I've got any money. "Evening," he says, "how can I help you?"

I take out the thin wallet I carry when I run, to put his mind at rest. "I'd like to buy a dozen red roses."

"You've come to the right place. We have some real beauties," he assures me and then hesitates. "But are you sure you wouldn't want something a little more interesting? I could make you up a nice mixed bouquet?"

"Thanks, but I can't go too far wrong with red roses," I point out. "And I'm in a bit of a hurry."

"You got it," he says, sounding a little disappointed. Then he smiles. "Roses are red, violets are blue, she'll love them, so she'll love you."

The guy sweeping up snorts derisively, and the girl sorting

ferns turns to me and says, "Forgive him. He's a nice man, but he can't help himself."

"Nothing wrong with a little poetry to break up the tedium of life," the florist replies with a defensive smile. And then, conspiratorially: "Tell you what, son. Meredith is gonna get your roses. Let me show you some truly special flowers that just came in, so that maybe next time I can talk you into a mixed bouquet."

I glance at my watch. "I really don't have . . ."

He's already opened the door of the cooler room and is ushering me inside. "It'll take two minutes, while she's clipping and wrapping your roses. You won't lose any time. Humor me. A flower of beauty is a joy forever."

I don't have it in me to be rude to a man who paraphrases John Keats and makes up his own bad doggerel. So I nod and walk in through the held-open door. It clicks shut behind us and we're alone in the cooler.

Big white pots on racks. Each pot is filled with a different type of flower. There's a long wooden table in the center, which I guess is used for assembling bouquets. It's not icy cold, like a meat locker. But it is chilly.

"I'm sweaty from running," I tell him. "This probably isn't such a good idea . . ."

But he's pulled a magnificent purple flower out of a pot and is holding it for my inspection. "Take a look at this baby. Just came in. It's called a Moon Shadow."

"Beautiful," I murmur. "Now I'd better go . . ."

"Take a whiff. You can almost taste the color."

I hesitate and inhale the Moon Shadow's aroma. Never smelled anything quite like it. It does smell like the very essence of purple.

The cloying, syrupy stench seems to flow up my nose and mouth and take up residence deep in my lungs.

I feel an urge to sit down. "I think I better be heading out," I say, and step toward the door.

"Absolutely," the little man agrees, but he's standing in my way. "Meredith, are his roses ready?"

I see that the girl who was sorting ferns has slipped into the cooler. She walks to the pots and starts spritzing them with a sprayer-gun. "Al is just wrapping them up now. One more minute."

I feel a little light-headed. The florist smiles sympathetically. "Sit down for a second, why don't you?" he says. "Al, bring over that chair."

The big guy with the Giants cap has also come into the cooler. He hurries over with what looks like an office chair, on wheels. "Here, buddy, take a load off."

What are they all doing in the cooler with me?

Who's minding the store?

Where did this leather office chair come from?

I register these questions, but most of all I know I have to get out of here fast. I force my legs to move. One step. Two. The shop workers don't try to stop me.

They just wait. I've almost made it to the door. I seem to be moving in slow motion. Feet are heavy. Muscles don't respond.

But my brain still works. No wonder the idea to buy P.J. flowers popped into my head right before I passed this store. It was planted. Some sort of telepathic suggestion. I fell into a trap.

I reach for the handle. But the door now seems heavy. I manage to pull it open an inch. "Help me," I mumble.

"Beacon of Hope, you're the one who needs to help us," the bald florist says.

3

I look back at the florist. Shake my head. "No."

"Yes," he insists. "Terrible things have happened. There's no time to lose. You're urgently needed."

"NO!" I scream, and with a tremendous effort pull the door open a little more. "Find someone else. I'm out of here."

The girl with the pierced nose steps over, raises her spray bottle, and squirts me in the face. My fingers instantly go limp on the handle and the door swings shut again. I start to topple and the big guy catches me on the chair. He wheels me over to the table, and then lifts me up onto it.

The exotic flowers in the cooler room seem to be blurring, melting, transforming. I'm surrounded by computer controls. Screens and dials and keyboards.

It's getting much harder for me to talk, but I gasp out, "No. Please. It's not fair. My life. P.J."

"I'm afraid there's no choice, my Prince," the florist says, injecting me with something as his two helpers strap me down. "Kidah was not able to kill the Dark Lord. Things have taken a frightful turn. Horrific. You're needed right away."

I gasp out a final question: "Where?"

"Why, there. With your mother and father. Or at least your mother. As for your father, that's part of the whole problem, isn't it? Now stop trying to move. Just hold still. Think of something nice. This will hurt, but it won't take long. Relatively speaking, that is."

He steps away from me, to some sort of master control panel.

, two assistants start punching keys and turning dials. The cooler is no longer cold. It's getting warmer. Hotter. Stifling.

The tabletop I'm strapped to starts to move. Swing. Revolve.

When I come up from that first revolution, I hear the explosion. Like a tsunami of sound. I see on a screen that a wall just got blown out in front of the shop.

"Sonic grenade!" the big guy in the Giants cap calls out in a worried voice.

"The Dark Army has found us!" the girl announces.

"We can't stop now!" the florist tells them. "We have to finish. Meredith, help me. Alazam, fight them."

As I complete a second revolution, I see that the big guy is unsheathing some sort of flaming sword. The florist and the girl are working at their computer consoles with great intensity.

I go down and up a third time. Whatever is spinning me is speeding up. Whirling.

I'm starting to get dizzy. Disoriented. Maybe it was the injection. I open my mouth to scream but no sound comes out.

The door to the flower cooler liquefies and a seven-foot-tall Dark Army cyborg steps in and points a gun at me.

Before he can shoot, Al chops him in half with the flaming sword. Torso and trunk are hewn apart at the hip, and blood spurts while circuits spark.

Now I'm spinning very fast.

More dark shapes pour into the cooler. One of them manages to wrest the sword away from Al and behead him with it.

A Dark Army monstrosity with a human body and an owl-like head shoots Meredith with a laser that comes streaming out of its yellow eyes. The blazing beam burns off her right arm to the shoulder. She screams, and then a second laser burst silences her.

I see the owl head swivel toward me. A blast streaks out but misses me.

I'm not just a moving target, I'm a whirling target that they can't draw a bead on. I try to follow what's happening, but I'm spinning so fast it's getting blurry.

The pudgy florist is spouting blood from some dire injury, but I see him dive toward Meredith's console where a green button is flashing.

A laser shot irradiates both his legs, but his momentum carries him the last few inches, and he bashes his fist decisively down on the green button.

A split second later he is lasered into cinders. The Dark Army goons start firing away at the complicated machinery all around the room. Screens melt and keyboards explode.

But jabbing down the green button must have finished some sort of crucial command sequence. Bolts of blinding emerald light shoot down from the ceiling and converge on me while I spin.

The last thing I see is a Dark Army goon firing a gun at me, and I feel a searing pain in my shoulder.

And then the green light swallows me up.

4

Propelled through a tunnel of blinding light, faster and faster. Barely conscious, but I feel the acceleration and I know where it must lead.

No one can survive this speed. I will crash out. Hit a wall. Atomize.

Side tunnels diverge in all directions at all times. Branches in a flickering labyrinth of green, white, and red. Up ahead, some sort of dark threshold looms.

Can this be the gateway to death? It seems to reach out for me. A dark tongue licks me in.

Ingested by a black hole?

In the large intestine of an event horizon?

I feel myself being torn slowly apart from all directions at once. Is this dismemberment by gravity? Evisceration by centrifugal force?

It's beyond agonizing.

Over the far edge of unbearable.

But I have to bear it because there's no way out. I'm screaming but there's no sound here and no one to hear me.

Death would be such a mercy. An escape. Please take me. Enfold me.

End it.

But it doesn't end. It only intensifies. Till everything but the agonizing pain fades to nothingness.

And then I'm out the other side of the excruciating inky hell, bursting through a golden membrane into some sort of bright cottony haze.

Particles. A quanta snowstorm. The dandruff of space-time. I'm sailing through it, head over heels.

It's warm. Soft. Salty.

Plop. Now I'm swimming in it. Floating in it. Sinking down into it. It's more than warm. It's hot!

The old survival instinct kicks in. A red alarm light begins flashing in my mind. Something is very wrong.

Because it's not snow. Nor did I tumble out of the tunnel of eternity into a swimming pool.

These are grains of sand, scorching to the touch. Beneath my head. Sifting through my hair. Covering me like an electric blanket that's short-circuiting.

It's a sandstorm! And once the sand buries me, all will be over! Another few seconds and I'll be too deep to ever fight my way to the surface.

One chance. Have to battle back to daylight. But which way is up? I could just be digging myself down deeper. I force my mind to work.

The fear of being buried alive helps me shake out the cobwebs. Yes, these are my hands, clawing upward. These are my legs kicking. My eyes are blinded by stinging sand. This is my mouth cracking wide open, wailing in agony.

One hand breaks through, and then my arm, and somehow I pull myself up and out of a desert grave. I try to gasp in oxygen, but what I'm breathing doesn't fill my lungs. I try to clear my eyes, but even as I wipe the sand away, I glimpse an orange-white sky so bright and burning with unfiltered glare that I can't bear to look at it.

I'm still in the shorts and T-shirt I went jogging in around the reservoir. The sand chars my skin.

I get to my feet, and I can feel the heat from the ground through my running shoes. Where am I?

An endless expanse of sand shimmers in the fierce heat of the blast-furnace sun. No trees. No buildings. No rocks. No shade. A spot of red falls on the sand.

Oh yeah, my shoulder. There's a nasty gash where the Dark Army ghoul shot me while I was strapped to the table.

I wonder if I'll bleed to death before I bake to death. I start walking. The sand blows in my eyes so I hold my good arm in front of my face. It blocks my vision, but there's nothing to see in a raging sandstorm. And even if the wind died down a bit and the sand stopped whipping at me, the solar glare would be blinding.

I'm lost, blind, and dripping blood.

But that's not what's really worrying me. There's another, deeper concern edging into my consciousness.

When I was on the table in the florist's shop, the Dark Army ghouls didn't only shoot at the people. They also fired away at the controls of the machines that launched me through time. They succeeded in killing the florist and his helpers, and they probably also did serious damage to the computer controls.

I'm pretty sure my mother and father didn't arrange for their son to be teleported back into a deadly sandstorm. I was probably supposed to arrive in some cushy palace chamber, just in time for a late-night snack.

So something malfunctioned; some key chronometer dial was probably incinerated by a laser. As I stagger through the sand, I can't help wondering how much alteration that might have caused to my trajectory. Did it significantly change the time and place where I arrived?

Suppose I'm not just a few miles south of the palace. I might have also arrived ten years later than I was supposed to, when humanity has completely perished.

The Dark Army may rule this bleak planet. Or the earth's declining condition may have been too much even for them. I might have arrived on a lifeless crag. I could be the only living organism left.

I stagger on. The soles of my shoes are melting—my feet feel like they're being slowly grilled. I lurch and almost go down. Blown sand blasts my arms and legs. There's no way for me to cover up. I try to turn my body so that my back is to the wind, but it's swirling.

I sink to one knee and scream as my weight pushes down and I can feel the skin of my kneecap singe.

Somehow I get back up and force myself onward. In desperation, I lower my arm and blink through the red-hot cloud of dust. There's something up ahead.

Is it a house? A cave? No, just a black rock. An ugly, misshapen boulder in the middle of a wasteland.

It will provide little or no shelter, and I'll never reach it anyway. It's too far, and I'm too weak.

But I have to try. Because I'm out of other options.

I stagger toward it. Every remaining volt of my life force is now directed toward making it to that boulder.

I keep myself going with visions of P.J.—she'll be back from the library now, planning her evening in the city. I wish I could knock on her door with my roses. I wish I could take her in my arms and tell her how much I love her, and warn her that the Dark Army may be closing in.

But I can't. While I'm dying in this sandstorm, she's probably heading out with the lacrosse player.

That thought pushes me on a few steps.

I think of Gisco. I wonder if he was involved in planning that little charade at the florist's. He knows how I feel about P.J. and he's a tricky fellow—the telepathic suggestion that brought me in the door could certainly have been his idea. I'll never get to ask him. And he'll never know what happened to me. Strange that two comrades who shared so many dangers together should end up so far apart.

The boulder is much closer, but I can't walk another step. I sink to my knees and crawl toward it, screaming each time my leg or palm presses the scorching sand.

Eko will also never know what happened to me. I guess Kidah's prophecies that I would marry her were wrong. I'm sure she'll get over it and find someone else. Her combination of beauty and brains, Zen calm and intensity, sexiness and vulnerability, is pretty irresistible.

Five feet from the boulder. Sand is coating the insides of my nose and mouth now, hot and dry in my throat. My hands and feet are flayed and fricasseed. I can feel myself slowly passing out.

I lunge forward and just manage to touch the boulder, and then I jerk my fingers away. It's smoldering hot. Great, I've managed with my last effort to crawl to the largest hot coal in a future Sahara.

I'm flat on my stomach now in the burning sand, too weak to

lift myself up to my knees. I slither and snake around the boulder, searching for some semblance of shelter. Is there a cave, a rooflike overhang, or even a small ledge that will create a tiny patch of shade?

I can't see anymore, but I can still feel. The sand does seem just a bit cooler. Or maybe I'm dying, and my senses are blinking out.

I'll expire here, unmissed and unmourned, hugging this humongous charcoal for all eternity.

I feel one last surge of rage at the pointlessness of it all, and then I sink away into the blackness of a final surrender.

5

Would *he like some tea?*

I don't know where I am or what's happened to me, but five telepathic words puncture the dark stillness.

I'm surely dead. Roasted in the hot sand. Mummified by the dryness. Desiccated, buried, and forgotten.

This must be the afterlife. Strange, I don't see any angels or hear any harp music. No hellfire, either. It's just black and quiet.

Does he take it with lemon?

Only one problem. It's hard for me to believe they drink tea in the afterlife, with or without lemon. I try to move. The only thing I can feel is my parched tongue, which slowly unsticks from the roof of my mouth.

I'm blind. Paralyzed. Insensate.

Of course it's not real lemon I'm offering to him. Citrus has been im-

possible to get for twenty years, since the last trees withered in Haifa. But it's a pretty good homemade substitute, if Morgan does say so himself.

"Can't see," I try to say. But the words don't come out. I can't open my mouth. Actually, that's not the problem. I think my mouth is open. But there's something in front of it, blocking it.

Then I realize that whoever's talking to me isn't speaking out loud. He's using telepathy. So I fire back: Help me. I can't move. I've gone blind.

He's being silly. His ocular equipment is perfectly functional. Morgan just had to cover him to hydrate him a bit. He was very dry. But what did he expect, taking a stroll on the crust in broad daylight? And he shouldn't try to move. He's still too weak.

It's weird being spoken about in the third person.

Something wet and sticky is slowly peeled off my face.

I can breathe more easily. And I can see again! Not clearly, but shapes and shadows.

Someone is moving near me. Not walking upright like a man. Scuttling. Uh-oh—is it a giant spider? Have I been taken prisoner by the Dark Lord, or one of his arachno-spawn? No, whoever is with me is not scuttling on eight legs but shuffling along like an ape.

I blink. It's a man. A little man, with bushy eyebrows and unnaturally long arms that seem to brush the floor when he walks, so that he looks like a gnomish chimpanzee. We're in some kind of low-ceilinged cavern.

Is he better?

A little better, I tell him. Thanks. Who are you?

Morgan. Who is he?

Jack. What am I doing here?

He's lying on my table.

I know that, Morgan. I've been making kind of a habit of lying on tables lately. I meant what am I doing in this hole or cave or pit or wherever the hell we are?

He doesn't like Morgan's hutch.

I like your hutch. It's fine.

But not good enough for him? Too small, maybe? Too dark? Just a Gorm, he mocks, living in a glorified latrine. Ah, but when he was dying on the crust, who saved his life? Thank you, Morgan. And thank you for offering him tea, Morgan. You could have left him to die and instead you rescued him, Morgan, and he's ever so grateful.

Uh-oh, a Gorm. I don't know exactly what that means, but I ran into one when I first fled Hadley, and it didn't end well. She pretended to be a Manhattan prep school girl, lured me to her fabulous penthouse, and almost devoured me. I'd better be very careful here.

I try to sit up. No good, I'm too weak. But I do manage to raise my head a few inches and peer around. The floor is dirt, covered by what look like plastic throw rugs. I see a small bed and chairs and on the far wall a bunch of mechanical equipment that I can't begin to fathom. It could be junk or it could be a supercomputer.

I take a breath and try to shake the cobwebs from my brain and the sand out of my ears. I've got to find a way to befriend this Gorm.

Look, I try to placate him telepathically, no offense meant. It's one of the nicest hutches I've ever been in.

He says it but does he really mean it?

Absolutely.

How many has he been in, I wonder?

The point is that your place is swell. But how did I get here? The last thing I remember is curling up next to a rock and preparing to die as the hot sand covered me.

Yes, but Morgan dug him out. When darkness comes, Morgan hunts. Darkness is the time to dig. Morgan brought him back and kept him alive and now Morgan wants to drink tea and have a nice chat.

Okay, you got it, let's have some tea. I push myself up with my arms and swing around to a sitting position. The room swirls and I feel dizzy, but I make it.

He wants to drink Morgan's tea, but he doesn't want to chat with Morgan.

Just my luck, I think to myself. Lured into a flower shop, attacked by the Dark Army, teleported into the far future, buried in a sandstorm, and rescued by a basket case of a Gorm with severe self-esteem issues.

You're wrong, I tell him, I'd love to chat. How's the weather outside?

Heat, lethal. Radiation level, lethal. Winds, lethal. Humidity index, lethal.

Wow, bad day, huh? What about tomorrow?

Worse.

How do you live in this?

Morgan lives under it. Morgan lives around it. The first rule of being a Gorm is survive at all costs.

Good first rule. What's the second rule?

Don't trust anyone. Here's his tea.

He carries an old teapot over and pours me a cup of brown liquid. I notice that he doesn't spill even a drop. Something tells me that in this parched wasteland, every molecule of moisture is precious. Next, looking proud, he uses a syringe to squirt in a little whitish paste that floats for a second on the surface of the tea and quickly dissolves. *That's the lemon substitute. Taste, please.*

I try a sip. It tastes like sweetened battery acid. The truth is I'd rather eat rain forest grubs than drink this guck. But my experience with the People of the Forest in the Amazon taught me to always appear to savor the local delicacy. I take another sip and force a smile. Yum. Best tea I've had in many a year. Well done.

The long-armed gnome beams back at me, and it's a surprisingly warm and chummy smile that lights up the corners of his crinkled face. *He likes Morgan's tea! On with the chat!*

He pours himself a cup of tea, takes a small sip, and waits eagerly for my next conversational salvo.

Why does the burden of making all the small talk at this mad tea party fall to me? Okay, let's see, we've exhausted the weather. Time to move on to politics. So, Morgan, I say, how goes the war?

He visibly tenses. Puts down his teacup so fast that he spills a bit. Starts to back away. *What war?*

The one between the Dark Army and the Dannites.

There's no war. Not anymore. It's over. And even if there still were a war, Morgan wouldn't take sides. Let the heroes fight for the crust. Bravo. Kill, kill. Morgan's just a little Gorm deep in his hutch, not bothering anyone, so no reason to hurt him.

Morgan retreats into a corner, places his long, trembling arms protectively over his face, and begins to alternately cringe and shiver.

6

The tea may taste toxic, but sipping it seems to have helped me recover. I feel a little stronger, and my thoughts are getting sharper.

I apparently just pressed some sort of major panic button. This Gorm has clearly lived through a titanic, hellish struggle, and he's still scared to death.

I walk over to him and take one of his quaking hands in my own. Easy there, Morgan. No one's going to hurt you.

He peeks out through his fingers. *They're not?*

No. I promise. And you're absolutely right. When the world goes crazy, there's no sense in getting involved.

Morgan isn't involved. No Gorm is involved.

I nod and smile at him reassuringly. That's wise. So, I take it Gorms are neither Dark Army nor Dannite?

The first rule of being a Gorm is . . .

I finish it for him: Survive at all costs.

Correct. It's much easier to survive when Morgan doesn't take sides. Anyway, no one wants a Gorm on his side. Not pure enough for the Dannites. Not strong and ruthless enough for the Dark Army. Just a Gorm in his hutch, not bothering anyone.

Makes perfect sense, I assure him. Come, let's sit back down and finish our tea before it gets cold.

As we walk back to our chairs I remind myself that the Gorm I ran into in Manhattan captured me and tried to turn me over to the Dark Army. She seemed to be doing it for money, rather than out of allegiance, but while Gorms may be nonaligned, that doesn't mean they aren't dangerous.

I study Morgan carefully. He doesn't look dangerous. He looks frightened, resourceful, long-suffering, and terribly lonely. I give him a friendly smile. Morgan, do you by any chance have any food in this charming hutch?

Sure, he says, brightening. *Wurfle egesta.*

Not the most appetizing name, but I hope for the best as I ask him telepathically, Are they any good?

They're fresh. I dig them up every night. The wurfles egest them and Morgan excavates them.

Okay, break them out.

He doesn't have to break them. They're bite-size.

No, I mean break them out of the closet or the refrigerator and let's eat them. I'm famished.

Morgan retreats to a corner of his hutch and pulls out a shovel. *Morgan doesn't store them in the closet. They reek. The only place to keep a wurfle egesta indoors is deep beneath the floor.*

Lunch is sounding less palatable by the second. But my stomach is rumbling and I have to eat something soon. You don't by chance have a piece of toast? I ask.

Morgan laughs. He's already tunneled a foot down. *That's a good one. Toast. He's very funny.*

Or a banana?

A look of almost religious veneration crosses his face. *Morgan has read about bananas. Genus* Musa, *family Musaceae. They were yellow and grew on trees, right?*

Look, old fellow, have you got anything at all in the larder besides wurfle egesta?

No, but here are some fresh ones, right where Morgan buried them last night.

A stench so noxious that it is almost visible slowly permeates the hutch, spreading out like a cloud of poison gas. It is so unspeakably rancid I can't compare it to anything I've ever come across, in all my travels to the ocean bottom or the dark heart of the rain forest.

Morgan hurries over and triumphantly deposits a handful of what look like immense rabbit droppings on the table. He sees my disgusted expression and grins. *If he wants to eat wurfle egesta, he needs to seal his nostrils.*

I think to myself that I might need to cut off my nose and my tongue, too, in order to go through with this.

Morgan demonstrates by clamping his nostrils tightly together with the fingers of his right hand while he uses his left to grab one of the odious pellets and pop it in his mouth. He chews vigorously for five seconds and then swallows and makes a strange face, like a mountain climber who's pleased at having successfully surmounted a deadly crag, but also horrified by what he's just done.

How is it? I ask.

Fresh, he replies. *Just egested last night.*

It's hard to imagine that anything this rank could spoil over time and become even more putrid. I know what I have to do now, and it takes every bit of courage and willpower at my command. You are the beacon of hope, I remind myself. I squeeze my nostrils closed, pick up the smallest of the dark pellets, and place it on my tongue.

The taste seems to punch right down through my throat to my guts, and land a walloping haymaker to the pit of my stomach which reverberates all the way to my bowels. Gasping and retching, heaving and snorting, I somehow manage to swallow the wretched thing.

How was it? Morgan asks expectantly.

I look back at him, and wipe tears from my eyes. I make a Herculean effort to look satisfied and even pleased. Very fresh, I gasp out to him telepathically.

Morgan looks back at me, sees the tears running down my cheeks, and bursts into laughter. *They're not exactly delicious, are they?*

No, I tell him, frankly they're bloody awful.

But they do keep Morgan alive, he says, *and the first rule of a Gorm is to—*

I add my telepathic voice to his and we finish the line together: *survive at all costs.*

And as we finish it, looking miserably into each other's eyes, we each grab another wurfle egesta, thrust it into our mouths, and commence chewing.

7

Does it hurt him?

That's the understatement of the year 3011.

Morgan will be done soon. Please try to think of something pleasant.

I look around. Mud walls, mud ceiling, mud floor. Don't be offended, I tell Morgan, but there's not much in this hutch to distract me from the pain.

He doesn't think Morgan has a light touch. He calls Morgan his friend but all he does is criticize him.

How can you act wounded when I'm the one having my shoulder sewn up by what feels like a blunt sewing machine? The acid bath was bad enough.

Morgan had to disinfect the wound before closing it.

A thousand years of technological progress has surely produced a disinfectant that doesn't sting. OW!

What does he mean, a thousand years of progress?

Careful, Jack. Don't blow your cover. Nothing, I tell Morgan. It's just an expression my mother used to use.

Morgan's dear old mother had some nice expressions, too. "Shut your mouth, keep low, run fast, hide dark" was one of her favorites.

Sounds like you had quite a childhood.

Almost done. These stitches could sting. Morgan advises him to please try to think of something cheerful.

Help me out, Morgan. I'm in a mud hutch under a wasteland. What's the most fun thing to do around here?

A Gorm gala. And we're having one soon.

A party? You're kidding me.

Morgan doesn't kid. Here goes. Be brave.

AAAAAAHHHHH.

Three more. Two more. All done. He's good as new.

What do you mean good as new? I'm gonna have a jagged scar there for the rest of my life. It'll look like I was sewn up by Dr. Frankenstein during an earthquake. And what's this about a party? I thought Gorms were timid, solitary souls, spread far apart to make themselves harder targets.

Correct. He's starting to understand Gorms.

No offense, but you don't sound like party animals.

Once a month, at the full moon, Gorms kick it, baby.

I stare back at gnomish old chimp-arms to see if he's kidding, but he grins and prances around with a few dance steps that look like they went out of style during the Roman Empire. Why? I ask, truly baffled.

Everyone needs a little fun, or what's the point?

I hear that, I tell him, thinking that I haven't had a happy moment in a thousand years. So when is gala night?

Tonight.

You're kidding. Where?

We have to start cleaning.

Here?

Morgan will introduce him to some very pretty Gorms. He might even get lucky and catch a snuggle.

I'm not really looking for one. There's a girl back home.

What happens in Morgan's hutch, stays in Morgan's hutch. Let's clean!

So we clean. And we mop. And we dust. And don't ask me how a mud hutch can start to look good, but by the time we finish scraping purple fungus from the bathroom walls, the ambience is markedly improved.

Morgan wipes himself down with an old rag and puts on a brightly colored, ill-fitting, and mismatched ensemble that makes him look like a color-blind court jester. *What does he think?*

You're the man, I tell him. I mean, the Gorm. But what I'm really thinking is that this party, however nutty, may be just the occasion I need to learn something valuable about the situation outside this burrow.

I take it from the few fearful comments that Morgan has let slip about the outside world that there was a war between the Dannites and the Dark Army, which terrorized everyone and wrecked the earth. If the Caretakers had won, they wouldn't have needed to send for me. So I infer that the bad guys must be in control.

But I need to know more. Is my mom trying to rally resistance, and is my dad still languishing in Dark Army captivity? Is there anything at all that I can do to help turn the tide? Or have I traveled forward a thousand years and arrived too late? Did the sands of time that almost buried me already sift over the King and Queen of Dann?

The hutch shakes. Uh-oh. What's that, Morgan?

Slingo! He's always the first. That's his ding-dong.

One by one the Gorms arrive, and Morgan ushers them down into his festive hole. As they shuck protective clothing and goggles, Morgan introduces them to me. *Lowell, Mingo, Hannah, this is Morgan's friend Jack.*

More and more guests arrive. I'm soon surrounded by a dozen suspicious Gorms. They clearly don't know what to make of me. *How did he get here?* they demand. *What does he want? Where did he come from?*

Hadley, I tell them, neglecting to mention that I'm also from a millennium in the past. What about you?

Oh, around these parts. Here and there. Near and far, they reply vaguely.

I can tell my presence makes them nervous, which isn't surprising since the second rule of being a Gorm is don't trust anyone. But before they can ask me too many more questions, Morgan switches on some sort of holographic device. Ghostly red, green, and blue streamers snake down from the ceiling, and colored lights whirl and flash.

Picture the weirdest costume party you've ever been to in your life and then turn the kaleidoscope so that every familiar feature and pattern is oddly distorted. As far as I can figure it, to be a Gorm is to be diminutive and weak, but one must also apparently be uniquely odd-looking.

There are noses as big as cucumbers and elbows that jut at right angles. There are eyes in back of heads and necks that can twist all the way around. The Gorms don't look like the products of genetic breeding experiments to produce super-beings. They look like fearful creatures who have spent so much time running and hiding that they've ended up with the collective junk heap of genetics.

The music starts. I assume it's music, though it sounds like heavy machinery malfunctioning. The Gorms start tapping their feet and circling their double-jointed necks. Pretty soon a bunch of them are dancing.

Morgan is leading a conga line, his long arms sweeping back and forth like an out-of-control skier.

They're drinking something they call shuffle, which makes them lose control, and a hutch full of drunken Gorms is not a pretty sight. What is shuffle? I ask the female Gorm who sits down near me.

Fermented purgation, she answers with a flirtatious smile. *Would he like some?*

I'll pass.

Would he like to dance?

Maybe in a few minutes, I tell her.

Flora is a very good dancer.

I'm sure she is—I mean I'm sure you are.

She can dance any dance ever invented.

I decide to try to use this conversation to find out something valuable. That's pretty impressive, I tell her. Did you learn to dance when you were a kid?

Not much else to do, hiding in a hutch day and night.

I know what you mean, I say with a smile. The war, right? Thank God it's over.

She looks back at me. *Flora doesn't talk about that.*

Neither do I, I say. Why dwell on things you can't change? The whole world in the grip of the Dark Army.

I'm looking into her black Gorm eyes. One is bigger than the other. *Let them have it,* she says telepathically. *Flora is just a Gorm in her hutch, minding her business.*

Absolutely right, I agree. Here, have another sip of shuffle. Say, Flora, do you think any of the Caretakers are still alive?

What? She seems alarmed. *Why?*

I shrug. Just curious. Those Dannites put up a hell of a fight. That queen—what's her name? Oh yeah, Mira. She was something. Do you think she might have survived?

Flora draws away from me. Her eyes narrow. *He's asking Flora questions because he wants information.*

Don't be silly, I reply. I was just making chitchat.

She starts to tremble. *He's using Flora to find out things. He's got an agenda. Flora doesn't know anything. Just a lonely Gorm who came to dance her troubles away.*

Then let's dance, I say to her, standing up and holding out my hand.

She hesitates, and asks suspiciously, *Really?*

Absolutely. No more questions. No agenda. Do you want to dance or not? I heard you were pretty good.

Her survival instinct clashes with her desire to dance, and then Flora violates the first rule of Gormdom and takes my hand and follows me out onto the dance floor.

8

In a minute we're spinning and twisting and Flora is indeed a really good dancer.

I, on the other hand, am not exactly known as twinkle-toes. P.J. used to always try to get me to dance with her at parties back in Hadley. I would make up excuses to avoid it. Sorry, sweetheart, don't like this song. Sore back from wrestling. Charley horse from football.

Now, as I dance with this Gorm, I can't help wondering who

P.J.'s dancing with in Manhattan. I bet that lacrosse player has all the moves.

I can just picture him at the Halloween party he was trying to set up in the Hamptons, sashaying over to P.J. in a cape and vampire fangs and holding out a hand to her . . .

From imagining P.J. dancing with another guy at a costume party, I blink and find myself doing the cha-cha with Flora. She smiles back at me. *He was far away.*

I was trying not to step on your feet—I always look that way when I dance. But you're terrific.

He was thinking about another girl.

Now why would you say a thing like that?

Flora can tell. It's okay. She leans close. *I'm a shape-shifter. I can be anyone he wants me to be.*

I like you the way you are, I tell her. In my limited experience, that's always a good thing to tell a woman.

No he doesn't. Let me make him happy.

But . . . don't you want to be you?

I will be me. And I will also be who he wants me to be. He and I both get what we want. Trust Flora. Think back to that girl he was remembering a few seconds ago.

I flash back to P.J., but I don't see her at the Halloween party dancing with the lacrosse player. I see her the way she looked when I took her to our junior prom. She was upstairs, dressing, and I was in the living room, talking to her dad. I heard footsteps on the stairs and turned. There she was, walking down the stairs in a blue dress, with her eyes shining, and I caught my breath.

Open up your mind and let Flora see.

I know I shouldn't do this. Private things should be kept private, and I have too many secrets to open my mind up during a Gorm gala.

Maybe it's the flashing lights, maybe the pounding music. I haven't drunk any shuffle, but I've smelled its fermented reek across the room. Or maybe the truth is that I miss P.J. and want her here, with me, even if it's just a bad carbon copy. For whatever reason, I lower my telepathic screens and let the Gorm see what I'm thinking.

Oh, she's beautiful. Flora will enjoy this.

My dancing partner's face rearranges itself. Black Gorm eyes lighten to hazel and glint back at me mischievously. The cucumber nose shrinks in on itself to a cute pickle and turns upward. The dull mop of flaxen hair becomes long and lustrous as it darkens to a gorgeous shade of auburn. Breasts swell, stumpy legs elongate, and Flora's frumpy outfit reconfigures itself into a form-fitting, shimmering light blue dress. It's P.J.!

I look back at her. Feel a tear welling in my eye. Before I know what I'm doing I take her in my arms.

The feel of her! The smoothness of her skin as I stroke her cheek. The sweet smell of her hair.

He likes this? The voice is P.J.'s but the inquiry, phrased in the third person, is unmistakably Flora.

I don't answer. Try to ignore the question. Don't want to break the spell. But I can't do this. I can't fake it this way. It feels cheap and somehow wrong.

P.J. hates this future world. Much as I enjoy imagining that she's here, with me, she doesn't fit in a hutch full of Gorms and it makes me feel guilty to pretend.

He doesn't like Flora this way?

It's not your fault. I'm sorry.

Want to try again? Is there anyone else?

I hate to admit it, but there is. And she is very much of this world. She would probably fit right in here—I bet she's drunk shuffle and boogied to this techno music. I close my eyes and imagine Eko, as she revealed herself to me on the Outer Banks. There was a moment when she abandoned her fighting guise, and transformed into her true self. Now, in my mind's eye, I picture her as the exotic beauty I flirted with in that beach house . . .

I lower my screens, and let Flora have a look, and I can almost feel her mind recoil. She lets out an earsplitting scream—the first sound I have ever heard a Gorm make with vocal cords—and staggers away from me.

The music shuts off. The lights stop pulsing. The shuffle-addled Gorms stop gyrating. They're all staring at us, alarmed. I guess that to be a Gorm is to be in a perpetual state of high alert. *What is it, Flora?*

He accessed a Priestess of Dann! she announces. *He knows her! He's been intimate with her! Flora could tell.*

There are frightened gasps as they surround me.

Intimate is too strong a word, I mumble back telepathically. We're just pals and occasional traveling companions. Really, there's nothing to be concerned about. Why doesn't someone turn the music back on . . .

Flora, what else did you see?

She's trembling, shuddering. *I saw blue ocean in the background, out a window. And clean skies. And a few minutes ago he was asking me about Queen Mira . . .*

Louder gasps. *Who is he? He can't be of this time. What does he want here? Morgan, where did you find him?*

Morgan steps forward and puts a protective hand on my shoulder. *There's no cause for worry. He was on the crust, lying unconscious. Morgan was looking for egesta and dug him up. He's not from the past or he would have told Morgan, because he's Morgan's friend. Right?*

I look back at him. Hesitate. Yes, I am your friend, Morgan, I say. And you're right, there's no cause for alarm. I admit I did come here from far away, and maybe I should have shared the exact circumstances with you, but the trip wasn't my choice. I'll leave now if you want.

My words don't pacify the mob of frightened muppets. If anything, they get even more agitated. *He wants to leave so he can betray us! He'll reveal our coordinates! We'll all die! Stop him!* Five Gorms grab me roughly.

I twist and squirm, but they're a lot stronger than they look. I start to feel panic-stricken myself. Who knows what a room full of drunk and paranoid Gorms will do to remove a perceived threat? Look, calm down, I urge them. I don't want to betray anybody. Just let me go.

More hands grab me. My legs. My wrists. My hair.

Sarajane, who is he? Wasn't there a prophecy about such as he?

A strange-looking Gorm—and that's saying a lot—steps forward. She looks like a hippie Medusa, with a long mane of unkempt gray hair and burning red eyes. She stands in front of me and the twin coal-pits of her pupils grow brighter till I feel the heat from them. A cherry-colored flame radiates from her sockets and dances over me. "Take off his shoes," she croaks in a low voice.

They pull off my track shoes and strip off my socks and see my missing pinky toe—the one the Dark Lord gnawed off in his Amazon compound.

The Gorms draw back, as if they can sense his evil, lingering presence in the scarred stump of my missing toe.

I try to make a run for it, but there's no place to go. I dodge and kick and somersault off a wall, but they grab me again.

The flame-eyed Medusa tilts back her head and emits a ululation. Then her fearsome face snaps forward and she intones telepathically: *He is the one of prophecy! For Esaki has written, a Prince of Dann shall come from the distant past, yea, nine fingers shall he have, and nine toes, and he shall bring doom to all who come near him!*

Terrified Gorm shrieks ring out.

Sarajane's red eyes bore in on me and she continues: *Death shall sit on his shoulders, and more death shall ride in the hollows of his ears. His true name is Jair, he will call himself Jack, but he might as well be called death, because rivers of blood will swallow up any fools who don't flee at the first sight of him!*

I guess a prophecy like that would put a damper on almost any social event, but it has a truly remarkable effect on a room crowded with paranoid Gorms.

There are half a dozen well-concealed secret exits to Morgan's hutch, and hysterical figures pry them open and crawl over each other to dive through narrow holes and clamber up chimneylike crevices.

One of them hurls something at my feet as he flees, and dark smoke billows. I breathe some of it in, and immediately start to pass out.

As I crumple to the floor, my last sight is of Morgan standing alone watching me in an empty hutch with holographic party streamers and an overturned bowl of shuffle.

9

H*e didn't trust Morgan.*

I blink awake. I'm lying on the floor. His long Gorm fingers are rubbing something under my nose.

He's a mighty Prince of Dann, who hobnobs with wizards and Dark Lords, but he was just using poor little Morgan.

Yes, I admit. I apologize. You deserved the truth. It was wrong of me. I ask your forgiveness.

Eating Morgan's wurfle egesta, drinking Morgan's tea with lemon, and lying through his clean white teeth.

They're not that clean. Look, I said I was sorry. You, better than anyone, should understand why I did it. The first rule of a Gorm is to survive at all costs. The second is don't trust anyone.

Now he's throwing the rules of being a Gorm back in Morgan's honest face! What about Morgan? Hello! Isn't Morgan here in this hutch, also? Did he ever stop to think that by coming here and accepting Morgan's hospitality, he was endangering Morgan? The Dark Army is hunt-

ing him. Now they're hunting Morgan, too! They will pop down into this hutch at any second, and it will be the neural flay!

Calm down. No one knows we're here.

A whole party of Gorms just found out.

But they're your friends, right?

Don't trust anyone. The Dark Army would pay well to find him. That's why we need to go now.

I focus on Morgan. He's exchanged his party jester outfit for a protective costume. Dark jacket. Goggles. Boots. There's a black rucksack next to him.

Got to get far away before they come.

I sit up. You really think your friends would sell you out to the Dark Army?

Morgan doesn't have any friends.

I take it you still haven't forgiven me?

His lips twitch. *No. But Morgan appreciates that his position is not an easy one. A Prince of Dann! The Dark Army will hunt him down. There's only one thing to do.*

What's that?

The Gorm leans toward me, as if feeling a need to whisper, even though we're communicating telepathically: *Just a Gorm in his hutch, but Morgan hears things.*

What kind of things?

The softest of telepathic whispers: *Not over yet.*

What? The war? I clamber slowly to my feet.

Morgan's not saying more. Dangerous to talk.

So my mother's still alive?

Not dead.

Then she's alive! Do you know where she is?

Morgan spreads out a map. This is not some futuristic high-tech holograph. It's an old-fashioned chart that could have been made before I was born. It probably wasn't, though, because geography was always one of my strong points, and there are many places I don't recognize.

There are also familiar names. Cairo. Jerusalem. This is the Middle East! Or at least what was the Middle East a thousand years ago.

I glance excitedly at the Gorm. Where are we?

His finger moves over the yellowing map and touches down. It looks to me like we're in what used to be Turkey.

And where do you think my mother is?

His finger moves again. I see Damascus. The Tigris and Euphrates rivers. The Al-Hawizeh marsh. I recall a news story I once saw on TV. Hey, wasn't that supposed to be where the Garden of Eden was located?

Just a legend.

And that's where mankind is making its final stand? Kind of ironic, huh?

The Dannites are hiding there for strategic reasons. It's become the most dangerous, inhospitable part of the whole planet. Even the Dark Army hesitates to go there.

But we're heading that way?

As soon as he puts on his gear. He gestures to a chair where some equipment has been laid out for me.

A few seconds later I'm all suited up. This stuff must be Morgan's spare kit—the sleeves of the jacket would be too long for your average orangutan. I lower the goggles over my eyes and suddenly Morgan's hutch is a dull green color. I bet these babies will protect me from the solar glare. How do I look?

If he wants to survive more than five minutes on the crust, he will do exactly what Morgan says.

You're the boss. Lead on. How long will our journey be?

Seven hundred miles through the most deadly terrain imaginable. We'll never make it. Foolish to even try. We're walking to our own certain and agonizing slaughter.

10

My pessimistic guide pushes a button and a sliding door retracts, and we start climbing steep steps dug into a shaft. Even through my protective suit, I can feel it growing hotter as we near the surface.

Are we gonna walk? I ask him.

Much too far.

Then we're gonna fly? I ask, remembering the antigravity suits that Eko taught me to use on the Outer Banks.

Seconds after he lifted off, a wurfle would swoop down and scromp him up.

What does that leave?

Chigga chigga.

What's that?

Best way to travel across the crust at night. Of course, a wurfle will still probably eat him.

If it happens it happens, I mutter, trying to match his glum mood. Eat me, digest me, and egest me.

We reach a rooflike barrier. I don't see any buttons or levers, but Morgan's hands move across it and it slowly swings open.

Heat comes flowing down the shaft like a dragon's searing breath.

We pull ourselves up and out, onto the brittle baking crust. It's night and we're wearing protective gear, but it still feels like we're walking across hot coals. Where are the chigga chiggas? I ask Morgan nervously.

Sleeping or procreating. You can never trust them.

Great, I say. What do we do till they show up?

Keep still. Try not to get eaten.

Sitting is out of the question, because the sandy ground is scorching. So we stand there and kick our boots when the thick soles get too hot.

Even though it's dark night and I'm wearing a jacket and goggles, I can feel the heat and sense the glare radiating up from the barren, microwaved earth.

The moon is out—the same beautiful moon I grew up watching in Hadley-by-Hudson a thousand years ago. The stars of the Milky Way are shining just as brightly as I remember them. Space is the same. The galaxy is lovely and unchanged. But our earth is a parched and empty kill zone.

Why are you out here with me? I finally ask Morgan. You say it's suicide and we'll both probably die. Why leave your hutch and come on this journey?

Had to leave. No choice. Dark Army is on the way.

But you don't have to take me on a seven-hundred-mile suicidal trek across deadly terrain. Why are you risking your life? It seems very un-Gorm-like. If you're acting out of friendship, I appreciate it, but I don't want your blood on my conscience.

He looks back at me. Raises his goggles. I raise my own. The night glare seeps up from the dark sand and makes us both blink. I see his big eyes looking back at me. *Tired of living like crud.*

I beg your pardon.

Hiding in a hutch. Eating wurfle egesta. Crud.

I admit it's a hard life. But you're surviving. Why roll the dice?

His eyes glint. *The Prince of Dann! If Morgan can bring him back, big reward. Delicious food. Clean water. Soft bed. Good night, Morgan. Thank you for bringing our Prince home. The Queen would like to sing you to sleep with a lullaby. Would you like another cupcake before bed?*

Nice fantasy, I tell him. But here's the reality. A lot of good folks have died on my account. The two people who raised me. A yellow dinghy that became a comrade. The governor of the free and wild state of the Amazon. Shot, tortured, blown to bits. If I were you, I'd point me toward the lost Eden and find a new hutch.

Morgan looks back at me a second more, blinks rapidly, and lowers his goggles. *When Morgan decides, he decides. And here come our rides.*

Not noble Arabian steeds.

Nor even a pair of mangy camels.

I follow Morgan's gaze and spot twin stains running parallel through the moonlight, as if two torpedoes are heading toward us just beneath the surface of hot dust. The smudges appear to be about ten feet long, and they are moving fast.

Are they sand snakes? I ask Morgan.

Giant unsegmented nematodes.

Worms?

Not parasitic.

I guess that's good news.

You have no idea. Parasitic nematodes were a blight for centuries, but they vanished in the great die-off three hundred years ago, when their hosts died. Dependency leads to extinction. These are the last worms left on earth. They're marvelous creatures in their way.

What way is that? I ask doubtfully, as the smudges draw near us. I see that they actually travel on top of the sand, but their color so perfectly matches the crust that they appear to be moving beneath its surface.

They're perfectly adapted to survive.

Survive what?

Almost anything. They're hermaphroditic. They can reproduce by themselves. They're cannibalistic. If hungry, they'll eat their own young. In fact, they can eat virtually anything—animal, vegetable, and even many minerals. And they have no vital organs. If a wurfle eats half of one, and the other half escapes, it can grow whole again in less than a week.

The two long brown bedroom slippers park themselves next

to us and lie stationary, with only their vacuum-nozzlelike mouths moving.

How come they don't eat us?

We're too big. Morgan will feed them what they love best—wurfle egesta—and they'll take us for a nice ride. He fishes some of the noxious pellets out of his jacket pocket and holds them out in either hand, as if offering sugar cubes to horses. The two loathsome worms shuffle forward and suction the food from his palms.

Okay, I say. You've fed them. What do we do now?

Climb on. Attach your suction gloves to their outer cuticle.

In a few seconds, I'm mounted on a giant nematode.

Is he ready to roll?

Ready as I'll ever be.

Hold on tight. If he falls off into a mud suck, he'll drown in hot slime.

Thanks for the warning. If I manage to stay on, is there anything I need to worry about?

If he hears a whistle and sees a big shadow behind him, it's a wurfle swooping down.

What do I do?

Let it eat him headfirst so he doesn't suffer. Hold on tight, Prince of Dann! Here we go!

The giant worm starts to slither. My fingers inch deeper in the suction gloves. At first, as the nematode coils and unspools across the crust, I'm in constant danger of falling off. But then I start to anticipate the odd rhythm of its motion. Also, like a horse that breaks from a trot into a gallop, the nematode gains momentum till it hits cruising speed and the ride becomes a bit smoother.

It makes a distinctive sound, a bit like a train going choo-choo. Or, I suppose, chigga chigga.

11

We travel fast and far. There are no red lights or stop signs to slow us down. There is only an endless expanse of dark and barren crust stretching away from us in all directions in the moonlight, like a becalmed ocean.

Dawn comes, and the temperature rises with the sun.

The nematodes stop and let us off, and then start to burrow down into the parched earth with a corkscrew motion. I can hear them digging, sawing through the hard-baked crust till they disappear from sight.

Morgan gets on all fours and we crawl down after them, snaking our way into the freshly dug shaft. We spend the next fourteen hours in a pitch-black wormhole, occasionally swallowing egestas, taking tiny sips of water from Morgan's thermos, and hiding from the deadly sun.

What makes you think my mother is still alive? I ask Morgan telepathically. Who did you hear it from? And do you know anything at all about my father?

Not safe to communicate during daylight, the Gorm warns me. *Wurfles hunt when the sun is up. They can sense thoughts. Morgan's hutch was shielded. Now we're exposed. Also, don't move around. Dark Army drones can spot movement beneath the crust. Quiet, quiet. Still, still.*

So I lie back against the rough hide of the nearest nematode and try to rest and block out the sense that I'm slowly baking in a subterranean brick oven.

The fourteen hours drag by, and finally we crawl out of our hole and resume our journey through the dark wasteland. No wurfles swoop down on us, but after about five hours of speed-slithering, the nematodes suddenly stop and remain very still. If unsegmented worms can look frightened, they do so.

What is it? I ask Morgan, who has dismounted and is furiously rooting around in his rucksack.

Glagour, he says, and I can sense his fear. *Heading our way fast.*

As if reaching the same dread conclusion, the nematodes suddenly begin corkscrewing themselves into the ground at a furious rate. They soon vanish.

Shouldn't we crawl down after them? I ask.

No use. They will go too far down. And they'll use their tails to completely seal the burrows with rocks and sand so the glagour can't follow. High heat. No air. We'd die.

I look back at him. Okay, so we can't escape. Next question— do glagour eat humans?

Can't eat him. No teeth. No mouth.

That's a relief.

Will attach to him. Imbibe him through membranes. Suck his body fluids first. Then the skin. Last the bones. Nothing left. Not a hair, not a tooth. No more Morgan. No more Jack. Drained and absorbed.

I feel myself tremble. What the hell are they?

Morgan has found what he's looking for. A couple of heavy black raincoats and protective pants. *Vivified offscourings.*

What?

Incarnated refuse. Put this on if you want to live.

I notice he already has the black pants on and is slipping on the jacket. I follow his lead. They're actually full-body suits, made out of some sort of thick synthetic material. As I pull on my pants I ask him, You mean the glagour are pollution that's come to life?

Morgan doesn't know if they've come to life, but they can move and find food and absorb it and replicate.

They sound pretty alive to me. Are you sure these suits will save us?

No. Zip it up. Any holes will let them in.

I seal it carefully. It's bulky, almost tentlike. Before zipping up the hood and face mask, I take one last look around. Something is blotting out the moon. Morgan, the moon is winking out.

The glagour! Seal his hood!

Okay, I'm fully zipped. Gloves. Booties. Pants. Jacket. Hood and mask. I can't see. What do we do when they come?

Lie flat and pretend you're part of the crust. Morgan wishes him good luck and a fast death if it comes to that. I hear Morgan's body thud onto the sand.

Good luck and a fast death to you, old pal, I reply, and I sprawl down awkwardly next to him. The synthetic suit absorbs most of the heat, but it's still like lying on a waffle iron. There's a thin breathing tube, which makes every breath an effort in frustration. Morgan, I'm asphyxiating and toasting.

Keep still. The more he moves, the longer they will stay. Morgan can hear them coming.

I can, too. A shrill, high-pitched whine fills the air. It sounds like a hundred dentist's drills descending on me. I try to remain motionless and become one with the crust.

Maybe the glagour will pass over us.

Something lands lightly on my ankle, with the impact of a Wiffle ball. Instinctively I try to kick it off. Big mistake. A second one lands. Then a third. Soon they come thudding down like hailstones.

But hailstones don't get hungry and move around. I can feel the glagour crawling over me. Searching for an opening. There must be thousands of them—it's like being buried under a blanket of blood-famished, whining mosquitoes.

I try to lie still, and to use what Eko taught me to empty my mind of all panic.

It's absolutely impossible. The prospect of being absorbed by living pollution is too much for me. There's no way to shut out the horrific feel of them squirming over every inch of my body. I start thrashing, and I hear myself screaming.

Next to me, Morgan also starts shrieking out loud. We don't try to communicate with each other or shout words or phrases—we're both beyond hysterical, making primitive, terrified sounds as we roll back and forth and occasionally knock into each other.

Minutes pass. Maybe hours. I'm not exactly sure how long I lie there howling and thrashing about. All I know is that at a certain point sanity begins to return in dribs and drabs, and I regain some control. Morgan, I ask telepathically, are they gone? Are you still there?

Still, still. Quiet, quiet. Could be a trick. They may come back.

So we lie still and silent. The heat from the crust is intense, and the breathing tube seems clogged. Finally I can't stand it any longer.

I unzip the mask and hood and look around. Morgan, I think they're gone.

So is one of the nematodes.

I turn and see that only one of the giant worms has crawled back out onto the crust.

What happened to the other one?

The glagour breached its burrow and absorbed it.

I hope it didn't suffer too much.

As Morgan's dear mother used to say: There is no good way to die, but there are many very bad ways.

Your mother had a way with words, I tell him.

A few seconds later we're both mounted on the sole surviving nematode, and it sets off into the darkness.

12

We speed-slither for hours. A sandstorm rages around us and we cling to our mount and tear through the heart of it. It's like tobogganing through a blast furnace.

As the storm ebbs, I see that the terrain has changed. Rock outcroppings poke through the sand and soon give way to great boulders which hunch in the moonlight. Hills and mountains rise in the distance, and soon the crumbling remains of towns and small cities appear. We pass silent urban graveyards where the sand has swallowed fallen skyscrapers, and the tops of minarets jut up like the desperate limbs of drowning swimmers between waves of gravel and rocks.

Damascus, Morgan tells me.

It seems incredible that a thriving metropolis stood here for millennia. Is Paris like this? I ask the Gorm. And then I hesitate. And what about New York?

Gone, all gone, he replies simply, and then he tenses.

Shadows scuttle around the ruins. Humans! Desperate women and children emerge from hiding places and hold out hands as we speed by. They're begging for food and they look like they need it—haggard faces, unprotected from the glare. Stick-thin bodies poking out of ragged clothes.

Can we stop and give them some water? I ask Morgan.

We can't help them, he answers. *They were fools to show themselves.* And then I hear true panic in Morgan's telepathic warning: *Get down! A Jasai!*

I see him duck his head so that he's practically kissing the nematode. Something he saw terrified him. I can't stop myself from glancing back at the beggars.

They're also reacting. Fleeing in all directions. Mothers pulling small kids along. But they only get a few steps. A tall man dressed all in billowing black, like the ghost of death itself, hurls himself at them from atop a boulder and for a moment in the moonlight I see his wild eyes. Then there's a tremendous explosion.

I duck my head and hug the nematode's back. The shock of the blast almost flips our mount, but luckily for us giant worms have extremely low centers of gravity. We're soon speeding away from the explosion. I look back and see that where the women and children stood, only a large, smoking crater remains.

What's a Jasai? I ask the Gorm. A Dark Army killer?

Dannite. They're a recent splinter group that appeared after the war against the Dark Army was lost. They want to force the end.

The end of what?

The human species. They revile humans.

But if they're Dannite, they are human, I object.

Yes, Morgan agrees, *they blame themselves for what's happened to the earth. According to their fanatical founder, humans are abominations in the eyes of God, responsible for every wretched thing that's happened to the once beautiful earth. Dann claimed that the planet could be saved and healed. Jasai preaches that Dann was wrong, and that humanity's last duty is to remove its own foul presence.*

So they're a suicide cult?

An annihilation cult. They don't want to just kill themselves. They want to take the entire human race with them. They believe that's the only way to atone for the damage Homo sapiens has wreaked.

I shiver, and almost slip off the worm's back. Has it really come to this? The human race so appalled by its own conduct that it's bent on exterminating itself?

The nematode gathers speed and we race through the darkness. The ruins fall away, and at the first light of dawn we come to what was once a marsh. The waters have long since dried up, and all that is left are the desiccated husks of reeds, and ghostly outlines of ancient water courses on gravel.

The nematode stops and we dismount.

What's the matter? I ask. Is the dawn spooking it? Is it going to dig a burrow for us to hide in again?

It refuses to go any farther, Morgan informs me. *And it also doesn't want to stay here.*

Why not?

Kill zone.

Offer it an egesta, I suggest.

Morgan takes a handful of egesta and holds them out in his palm.

The giant worm shuffles close, obviously hungry and tempted to accept a hearty breakfast. Then it reconsiders. The nozzlelike mouth twitches and shuts tight.

The nematode turns and begins to slither back the way it came, leaving Morgan and me all alone in the ruined earth's most feared kill zone.

13

Morgan gives me a laser blaster from his rucksack, takes one for himself, and we set out across the wasteland. The stock of the large gun feels good in my hands, but it worries me that such a weapon is necessary.

What am I supposed to shoot? I ask him.

He doesn't want to know.

I do. Forewarned is forearmed. What's hunting us?

If the legends are true, there are swarms of mutant locusts, which emerge from the ground and eat everything they set upon, and then each other. And there are lizards as big as dinosaurs, which hide themselves in dunes and remain motionless for weeks until something eatable passes by. Worst of all are the hairy red desert goliath scorpions. Just one sting and all your blood turns to—

Okay, I cut him off. You're right. I don't want to know. What's the good news?

The heat will kill us before the locusts or the lizards.

Unfortunately, Morgan wasn't exaggerating. Soon we're baking. Then we're frying. And we start quarreling.

Morgan, I tell him, I can't take much more of this.

Gorms don't like to hear whining when they're dying.

Allow me to point out that you whine constantly. It's your distinguishing feature. Along with low self-esteem.

Morgan was doing fine, happy and safe in his hutch, till the mighty Prince of Dann came traipsing along.

I didn't ask you to bring me here. This was your bright idea. Now what are we going to do to get out alive?

As Morgan's mother used to say: Stop thinking! Shut your useless mind up and conserve energy.

No offense, but your mother sounds like a horror show.

Morgan wheels around, his gun aimed at my chest. *Never say bad things about Morgan's mother.*

I point my own gun back at him: Don't tell me not to think. One of us is going to have to find a way out of here, and I don't think it's going to be you, or your mother. And don't point that gun at me. We both know you'll never shoot.

Morgan raises the gun and fires. A blast of searing energy erupts from the muzzle and passes inches over my left shoulder.

I sense something and whirl around. Ten feet from us is a red hairy scorpion, with twelve eyes and a humongous stinger poised to strike. It's as big as a tank, with a bright crimson carapace for body armor. Morgan's laser blast bounces off its shell like sunlight from a car hood.

The pronged tail sweeps toward me and I somersault out of the way. *Don't let the telson touch him. His blood will congeal in two seconds.*

The venom-dripping barb swings at my legs, and this time I vault over it. I don't want my blood to congeal, I assure Morgan. I like it in liquid form. What can we do to kill it? Your lasers aren't even giving it a headache.

Take out its eyes!

The scorpion must have heard that. It pivots like lightning on its eight legs, opens its hideous mouth, and sprays a cloud of acid at Morgan. The Gorm dives out of the way, dropping his black rucksack on a rock. The sack and the rock it lands on sizzle and melt in the acid bath.

I raise my gun and circle, looking for the monster's eyes. There are plenty of them, as big as motorcycle headlights—I see a pair high up on its head, and five pairs lower down. I blast away, and they glow and explode.

Morgan also starts firing, and in seconds all twelve eyes are gone. The venomous arachnid rears up and hisses in agony and rage. Blind or not, it still senses exactly where we are. Every time I take a step, it scuttles to cut me off. I spot bristly hairs hanging from its abdomen—they must function as sensory organs. Morgan and I remain completely still as the scorpion probes the air for us.

Okay, we blinded it, I tell Morgan, but we still can't move. How do we finish it off?

Sonic grenade, he says, taking one out of a back pocket. *The problem is Morgan doesn't throw very well, even when he's calm.* I see that his long arm is shaking with fear.

The good news is you have a relief pitcher from Hadley ready in the bull pen, I tell him. Toss me that grenade.

Once Morgan activates it, we'll only have twelve seconds to get away. Are you ready?

As I'll ever be.

Morgan flips a tiny switch. The sonic grenade starts to hum and glow. He tosses it to me. I won't have any problem nailing the scorpion at close range. But as soon as we start running to escape the explosion, the scorpion will chase us. If we manage to escape the grenade's blast, the scorpion will, too, and then it will chase us down.

Ten seconds! Nine. Throw it.

Don't start running yet, I warn Morgan. I've got an idea. I slide-step to my left, dragging my foot. The scorpion instantly detects the movement and comes after me, opening its fearsome jaws to spit acid.

I jump high and fire the grenade into the monstrosity's mouth and far down its throat. *Run,* I tell Morgan.

The Gorm is already sprinting away. I follow him.

The scorpion comes right after us. Our sudden takeoff opened up a little daylight, which the eight-legged giant immediately begins to close. I can hear its pincers scuttling over the crust, gaining ground.

It's coming! Six seconds. Five. Run faster.

I was always a fast runner. Fastest in my school, in my town, in my county. I once gained three hundred and forty yards in a football game. I fly into full sprint.

Morgan pulls farther away from me on his short legs. *I SAID RUN!*

I am running! How did you get to be so fast?

As Morgan's mother used to say: Fear all, flee fast, live long. Two seconds left. One. Down!

The Gorm dives headlong onto a dried-up streambed, and I follow him. As I slide, the scorching gravel burns my face and torches my chest through my protective suit.

The sonic grenade EXPLODES. It sounds like a bottled thunderclap. Gray-black dust rises like a shroud. I see the crimson carapace torn apart from the inside as pieces of legs, pincers twitching, fly by me.

I get up, and Morgan does, too. The dead scorpion is lying on its side, like an overturned brick house, some of its remaining legs still thrashing.

Well done, I tell Morgan, thrilled with our victory. Those things are nasty. How'd you like that sonic grenade fastball down the middle?

We lost our water, the Gorm replies miserably, ever the pragmatist. *It was inside my rucksack. We can't survive more than two hours without it.*

Then let's turn back.

Impossible. We've already come too far.

What does that leave?

Not much. Our only chance is to go forward. We have to find the stronghold of Dann before the sun kills us.

14

This is how it feels to die in a desert. At first you fear it, and then you just hope it will happen quickly.

We are walking over crust so dry and hot that it might as well be a bed of cinders. Nothing grows here, and nothing has for a long time. There are no weeds or bramble, no husks of reeds or tree stumps.

Was the Garden of Eden really here, thousands of years ago— a leafy glade between beautiful rivers with the tree of knowledge hanging with tempting fruit? As I trudge along, I can't help feeling a tremendous sense of guilt at how we screwed it all up. I don't know if I believe in the Eden myth, but in a sense the whole world

I came from was like a lush garden, with clean skies and fish-filled oceans. And now there's nothing left but gravel.

I am sweating and slowly roasting inside my protective suit, like a self-basting chicken. The sun is up, and even though my eyes are half slitted shut the glare is blinding me through my protective goggles. My boots are catching fire—I can smell burning rubber and see tiny plumes of smoke rising from the soles. Morgan, how can we possibly find the hidden fortress of Dann when we can't keep our eyes open?

Morgan would like to be back in his hutch, eating his wurfle egesta and sipping his lemon tea. A cruddy life is better than a miserable death.

I can't argue with you there, I tell him. Sorry I brought you to this fate.

Not his fault. Morgan made his own decisions, lousy as they were.

No, it is my fault. I do this to everybody I meet. At least it's over. There's a girl in Manhattan I wish I could say goodbye to, and a big dog somewhere in South America. I hope he's eating for both of us . . .

Morgan suddenly stops walking and looks around.

What is it? I ask. Not one of those hidden dinosaurs?

He raises his laser blaster. *Possibly . . .*

The ground beneath his feet erupts as a concealed ninja, dressed in black with a birdlike mask, bursts upward from beneath the gravel and slices Morgan's legs off at the knees with a laser scimitar.

Morgan shrieks and fires his gun but it's hard to get off a good shot when your legs have just been hacked off.

For a second I'm stunned. Then the ninja swings his scimitar at me, and even though I'm weak and blinded by the glare, Eko's training takes over. I dive-roll out of the way and shoot my gun at him as I'm upside down.

The ninja blocks my blast with a deft parry of his scimitar, which acts as a light shield. He swings at me again as I regain my feet. This time I reverse direction and dart toward him. I slip inside the downward arc of his scimitar and sock him in the jaw.

He goes over backward, and I start to raise my gun to finish him off. Then the crust beneath my feet explodes, launching me high into the air. I fall back hard to the ground, and land on the crown of my head.

When I get groggily to my knees I see that it's another ninja, come to help his friend. No, check that. Two more black-clad ninjas have come as reinforcements. So now there are three, all with weapons at the ready.

No way I can fight them. I'm exhausted and reeling from the head injury. I crawl across the crust to Morgan, and cover him with my body. I throw away my gun, and grab Morgan's and toss it away also. Then I raise my hands in the air and wait.

The ninjas advance slowly from three sides, scimitars raised to slice me in half. Each of them moves gracefully, with the circling shuffle steps of a boxer. Their dark eyes glitter menacingly out of birdlike masks. As I lie there in helpless fear, waiting for the end to come, I suddenly remember something.

This is exactly the way Eko looked when she first jumped down at me from the ceiling of the barn on the Outer Banks! She had the same shuffling step, the same birdlike mask, and even the same dispassionate look in her eye! These ninjas just might be the guardians of the hidden fortress of Dann!

I rip off my mask and goggles. Toss them away. "Don't kill me, I'm on your side. I'm one of you!" I shout, or at least try to shout. My throat is so dry that the words get sandpapered and come out in a whisper.

The ninjas circle closer, weapons poised to strike.

"I'M JACK DANIELSON," I shout out again. "THE BEACON OF HOPE! DANN, DANN, DANIELSON. DON'T YOU GET IT?"

But they don't get it. I can feel the heat from their laser weapons. They're almost within striking distance.

I try one last time. "I'M CLOSE FRIENDS WITH EKO. BUDDIES WITH GISCO THE DOG. AND I'M A GODSON OF KIDAH, THE GREAT WIZARD. I CAME HERE TO FIND MIRA, MY MOTHER."

That does it. They stop, or at least hesitate.

It's true, Morgan shouts out telepathically, while lying on his back, writhing in pain, and slowly bleeding to death. *You idiots just attacked your own last hope. He is the Prince of Dann, come home to save his father and defeat the Dark Army.*

The leader of the ninjas steps forward. He holds his scimitar high, ready to swipe down. *Prove it or die.*

Morgan looks up at him. *You must know the prophecy of Esaki. Look at his hands and his feet.*

I shuck my gloves and rip off my boots and dance around in agony on the blistering crust as I show them my missing finger and toe.

They look me over, and I have the strangest sense that they are probing my scarred wounds with their minds, and somehow sensing Dargon and the Dark Lord.

Then, of all the odd things that have happened to me in this nutty future world, the very strangest occurs. They don't hack me apart with their scimitars. Rather they bow to me. Actually that's not a strong enough word. They drop their weapons and sink to their knees and touch their bellies to the crust, prostrating themselves. "Forgive us, Young Lord," their leader says. "We didn't know you. All hail the mighty Prince of Dann!"

✳

15

The mighty Prince of Dann is flickering like a candle in a windstorm. It could be exhaustion, dehydration, or sunstroke, or perhaps I'm experiencing a delayed reaction to being slithered over by living pollution, clashing with a giant scorpion, and bashing my head on the crust. For whatever reason, I'm fading in and out.

Morgan is in even worse shape. I hear his pitiful wails, voiced and telepathic, as we are carried down dark, sloping passageways. The Gorm thinks he's dying, and apparently he doesn't intend to expire quietly. I wish I could help him, but I can barely keep my eyes open.

There's not much to see. I now understand why the last fortress of Dann has remained hidden—not only is it in a kill zone but it's also completely subterranean. We're already far beneath the crust, and still descending.

I knew that people could be shape-shifters, but I didn't know places could do it. But unless I'm delirious, the cave chambers shift their appearance constantly as we pass through them. Now they appear to glisten with ice, now they're damp with water, now they're sandy. Doorways we hurry through seal up behind us, and high ceilings lower as if to bury us and stop just above our heads.

It's a constantly shifting labyrinth, a maze that reinvents itself every few seconds. Even if someone discovered the surface entrance, he could never thread his way down to its heart.

I start to glimpse people at the edges of chambers. Some of them are dressed like ninjas, with weapons and masks. Others look like priests and priestesses in white robes. They cautiously emerge from the shadows to have a look at us.

Morgan has become quiet and still. He's lost a lot of blood, and only the fact that his long arms are trembling gives me hope that he's still alive.

A white-robed figure walks up behind us. I see a short man with a strong face and large gray eyes. He reminds me of a male version of Eko.

Help my friend, I beg him telepathically with my last energy. I hold out my arms to the Dannite priest. *He's in shock. He's lost blood. He's dying. He saved me, and since I'm your prince you have to save him.*

The man in white reaches out and touches me on the forehead, and it relaxes me. Then his finger flicks down to my neck, and I black out.

I am floating through darkness.

Now I am suspended in a bath of cool air.

A blind old witch of a woman with long white hair and a horribly lined and pocked face is sitting before me, surveying me with sightless eyes. She doesn't touch me, but I feel her mind reaching out to my mind, searching for an open door or window.

I try to protect what's mine, but I'm too weak to keep all my screens up. She's a telepath extraordinaire, quick and powerful, and she finds an opening and slips inside. I feel her tiptoeing around in the library of my recollections, trying to authenticate me or debunk my story. She takes down a volume from this shelf and reads a bit and moves on. She works her way backward to my childhood, and then to my earliest memories from infancy.

Are these my own thoughts or am I somehow seeing myself through her? A child cries at night, and a woman in a nightgown hurries in and tries her best to comfort him. It's my bedroom in Hadley, and I'm standing in a crib, wailing like a lost soul. The woman who raised me as my mom strokes my face, but she can't quiet me. The infant in the crib is in terrible pain, there's an absence in his tiny heart that no amount of comforting can lessen.

But then something does lessen it. Something makes the pain

and loneliness dissolve. It's a soothing sound, soft and lovely and familiar.

I'm lying on my back in some kind of hospital bed. It's dark in the room, but there's a tiny light on by the door. A woman stands near me. She's very beautiful, with long and lustrous black hair and eyes that appear to shine brightly one moment, and fade almost to nothing the next.

Mira. She's singing the lullaby I heard atop the Andes, when she stirred the winds to save me. She senses that I've opened my eyes, and steps forward.

I have anticipated this moment for a long time. What should I say to the woman who abandoned me, and sent me back a thousand years to live a childhood that was a lie? Should I demand an explanation? Vent my rage at her for messing up my life?

Now that the moment is at hand, I look back at her and open my mouth. I'm still very weak, but I force out a single word. "Mom?"

She takes my hand and smiles down at me, and begins to weep silently. Her tears fall on my cheeks, or perhaps I'm crying, too. She bends and kisses me softly on the forehead, without ever stopping her sad and lovely song.

✳

16

A grandmotherly woman with white hair to match her white robe slips into my room with a deep bow, and begins spoon-feeding me breakfast.

"You don't have to bow," I tell her with a smile. "A simple wave hello will do."

She doesn't smile back or say a word. She looks a little frightened to be alone with me. I guess the prophecies make the Prince of Dann out to be a big deal.

"How's my friend?" I ask as I gulp down cereal. I'm famished. Even though these brown flakes have the flavor and consistency of cardboard, compared to wurfle egesta they're divine. "Are you taking care of the Gorm? At least give me a nod to let me know he's still alive."

She pauses and looks at me, but says nothing. When I finish the last spoonful of cardboard flakes she backs out of the room, bowing deeply.

I try to sit up, but I'm too weak. Time passes.

Then the door opens and my mother floats in. She moves even more gracefully than Eko. Her long black hair sweeps behind her like a cape.

She closes the door so that we're alone, and walks over to my bed. "How do you feel?"

"I'll be okay." This isn't like our tearful reconciliation the previous night, when I was floating in and out of consciousness. Now I'm wide-awake and full of questions. But she doesn't say anything, and I'm not sure where to begin. "How's Morgan?" I finally venture.

"The Gorm?"

She doesn't say it contemptuously, but I sense that the Dannites look down on Gorms.

"That's right, my Gorm friend who saved my life."

"He's stabilized."

"Please take care of him."

"We are," she promises. "He saved more than just your life. If you had died on the crust, it would all be over." She steps closer and her voice drops. "If I had lost you a second time, I would have just given up."

"You didn't exactly lose me the first time," I point out, my tone hardening a bit. "You sent me away."

"True," she whispers. "I had studied the mysteries of Dann for years—the secrets of disciplining my mind against any eventuality. But when it happened I couldn't control my grief. The night they sent you back, I tried to kill myself. I walked alone and unprotected on the crust, picturing you being raised by another woman, wondering if I had done the right thing."

"Why did you do it?"

"The prophecies were clear. You and you alone could find Firestorm and save the earth." She sits down on a chair next to my bed. "I know you have many questions. Go ahead and ask. I promise I'll tell you the truth."

"Why didn't you let me grow up first, and then send me back? I couldn't find Firestorm when I was a baby."

"The Dark Army knew the prophecies about you. They started hunting for you the day you were born, in a world stripped barren of hiding places. Our scientists had just made the discovery that opened the door to time travel. The Dark Army hadn't made that breakthrough yet. We knew if we sent you back right away, your guardians would have a few years' head start. They could use the time to wash you clean, to hide you in a wild and overpopulated world."

I nod. Her answer makes sense. I plant my palms on the mattress and sit up with a great effort.

"Don't tire yourself out, Jair," she whispers, gently propping a pillow behind me. "You need to sleep and regain your strength. We have important work to do very soon."

"My name is Jack, and I'd rather talk. It's not every day you get to ask your mother the secrets of your life."

She gives me a sad smile. "I see you're as bullheaded as your father."

"He's the one who made the decision to send me back, right?"

"We both made the decision, but I would never have had the strength to carry it out. Your father has an iron sense of duty."

"An iron sense of duty and he's also bullheaded? Does he have any redeeming qualities?"

Her smile brightens. "He's strong, wise, gentle, and kind. A sense of duty, Jair, is not a character flaw."

"Mom, my name's *Jack*. It rhymes with *sent back*. If my father had such an iron sense of duty, why didn't he journey back into the past himself and find Firestorm? If I was the only one who could do it, why didn't one of you come back with me, to raise me till I was ready?"

"We would have loved to go back with you," she says. "But when time travel first became possible, the crossing was perilous. Your father has a weak heart. Our doctors feared that he would not survive the journey. I was needed here, to take over the struggle and lead the Dannites if anything happened to him. And there was another reason: the Dark Army knew us both well. They could have scanned whole continents and found us. We sent you back with two guardians who the Dark Army couldn't trace. They were able to make the journey safely and shelter you for years."

"Yes." I nod. "They handled the whole charade with great skill. My entire childhood was a highly successful deception. Well done, Mom."

Mira gives me a pained look, and replies in a low, serious voice. "I understand your anger, but there was no choice and we all paid a price. I suffered for years. You grew up living a lie. And your father was captured soon after you were sent back. The energy pulse required for time travel betrayed his position to the Dark Army. I've carried on the fight alone, while he's suffered terrible tortures. Now time has run out for all of us. The Omega Box has journeyed to the past and joined the Dark Lord."

I would like to keep the conversation focused on my own grievances, but I can't stop myself from asking: "Who or what is the Omega Box?"

"Both a who and a what. It's a living doomsday device, built by the Jasai cult, with the power to wipe out all human life. The Omega Box was originally a machine, but it's developed a consciousness and a will of its own. It's thrown in its lot with the Dark Army. It wants to help them damage our earth in the past, so it can rule with them in the years to come."

"So it's gone back in time to help the Dark Lord?"

"Yes, they're working together. The past world is being damaged at an accelerating rate, and Kidah cannot stop it. That damage a thousand years ago is having a ripple effect on this world. No human can survive much longer in this living hell, but the Dark Army mutants grow stronger and more numerous. They are now poised to achieve final victory, so they no longer have any need for your father. The date of his execution has been set."

I look back at her and whisper, "When?"

"Five days. Will you put your anger aside and help me get him out?"

I look up at her face and see fierce determination. She's the Queen of Dann, and a loving wife, and she means business.

"I'm sure he's under guard, and the Dark Army has him locked up in a pretty secure spot," I point out.

"Yes, they have him in the tower cell of the Fortress of Aighar." She almost shivers as she says it. "But every dungeon has a doorway. The fate of the world, past, present, and future, depends on our saving him. You are the beacon of hope, my son. You hold the only key."

17

Deep in the heart of the labyrinth, my mother and I plan a daring prison break.

I still have a million questions for her, not to mention tremendously mixed-up emotions of anger and sympathy, suspicion and closeness, but there's no time for any of it. There are five days left before my dad's execution. Every hour is precious.

All of the remaining resources of the forces of Dann are at our disposal. This will be a make-or-break mission—the Dark Army has won the war and is closing in on this subterranean fortress. In a week or two, my mom informs me, Dark Army drones will locate it and crust-penetrating bombs will pulverize it. "However well we hide, no matter how deep we dig, their snake missiles will create earthquakes that turn our last hideout into a final tomb for mankind," she explains. "I would rather die trying to save your father, and at least go down fighting."

I'm growing stronger by the hour. Whatever they're feeding me must be packed with vitamins and nutrients. Six hours ago I could barely sit up in bed, and now I hurry alongside her through seemingly endless corridors as we consult one strange expert after another.

There is the computer wiz, who looks to be about fourteen years old. He strokes a watermelon-size orange sphere and holds his hands to either side. I'm reminded of the way Eko used a blue cube to forecast the weather and check for dangers on the Outer Banks.

But this orange sphere is clearly some kind of supercomputer that requires a very special ability. Orange light from the sphere envelops the boy as my mother asks questions.

"Show us the Fortress of Aighar," she requests.

Tangerine beams flash out through his eye sockets, mouth, and nose. They coalesce into 3-D images that rotate in midair. A hulking, grim structure takes shape; it looks like a medieval castle built by a mad rocket scientist.

Instead of a moat with a drawbridge there's a flowing river of what appears to be gaseous red acid that licks upward at the castle's metallic walls. Those walls soar to incredible heights, and are topped with crenelated escarpments that have the ability to move—so many teeth ready to take a chomp out of unwanted airborne intruders.

At the apex of the castle, inside the jawlike circle of embattlements, is a small, windowless tower. On its roof squats a guardian gargoyle with crimson eyes.

"Where is the prisoner now?" my mother asks.

The castle tower lights up bright green.

For a moment I imagine my father in that tiny windowless prison, no doubt bound and blindfolded, counting down the hours to his execution.

"Show us the route," my mother commands.

The fortress dwindles in size and recedes into the background as the hills and mountains that encircle it become visible. The view of the surrounding terrain telescopes till a vast plain appears, and beneath that desert a purple light flickers. I understand that the purple light signifies our current position. We must find a way to cross these formidable mountain barriers in five days if we are to rescue my father.

Next, my mother and I pay a visit to the white-haired crone of a telepath who probed my mind earlier. The old woman appears to be sleeping in a chair, but when my mother says, "Rachel, we need you," her lips turn up in a smile.

"Throw your mind to the Fortress of Aighar," my mother

says. "But be very careful—they mustn't feel you doing it. Seek out the King, in the castle tower." Mom pauses, and her voice becomes a tense whisper: "How is my husband? Has he been driven mad by their tortures? Will he be able to help us if we can get to him?"

The old woman's head rises from her chin, and then she goes into a deep trance. She sits frozen, barely breathing, as minutes crawl by. When she finally snaps out of it with a shudder, she nearly tumbles off her chair. My mother catches her and holds her.

"They have powerful telepaths guarding him," the old woman rasps. "They have spun a mind web around him. It would have been risky for me to try to find a way through. Light as my footsteps are, they would have sensed me."

"Did you pick up anything useful?" my mother asks in a soft whisper. I get the feeling she had checked on his condition before, and is a little afraid to hear an update.

"The King still lives," the telepath answers. "I'm sorry, my Queen, to tell you this, but I sensed great pain, a level of suffering that verges on madness. Even if you find the King, I'm not sure if he'll be able to help you."

"Thank you, Rachel. You're not responsible for what you see. Go back to sleep." My mother strokes the old woman's mane of long white hair, and then leads me off at a fast clip. "We must make plans with the Warrior Circle who will help us on our journey."

"Fine, let's go meet the warriors, but there's somebody I need to check on first," I tell her. She protests that there's no time to waste, but I insist.

A few minutes later we enter Morgan's room. He's been fitted out with two artificial legs that look remarkably lifelike. I notice that his long arms are trembling, even though he's supposed to be under deep sedation.

I hurry to his bedside, and touch one of his quivering wrists.

"Rest easy, old fellow," I whisper. "You fought bravely and gave us all a chance."

Can he get Morgan some pudding?

The thought is so weak and unexpected that I almost miss it— it's the barest puff of thought breeze, a telepathic leaf spinning through murky haze.

Was that you, Morgan? I ask. How can you think about pudding? You're supposed to be unconscious and near death.

Chocolate, please.

Okay, I'll see what I can do.

One closed eye opens a crack. *And he owes Morgan a lullaby. Morgan has never heard a lullaby.*

Didn't your mother ever sing to you?

Sleep light, learn from your nightmares, wake fast and run! she used to say. Never any singing.

Okay, chocolate pudding and a lullaby. I'll do my best for you. Try to rest.

I head out and confer with my mother and a doctor in the corridor. "Will he be able to walk again?" I ask.

"He'll be able to do whatever weird things Gorms do," the white-robed medic assures me. I sense a slight contemptuousness in his tone, as if he thinks it's beneath him to be taking such good care of a Gorm.

"What Gorms really like to do is dance," I tell him. "So I want you to personally make sure he can get down and boogie with the best of them. Got that, doc?"

The doctor looks back at me, very surprised. "Yes, my Prince. I'll do what I can to get him dancing again."

"Also, he needs chocolate pudding. It's a matter of the utmost urgency."

His eyes go wide and he hesitates. "I will make sure he gets some. But what he really needs is sleep, and he's not responding to our strongest sedatives. Gorms are so paranoid that they're hypertense—you can't knock them out chemically without killing them."

"I know what will put him to sleep," I say. Then I turn to my mother and whisper a few words.

"That's crazy," she responds. "To a Gorm? Jair, we don't have time. Every second counts."

"He saved my life," I tell her. "This is the first favor I ever asked of you, Mom."

I don't think she's used to being called Mom. She looks back at me and then walks into Morgan's room.

I glance through the window and watch the Queen of Dann find a spot near the Gorm's bed, and begin singing. Her beautiful, sad voice swells and ebbs in a lullaby gentle enough to stir winds at the pinnacle of the Andes.

I see a slight, contented smile flicker across Morgan's face as his arms stop trembling and the old Gorm slowly drops off to sleep.

18

You need to choose a weapon. Right this way."

I follow a short, muscular man with a bushy mustache into the armory. An assortment of deadly devices hangs floor to ceiling on wall racks, glinting in the low light like Christmas tree ornaments.

The armorer strokes his mustache and smiles—he's a man who clearly likes his job. "Those are the guns," he tells me. "Short-range blasters, electron beam rifles, and Dark Matter cannons. Here are the explosives: neural paralyzers, axon atomizers, and the 'Big Poppers'—when they go off you'd better lie flat and keep your head down. Take a couple of them," he suggests, handing the small bombs out like hard candies. "You never know when you're going to need a big pop. Now come check these out."

My mother stands by the door, watching me, and an amused smile flickers across her face. The Queen of Dann is apparently one mother who doesn't seem to mind if her son plays with guns.

I follow the armorer to the far wall, where hundreds of handles and shafts are stacked on shelves like different-size baseball bats. "These are all laser hand weapons: swords, scimitars, maces, war hammers, and clubs. Try this one. It's my personal favorite."

He passes me a long blue shaft. I slide my hand up and down it, searching for a switch. "How do I turn it on?"

The armorer looks a bit embarrassed for me. "Sorry, my Prince. I should have explained. Concentrate on the handle and will the blade to appear."

I hold the blue shaft and focus my mind on it. Okay, handle. This is the mighty Prince of Dann, about to go into combat. I need a weapon with a serious blade. What have you got?

As if in answer, a blue flame shoots out of the handle and hooks sharply. It's a sapphire scimitar, weightless as the wind, with a ten-foot shimmering laser blade!

I sweep it through the air and one of the armorer's assistants leaps out of the way and bangs his head on a low shelf.

"I know you wouldn't have hit me, my Prince," he apologizes, rubbing his head. "It's just that it's such a small space and we have had some accidents."

"I understand," I tell him. Then I turn back to the armorer. "I'll take it. Do you wrap it up or do I carry it out?"

"Stick it in your belt. It's yours now. But make sure you retract the blade first," he says with a smile, and leads me toward the door.

My mom joins us as we head out of the armory. "This is the first time I've seen you look happy, Jair," she teases. "All it took was a scimitar."

"And a couple of Big Poppers," I tell her. "I always wanted my own arsenal. Now, where are those warriors?"

"They're waiting for us . . ." she starts to say and then pivots with incredible speed as a warning shout rings out from a guard at the far end of the passageway. A man has burst by him and is running toward us, dressed all in black. My mother grabs the blue scimitar handle from my belt and hurls it end over end at the dark-robed man, who is still thirty yards away.

He sees the weapon spinning at him and tries to duck out of the way, but the scimitar flies with tremendous speed and accuracy. The blue blade flickers on, and the scimitar chops him nearly in half.

As he falls, the black ninja's hands move across his chest, and he shouts out, "Death to mankind!"

My mother dives toward me and tackles me hard. I fall facefirst, and the armorer jumps on top of me.

There's a tremendous explosion that sends a fireball of energy shooting down the corridor. It would have killed us for sure if we were still standing, or if the assassin had gotten any closer. I feel it pass over me, singeing hair off the back of my head.

Then the fire and the noise are gone, and we get slowly to our feet.

The armorer who shielded me with his body looks a little shaky. I'm pretty sure his back was scorched by the fireball, but he's too proud to complain.

Guards run up to check on us. "I'm so sorry, my Queen," the leader of the bodyguards apologizes. "He should never have gotten so close."

"There's no way to prevent it."

"Who was he?" I ask my mom. "Has the Dark Army found us?"

"No, he's one of ours," she admits. "A Jasai. The cult is spreading like an infection through our ranks." She pauses and then adds sadly, "It's our own fault things have come to such a pass that trusted followers of Dann are willing to believe the world would be better off if humanity were extinguished."

19

The bodyguards lead us quickly from the scene of the blast, into a nearby chamber. The Warrior Circle of Dann is waiting for us, twenty ninja priests, dressed in colored robes and wearing birdlike masks. I wonder if Eko belonged to this secret society—something tells me she might have even been its leader.

They bow to us and my mother returns their bow. I follow her example. These are the guys and gals who are going to keep us alive during the next few days, so I'd better stay on their good side.

When I straighten up, I see that a ninja in a scarlet mask has stepped forward holding a small metal sphere. He hurls it at a wall, and the sphere shatters. A purple gas seeps out of its cracked shell and filters up the chamber's wall. In seconds it transforms the rock face to a vivid, topographic map that illustrates the priest's words as he describes what lies ahead.

"It is two thousand miles to the Fortress of Aighar," he says. "To have any chance, we must leave tonight. Advance parties have already been dispatched to prepare the way for each of the three stages of the journey."

A red line begins to trace our route across the map on the cavern wall. "The first leg will take us across flat desert. We must travel day and night, and risk discovery and instant annihilation

by Dark Army drones and orbiting scanners. The other principal
dangers will be gravel storms, giant scorpions, and a swarm of locusts that has filled the sky from the dry oasis to the hills."

The red line extends to the end of the flat plain and slowly begins to climb. "When we reach the hills, things will of course become much more difficult. The flying snakes have just hatched
and clouds of glagour are descending to feed on the venomous spawn. Glagour, my Prince, is a type of predatory living
pollution—"

"I'm familiar with it," I tell him, recalling how I lay cringing
and shouting hysterically as hungry sludge rolled back and forth
over my body.

"If we successfully surmount the hills, we will reach the
mountains of Aighar. Constant seismic activity coupled with sea-
sonal ice storms will make this last segment of the trip by far the
most perilous. As we draw closer to the Dark Army, the number
and lethality of their drones, scouts, traps, land mines, and other
security devices will increase exponentially. Our only chance is to
travel the final two hundred miles deep underground."

The red line on the map dips beneath the surface of the mountains. "There is a cave system threading far beneath the mountains. We can follow it to within twenty miles of the fortress, and
emerge right here, with enough time still remaining to save the
King . . ."

The red line stops moving, and I see the familiar, hulking
Fortress of Aighar looming over the mountains.

"Thank you, Donnerell," my mother says. "You have given us
a chance. There's not a second to lose. We must leave at once—"

"Wait a minute," I say. "Excuse me but didn't Donnerell leave
out the most important part of the whole mission?"

No one responds. They're all looking at me.

"Let's say we somehow survive the locusts and the flying
snakes, not to mention the ice storms. How are we going to cross
the last twenty miles and rescue the King?"

They're all staring at me like I just asked the stupidest question in the history of Danndom.

"Let's take this one step at a time," I suggest. "We follow the cave system and emerge near the fortress in darkness. Who's going in to try to save the King?"

"The fewer the better," my mother tells me. "The two of us will go in alone."

"Fine," I agree. "Let's keep it in the family. But what's the plan of extraction? They're not going to just invite us in and let us have him, right? We're going to have to do something pretty smart to get him out."

I stop and look around. They're still staring at me as if I'm missing the most obvious thing in the world. "There's an acid moat," I remind them, "and the metal walls of the castle appear impossible to climb. I assume there are guards, scanning devices, booby traps, and some kind of hell-troll on the roof. My dad may be insane and incapacitated. How are we going to get into the castle, find him, and carry him out, without being spotted?"

My mother looks a little embarrassed. "Jair, of course you know the answer to that."

"My name is Jack, and no, I don't."

She smiles. "But you must. *You* are the answer to that."

20

I look back at my mother, and at the circle of silent bird-masked warriors. "What do you mean I am the answer? How do you figure that?"

"The only way in and out of the dreaded Fortress of Aighar is with the Blue Star of Dann," my mom says. "It will cloak us for a few hours with invisibility, and shield us from Dark Army scanners. Now, where is the Star?"

"Good question," I agree, looking around at the rookery of ninjas. "Why don't you start by telling me what the Star is, and then we'll get into what happened to it."

She looks impatient, but then she nods and launches into a quick explanation. She tells me how the Blue Star was found by Dann himself, during his years of wandering in the northern polar regions. The last of the ice cap was melting, the world's climate was on a fast path to ruin, and Dann was trying to figure out some way of reversing the damage. Then he found the Star.

"Where was it hidden?" I ask, drawn in by the story.

"Rumor has it that the Star was encased in the very last melting glacier," she says softly, "and it lit up as he drew near. Some say it was the shining heart of the polar regions of the earth, crying out for redress."

"Okay, I can wrap my mind around that," I say, remembering when I held Firestorm in my hands and felt the power of the oceans. I also recall the hidden valley in the Amazon, and how the tallest stone monolith there seemed to be the very incarnation of the spirit of the forest. "Now I know what the Blue Star of Dann is, or was. What happened to it?"

"It was passed down from generation to generation among the leaders of Dann," my mother explains. "It's very small and easy to conceal. It can remain quiescent upon command, and is nearly impossible to detect. It was hidden in necklaces and boot heels, amulets and weapon handles. For many years your father kept it in a tiny silver box around his neck. Several times the Dark Army almost captured it, but we were always able to keep it from them."

"Did they finally get it? What did my father end up doing with it?"

She gives me a sharp look. "Why, he sent it to you, of course.

Actually, he had already been taken captive. But we had the Star and he was able to smuggle a message out that we should send it back to you. We know your guardians received it, and hid it in a piece of everyday apparel."

As I listen to her, the horrible truth begins to dawn on me, and I feel sick.

"They put it in a watch," she continues, "and made sure that when you were ready to search for Firestorm you would find it."

I swallow and nod. "Okay. Listen, Mom. I've got some bad news . . ."

"We know you did find it," she finishes, "and that you used it several times to save your life. Now, where is it, Jair? I don't see a watch on your wrist, so I assume you removed it from that casing and concealed it in a new hiding place. I commend you for your caution. The Blue Star is not only priceless and irreplaceable, but it's also our last hope of rescuing your father and saving the earth." She smiles at me. "Tell me, son. Where is it?"

I look back at her. "I don't have it."

"You concealed it by hiding it on the Gorm for safekeeping? Brilliant! Is that why you wanted to check on him?"

"No," I mumble, "it's not on the Gorm."

She looks at me. "Then it must be in his hutch. We can send a warrior to fetch it. Or did you hide it during your journey?" She steps forward and grabs my shoulders. "Tell me where it is. Every minute is crucial."

I take a deep breath and look right back into her eyes. "I threw it away."

Her eyes widen. "What?"

"I took the watch off my wrist and threw it away."

"No. That's impossible. I don't believe you."

"In retrospect, maybe it wasn't my smartest move."

Her face tightens. Then her fingers begin to dig into my shoulders, and I see panic in her eyes. I also notice that the ninja warriors are standing up. If it's possible for men and women in birdlike masks to look shocked, they do. "Where did you throw it?" she demands in a tense whisper.

"I'm not really sure," I admit. "I flung it into a bend of a river somewhere in the Amazon Basin a thousand years ago. It lit up brightly when it hit the water, and then it sank out of sight. I'm sorry, but it's gone. Now it's just a fancy night-light for piranhas. Maybe we can rescue Dad without it . . ."

It's not fun when the Queen of Dann loses her temper. Her voice rises as her fingers dig into my arms. "We can't possibly rescue him without it!" she announces. And then she completely loses it and erupts: "HOW COULD YOU DO SUCH A STUPID THING! THROW OUT THE BLUE STAR OF DANN! TOSS AWAY ALL OUR HOPES! GIVE UP YOUR LEGACY! NOT TO MENTION CONDEMNING YOUR FATHER TO A PUBLIC NEURAL FLAY!"

Anger comes to my rescue. I free my arms and push her away hard enough to make her stumble back. My own voice booms through the council chamber. *"I'LL TELL YOU WHY I DID IT. Because you and my father were still controlling my life, ruining my life, even though you sent me away. No, that's too kind a word. Abandoned me. Lied to me."*

"I never lied to you—" she objects.

"Even worse, you found two people who would tell me the lies you concocted. Everything I tried to do, everything I was proud of or thought was my own—the friends I had, the girl I loved, the life I built for myself—got torn to shreds by your lies. And it keeps happening. The Dark Army chases me, they kill and kidnap people I love, they haunt me. And you're just as bad. You think nothing of sending your operatives to pretend to own a flower shop, spray me with nerve gas, and teleport me a thousand years into the future so I can do your bidding. Well, Mom, I guess I was just tired of being lied to and controlled. Call it teenage rebellion. You're damn right I threw it away. Take some responsibility."

We're facing each other, breathing hard. I guess some of what I said must have gotten through. She nods and says softly, "All right, Jair. But even so, the Blue Star of Dann!"

"I didn't know what it was," I point out in a slightly softer voice. "My guardians never told me. Maybe they were going to when I got older, but when the Dark Army showed up things happened in a hurry. And there was no explanation in the box where I found it. Gisco and Eko saw me use it and never told me what it was."

"Of course they didn't. To name the Star of Dann or discuss it openly was to expose the secret to the Dark Army."

"Well, I didn't know what it was. How could I know?"

My mother looks back at me. Seconds tick away. "You knew it was from your father," she finally replies. "The only thing you had from him. That should have been enough."

"Well, it wasn't. Anyway, it's gone. We have four days to save Dad. What's Plan B?"

She lowers her head. "There is no Plan B. The Blue Star of Dann was our only hope. All is lost."

PART TWO

21

The car carrying the four Barnard girls turned off the road toward the Sound in the late afternoon.

They stopped at a black iron gate and spoke their names into an intercom. The gate swung open and they drove down a winding driveway with trees on either side. They rounded a bend, the trees gave way to a lush lawn, and the house rose in front of them in all its glory.

P.J. and her three friends gaped at its height and sprawl, its swimming pool and tennis court. Two servants were busy setting up a gazebo on the perfect grass of the football-field-size backyard that sloped down like an emerald carpet to the strip of private beach at the water's edge. Daphne, the drama major, let out a whistle. "I heard Scott was loaded, but check this out!"

They pulled to a stop on a circular driveway. P.J. stepped out onto the gravel, and as if on cue the band began to play. Electric guitar music competed with the sound of the nearby surf.

The purple light of the sinking sun glittered off brightly colored streamers hung from willow trees. Ghoul and goblin masks had been attached to a fence and their gaping eyes seemed to wink and move in the fading light.

Fifteen minutes later the girls were in their costumes, sipping daiquiris dispensed at a bar on the back porch. They knew some of the other guests, and made polite chitchat as the first brave couples started to dance.

Their host came strolling across the grass dressed as a vampire, with a black cape, a red trident, and gleaming plastic fangs.

He used his trident to jab a friend in the back and to salute a pretty girl, and it was possible to recognize the stick technique of an All-Ivy lacrosse player.

"Hi, girls," he said to the four witches. "Halloween came early this year. Thanks for driving out to my humble home away from home."

"Scott, your humble home away from home is like Xanadu squared," Daphne said with a more-than-friendly smile. "You've blown your cover."

"Yeah, it kind of makes it hard to share a teeny dorm room, especially with a roommate who doesn't bathe," he agreed with a laugh.

"I'll tell Zack you said that," Daphne threatened, "unless you dance with me later."

"Zack already knows he stinks," the handsome vampire responded, ignoring the flirtation, and then his focus narrowed to one of the witches.

"Hi, P.J. Looks like you're ready for another drink. You've got to try the Long Island Iced Teas. I think they were invented a mile from here."

The other three girls exchanged glances and soon drifted away, leaving the vampire alone with the prettiest witch in the coven.

P.J. turned down the drink, but she couldn't resist an invitation for a private tour. He led her away from the party, across the sloping lawn to the sand. The footing on the dune was treacherous, and he put his hand gently on her back to guide her down to the water's edge. "I'm glad you came," he said. "I threw this party just to get you here."

She rewarded him with a smile. "I'm sure you say that to all the girls."

"It's true," he told her. "I didn't think you'd come. You haven't been returning phone calls."

"Sorry," P.J. said. "I've been very worried about someone."

"Your high school boyfriend?"

She nodded. "He's . . . disappeared. Without a forwarding address."

"His loss is my gain," Scott observed. And then, sensing that she was profoundly worried, he quickly became more sympathetic. "Can't you check with his parents?"

"He doesn't have parents."

"You mean he's an orphan?"

"His mom and dad died in an accident a year ago. He's all alone."

"Wow, that's really messed up," Scott said. "But I bet there's some simple explanation. I only met him once, but he struck me as someone who could take care of himself. He probably just got the wanderlust and took off for a while. Anyway, you're gonna worry yourself sick. Take a night off. Okay?"

"I'll try," P.J. promised, looking into his compelling dark eyes. "Those fangs aren't real, are they? You look ready to bite me."

"I might later," he told her softly. "You look good enough to eat. But first I want to dance with you. And I have to warn you, I'm not a very good dancer. So I think we both need to stop by the bar and sample those special Long Island Iced Teas."

✳

22

The two of them stood on the porch looking out at the party as the bartender mixed their drinks. Dozens of costumed college students stood on the lawn, mingling and sipping drinks and dancing to the pounding music. "Does anthropology help you to understand our need for ridiculous parties like this?" Scott asked.

P.J. turned to look at him. "How did you know I was taking anthropology?"

"You told me at that Greek restaurant."

"I swear I never did. You must be stalking me."

"You just don't remember telling me because you were flirting with so many boys that night."

"My boyfriend was there, so I seriously doubt I was flirting with anybody," P.J. said.

"Well, he's not here, so tonight you can flirt with me." Scott took her hand and turned her palm up. "Did you know that vampires can read fortunes? Let's see. You will meet a handsome lacrosse player. He will be a lousy dancer but a good kisser. And he's batty about you."

P.J. smiled and gently pulled her hand away. "I have to tell you the truth. I'm flattered and I like you. But I don't think I'll be kissing anybody tonight."

"I appreciate your honesty, and I won't put any of my lame moves on you," Scott promised. "They probably wouldn't work anyway. It's just nice to have you here. Looks like our drinks are ready."

The bartender passed them their iced teas. As P.J. stepped away with her drink, the bartender gave Scott a tiny nod. In return, a rolled up twenty-dollar bill was deposited with a deft flick of the vampire's long fingers into the bartender's tip jar.

P.J. sipped the cool drink as they walked out onto the lawn. Scott recaptured her hand, and used it to guide her toward the band. A stunning blonde in a short skirt slipped up on Scott's other side, bumped him, and smiled at him beneath her pixie paint and glitter. She had a killer body and not much clothing to hide it, and Scott gave her a long look. But then he turned his attention back to P.J. and said, "Okay, witch girl. Want to make a little magic with the prince of darkness on the dance floor?"

"Your lines are truly hokey," she told him, as they left their drinks on a picnic table and waded into the sea of gyrating bodies. Then they were dancing, moving together to the pounding beat in the perfect autumn night.

His hand stroked her hair. "Let it go," he advised.

"What?"

"Enjoy yourself for one night. You're allowed."

"Sorry. I'm trying. It's just so unlike Jack to disappear. If he was going on a trip he would have told me. I could call the police but I have no evidence that anything is wrong, and—"

"And I said let it go," Scott reminded her, and then glanced past her.

The pixie had reappeared and was dancing near them, doing a sultry solo while looking straight at Scott. "Looks like you have a fan," P.J. whispered. "You can dance with her if you want."

"Why would I?" he asked. "I'm dancing with the person I want to be with. Come a little closer, P.J."

The band began a slow song, and for a while they danced at arm's length. Then Scott gently pulled her in, and his cape billowed around them. P.J. tucked her head against his chest, and his head lowered to her neck. He nipped her playfully with his fangs. "Hey," she said, looking up into his gleaming black eyes, "no biting."

"Then be sweet to me," he whispered. He kissed her on the lips so quickly and smoothly that it took her by surprise. P.J. was surprised to find herself kissing him back, and they swayed together, his hands setting a rhythm for their bodies, their tongues touching.

She broke away before the song ended. "That's enough. I feel a little woozy."

"Yeah, for an autumn night it's hot here on the dance floor," he agreed. "Let's get our drinks."

He led her back to the picnic table and handed her her drink. "Here's to letting go for one evening. Cheers."

She took another sip. "I feel a little light-headed."

"Sit down," he advised her, pulling her toward a bench. But before he could sit next to her the blond pixie danced over and captured him with a pink lasso.

"Excuse me," she said to P.J., "can I borrow your vampire?" Without waiting for an answer, she tugged the protesting lacrosse player out onto the dance floor.

Daphne sat down next to P.J. "Having fun?"

"Yeah. And feeling a little guilty," P.J. confessed.

"You're hopeless. High school boyfriends are great when you're in high school. There comes a time to move on. And Scott is hot. Not to mention rich. Go for it, girl." She looked at P.J. more closely. "Are you okay?"

P.J. blinked. "Yeah, I'm fine. I guess I'm just tired."

"Well, wake up, 'cause here comes Dracula. Three's a crowd so I'm out of here."

Scott had extricated himself from the lasso and came hurrying back. "Sorry about that. I don't even recognize that chick but she sure seems to know me. This is a great song. Want to go back out? I promise no more biting."

"To be honest, I'm not feeling so well," P.J. told him.

"Sick?"

"I don't know. A little dizzy."

"Come," he said. "I'll take you to a place where you can lie down and rest."

23

It was much quieter inside the house. The pulsing music sounded distant as Scott led her through the ground floor, past servants and bartenders. They climbed the stairs to the second floor, and all was silent.

The bedroom he led her to was at the end of a hallway and faced the ocean. P.J. tripped, and he caught her.

"Sorry," she gasped. "My head is spinning. I hate to take you away from your own party."

"It's okay," he said, reaching back to lock the door behind them. "Lie down. Close your eyes."

P.J. lay on the bed and shut her eyes. She felt him sit down next to her and prop a pillow under her head. "Let's unbutton this a little so that you can breathe," he suggested, and his hands moved over her blouse.

She tried to roll away, but she was dizzy and he sounded genuinely concerned. "Relax, I just want to put you to bed. You don't need this skirt, either."

She felt him stand up off the bed and thought he was going back down to the party. "Thanks," she murmured.

She heard a clink as his belt buckle hit the floor, and forced her eyes open. He had taken off his clothes. "I'm just going to lie next to you," he whispered.

"No," she said, and tried to get up.

Suddenly he was on the bed with her, his hands moving over her body. "We could be so good together. You must know I'm crazy about you."

"NO!" she shouted. "HELP!" Or at least she tried to shout. But the room was whirling and her tongue felt swollen.

He pinned her down with the weight of his body. "Stop fighting. Just let it happen."

"NO," she said again, and tried to scratch him, but he was too strong for her. She thought of Jack and made one last effort to kick free, but she only succeeded in knocking him backward.

"Bitch. You've been teasing me since we met," he growled, and slapped her. "Now it's my turn." He started to climb on top, and that was when the door burst inward.

A shadowy figure darted into the room, grabbed Scott by the arm, and pulled him off P.J. with so much force that he spun hard into a wall.

P.J. blinked. She was half-conscious, fading in and out. She saw Scott get back to his feet and say, "What the hell?" and raise his fists. He stepped toward the person who had come to save her.

P.J. turned her head toward the door and saw that it was the blond pixie. She was at least a foot shorter than Scott, but she didn't back up as he advanced. Instead, she launched herself into the air and executed a snapping kick with her right leg. Her foot smacked into Scott's chin and knocked him across the room.

He slumped to the floor, unconscious.

The pixie hurried over to P.J. and stood for a second, looking down at her. "Look at you," she whispered and there was anger in her voice.

"Thank you," P.J. managed to whisper.

"Don't thank me. We've got to get out of here fast. Can you walk?"

P.J. tried to shake her head, but she couldn't even manage that. She felt herself starting to black out. The last thing she remembered was being hoisted up onto the pixie's shoulder, as a voice that sounded somehow familiar muttered, "Jack deserves so much better."

24

The small Long Island airport was closed for the night. A gray van pulled up outside the chain-link fence and flashed what appeared to be extremely bright high beams. A section of the metal fence glowed red and then melted away into the dust.

The van drove between the dark hangars till it reached the last one, and then the van's door opened and a shadow flitted out and entered the low-slung building.

A few minutes later, a small single-engine Cessna taxied out with its lights off.

P.J. blinked back to momentary consciousness as she was lifted out of the van. She turned her head and saw glitter on the cheeks of the person carrying her, and recognized the pixie. "Who are you? Where are you taking me?" she gasped. "NO! STOP! I DON'T WANT TO GO!" She began to struggle and kick.

The pixie's hands moved on P.J.'s neck, feeling for a pressure point, and then two fingers dug down. P.J. immediately stopped kicking and was carried the rest of the way to the waiting plane and quickly strapped into a seat.

The takeoff was accomplished in darkness, from a moonlit landing strip into a cloud-cloaked midnight sky.

The pixie flew the small plane out over the Atlantic and headed south. When it was far from land, she stroked a small yellow sphere mounted over the controls. A yellow flame flickered from the sphere, and she leaned forward, as if communing with it.

P.J. woke a second time as the yellow nimbus played over the cabin's walls. She felt a bit more clearheaded, but at the same time she knew she must be hallucinating.

As P.J. watched, the blond pixie seemed to stretch and change color and shape. Blond hair turned dark. Short legs grew longer. White skin darkened to olive, and Caucasian features altered to Eurasian. The pixie's girlish body filled out in sexy curves.

P.J. studied the beautiful woman in the pilot's seat and whispered, "I've seen you before. You're Eko."

"Be silent," came the curt reply. The woman's attention was focused on the aircraft controls.

The single-engine Cessna had been plowing into a stiff headwind at just over one hundred miles per hour. The yellow glow played over the inside of the narrow cabin, and then seemed to radiate through the walls and glint off the aluminum exterior as the old two-seater transformed.

The riveted aluminum sprouted a layer of soft skin that blistered into hundreds of discrete panels, angled in different directions to break up radar. The strut-braced wings retracted into a batwing shape. The single piston engine went silent and stopped emitting heat, but even as it seemed to be shutting down its thrust increased exponentially.

P.J. watched the dials as the plane sped up to two, then three, then four hundred miles per hour. P.J. and Eko climbed higher into the night sky. Their ride had been choppy, but now it became as smooth and silent as an eagle gliding majestically over the shadowy earth far below.

"What's going on?" P.J. demanded.

"Just go back to sleep," Eko told her.

"I was drugged, wasn't I? Scott . . . ?"

"He gave the bartender a pill to slip into your drink. I'd guess GHB. It's a general anesthetic and a date rape drug. Nice people you hang out with."

"I have a terrible headache."

"You'll feel worse before you feel better. Sleep is the best thing for you now."

"I don't want to go to sleep. I want to know what's going on. What am I doing in this plane? Why did you save me? You don't even like me. And where are you taking me?"

Eko glanced at her. "I really don't think you could handle the answer."

"Don't patronize me," P.J. told her. "I may have done a few dumb things at that party, but I can handle the truth, and I have a right to know where we're headed."

Eko glanced down at the controls and thought about it for a good ten seconds. She finally answered: "The Amazon."

P.J. grimaced. "Oh no."

"Oh yes," Eko assured her. "Every hour is precious. We're about to break the sound barrier. We should arrive before dawn. Lie back and try to sleep."

P.J. looked back at her and responded softly but strongly: "You wouldn't have come for me it you didn't need my help. With all your powers, I can do something you can't, and it must be important. So if you don't want me to fight you every step of the way, you'd better tell me what's happened. Is Jack okay? Will he be there to meet us?"

25

I still don't understand why you needed me," P.J. said as the bat-winged plane hurtled silently through the darkness, thirty thousand feet over the Leeward Islands. "Why didn't they just send Jack back in time to find the watch?"

"Because the trip might have killed him," Eko told her. "The passage through time puts tremendous stress on the heart and the central nervous system. A human body needs time to recover. Jack made the jump forward less than two weeks ago. If he tried to come back too soon, he could have a stroke or a heart attack. Even if he made it back and found the watch, he could never have returned with it to the future again, where he's urgently needed. So bringing him here wasn't an option. You're the only other person who knows where the watch was discarded."

"*But I swear I don't know,*" P.J. almost shouted. She got control of herself. "Jack and I were talking and winding our way through river channels. My mind was on getting out of the Amazon, taking a hot bath, and heading home. I wasn't watching where we were going. I couldn't find that bend in the river again in a million years."

"You'll find it," Eko promised her.

"*No I won't.* I can't. Look, I'd help if I could. I admit I don't particularly like being kidnapped by you—"

"I saved you from being raped."

"That's true. Thank you. And then you kidnapped me for your own purposes. And when I said I didn't want to go, you knocked me unconscious."

"They're Jack's purposes, too," Eko pointed out.

"*You want them to be Jack's purposes,*" P.J. fired back. "From what he's told me, he's been as helpless in all this as I am now. He didn't want to go off to find Firestorm. He was forced to go to the Amazon to try to rescue me. And I bet he didn't willingly jump into a time machine a week ago. Why don't you just admit it— you guys hijack our lives for your own purposes and find self-serving ways to justify it."

Eko gave her a tiny smile tinged with admiration. "Nice speech. You must be feeling a little better."

"My head still aches," P.J. admitted.

"Drink some water. Here's a thermos."

"Thanks." P.J. took a long sip.

There was a moment of silent connection between the two women that surprised them both.

"I guess it was pretty stupid of me to get tricked that way," P.J. said softly. "You want a sip?"

"Sure. Thanks." Eko took the thermos from her. "It wasn't your fault. Men are not to be trusted. Now or a thousand years from now, most of them can only think about one thing. Then again, their simplicity makes them much easier to manipulate."

P.J. took the thermos back and swallowed a big gulp of cold water. "I bet you're good at manipulating them."

"When I need to be."

"Have you had lots of . . . 'boyfriends'?"

"Do you mean have I slept with a lot of men?" Eko asked with a smile.

"Have you?"

"Not as many as I'd like."

"Meaning you haven't slept with Jack?"

Eko turned her head and looked at P.J. The beautiful gray eyes glittered.

"But you'd like to," P.J. whispered. "I bet you'd do anything to manipulate him into your arms, and I bet you could justify that as part of some cosmic necessity. I feel sorry for you. You lie to yourself about the things that are most important."

Eko didn't reply right away. She touched the controls, and the plane began to descend through thick cloud cover.

"The notion that I even have to justify anything to you is absurd," she told P.J. "It may be hard for you to accept this, but your life is insignificant and utterly meaningless when the stakes are considered. As for Jack, he's fulfilling his destiny. He was born to a family, a fate, a role, and he must accomplish that task."

"And, of course, part of that task just happens to be marrying you?" P.J. suggested quietly.

"It is written that if we save the earth, we will rule together in a new Eden. Our descendants will be as numerous as the sand grains."

"You're nuts," P.J. told her. "And you're also wrong. People have the right to choose."

The dials showed that they were already down to twenty-five thousand feet. The clouds completely screened their window.

"We're almost there," Eko told her. "I understand now why Jack liked you. Part of it, of course, was nostalgia for his lost childhood. You represent an innocent time that he knows he can never get back, but he still craves. But you're also strong and smart and I think you really do love him. Unfortunately for you, the more you try to hold on to each other, the more you both will suffer. You're going to have to forget him."

"I can't and I won't."

The plane darted out of the clouds. They were high over the Andes. Dawn had broken, and golden sunlight was spilling over the crags and slowly seeping into the valleys like yolk from a cracked, magical egg.

"I can help you forget him," Eko said.

"How can you do that?"

"By getting inside your mind."

P.J. looked back at her and fear showed plainly on her face. "No way. I don't ever want you inside my mind."

"I'm afraid there's no choice," Eko told her. "That's how we're going to find the watch."

26

The emerald carpet stretched as far as P.J. could see in all directions. As the plane flew lower, the green became flecked with glinting sequins connected by silvery threads—the lakes and rivers of the vast Amazon Basin.

P.J. was feeling stronger, and she tried to hide her recovery from Eko. She didn't know how she could fight off this powerful woman from the future, but the prospect of a stranger who was also a rival invading her mind and possibly changing her memories was terrifying.

As she slumped down in her seat, feigning exhaustion, P.J. tried to figure out a way to resist. She clearly didn't stand a chance with just her bare hands, and there was nothing resembling a weapon in the plane's tiny cabin.

Suddenly, the seamless green tapestry below was riven by an impossibly wide, black gash. Even from this height, the dark body of water looked like an inland sea that had somehow been squeezed and elongated. But it was not a sea or even a great lake—it had two banks and flowed from one horizon to the other. "What is it?" P.J. gasped.

"The Amazon River," Eko told her.

"I've never seen anything like it."

"There is nothing like it," Eko agreed softly.

P.J. glanced quickly at her. Sadness rang in Eko's voice, and as she looked down at the mighty river, her impassivity slipped for a second and regret and longing showed clearly on her face.

"What's the matter?"

"Nothing," Eko answered quickly, dabbing some moisture from the corner of an eye. "It's just . . . the scale of it is so awesome. It's got greater river flow than the next eight largest rivers combined," she mumbled, using her storehouse of facts to try to mask her lapse in self-control. "If you go to the mouth of the Amazon, and then sail out of sight of the coast, you can still drink. That's how much fresh water is discharged into the ocean. Remarkable, isn't it?"

"You look so sad."

Eko returned P.J.'s gaze and nodded.

For the second time, there was a connection between the two women. "It's of no consequence," Eko muttered. "You wouldn't understand."

"You hate to show emotion because you think it's a weakness," P.J. observed, looking back into the glittering gray eyes. "But it's not. It's who you are. So tell me. Is it something about Jack? Or your childhood? Did you grow up on a big river like this?"

Eko hesitated and then whispered, "The opposite." She

looked down at the wide ribbon of dark water and added softly, "If you could see my world. A scorched wilderness of sand and gravel. Mothers and children dying for lack of a drink of water. And then you look down . . . and see . . . what our earth once had to offer . . ."

"And that's where Jack is right now?" P.J. whispered back. "In that dying future?"

"Trying to change things."

"If we find the watch, there's a chance that things might turn out differently?"

"If we don't find it," Eko said, "it's over."

The plane swooped lower over the glistening black river. A flock of brightly plumed birds broke through the tree cover of the near bank and made a rainbow streak of color as they flew out over the dark river.

"Okay," P.J. said, "I'm willing to try to help. But I need some kind of guarantee that you won't hurt me or erase what's mine."

Eko looked back at her. The gray eyes hardened, and the beautiful face regained its sphinxlike demeanor. "There can be no bargaining between us," she said. "You will help me because you must, and I will do what I need to do. That's all."

Eko stroked the yellow sphere and the bat-winged plane transformed again, but not back into a Cessna. They were now so close to the river's surface that tiny windblown waves were visible. The wings came together and twisted beneath the body of the craft to form a steel skirt. The engine began blasting a pillow of air down at the water below, while at the same time propelling them forward horizontally at great speed.

They were now in a futuristic hovercraft, sleek, silent, and perfectly suited to this watery world. They skimmed over the four-mile-wide Amazon, heading swiftly upriver. Eko soon steered them off the main channel, and they began threading their way up its tributaries.

Occasionally they passed a small village, but it would have

been hard for even the keenest lookout's eyes to spot them. The skin of the hovercraft had a chameleon-like quality that allowed it to match the color of the water, and they were traveling silently and at great speed. The tributaries gave way to smaller rivers, and then to snaking streams, until they finally reached a watery cross-roads.

Eko brought the hovercraft to a stop near a bank, and they floated beneath overhanging trees. "This is as close as I can bring us," she told P.J. "Only you can get us closer. Do I have to force you to do this?"

P.J. did not have to pretend to be panicked—she was truly terrified. She merely gave in to her own building hysteria, and began shaking and hyperventilating. "No, I don't want you to force me," she gasped. "I'll do what you say. But I'm afraid. Can I lie down and go to sleep, and pretend it's . . . like an operation in a hospital?"

She half closed her eyes and stretched out on the seat, and then leaned back even farther so that her head touched the control panel. Suddenly P.J. spun and grabbed the yellow sphere. She wrenched it off its base, jumped to her feet, and held it over her head. "Don't make a move or I swear I'll break this into a million pieces."

Eko stood to face her, her eyes flicking from the sphere to P.J., estimating distances and microseconds of reaction time. "That's just a guidance system," she said. "Don't make this harder than it has to be."

"I sincerely doubt that it's just a guidance system. I watched you use it to make the plane change shape. I think you need it to accomplish this mission, and I bet there aren't too many of these gizmos available in the twenty-first century. Right now you're thinking that maybe you can grab it out of my hands. Are you sure you want to risk that? I've seen you move and you're super-fast, but I can smash it in an instant. So sit back down."

Eko studied P.J.'s face, gauging her strength and resolve, and then she sat back down. "Okay," she said, "I can see that you were playing possum, and you're stronger than I thought. And you're right, I do need that to complete my mission. You've been very clever. But where do we go from here?"

"I want to help you find the watch and save your world, and I especially want to help Jack. But we'll do it my way."

"What way is that?" Eko asked.

"A swap. You go into my mind, and I go into yours."

"That's impossible," Eko told her. "You know nothing about telepathy."

"Any road that can be walked down one way can be walked down the other way, too. I'm sure you can find a way to manage it, since the hopes of the future are at stake."

27

The two women sat on the floor of the hovercraft, facing each other. P.J. still held the yellow sphere in her right hand, ready to dash it to the floor in an instant. It seemed to throb with a faint golden pulse that covered them both in a warm glow.

P.J. felt her mind being unlocked and entered. As the doorway to her earliest memories was breached, she felt herself passing the other way . . .

Running. A little girl on unsteady legs, fleeing across a dark wilderness, trying to keep up with a frightened woman who clutched her by the hand. The young girl had seen her father die, and now her mother was badly wounded. There was the horror of being hunted.

A dark mouth opened and enveloped them. A cave. They ran

into blackness, and suddenly they were no longer alone. Glittering eyes studied them. Hands aimed weapons at them. But these weren't the monsters of the Dark Army. These were humans, dressed in white robes.

"Take my daughter," the woman gasped. "Please . . ."

And then there was a horrible double scream—a woman dying in agony and a little girl wailing as she sensed that she was suddenly alone in the world.

That double scream billowed into long white robes. Girls and boys. Acolytes. Learning the wisdom of Dann, and the disciplines of the priesthood.

One dark-haired girl sat by herself. Meditating alone. Fasting while the rest of them ate. Learning to fight in ever more complex movements of punches and kicks, pirouettes and leaps. Practicing the kata over and over through the stormy night when the loneliness was the worst.

P.J. had never felt such loneliness—it was a live thing, gnawing inside the girl's stomach. No family and no friends, no one to hold as the thunderstorms howled and ice storms belted down on a desolate, war-racked world.

And even as P.J. sat, watching the lightning lash the mountains through that solitary girl's eyes, she was aware of another little girl in a very different place and time, walking down the stairs of a dark house.

Step by step. As shadows moved on the white walls.

Those were the shadows Eko saw through little P.J.'s expectant eyes as she left the warmth of the coverlet, and moved from the cozy bedroom with stuffed animals and a night-light, down wooden stairs that creaked, to a living room with a tree in the middle of it.

The smell of pine. The pile of boxes arranged carefully. Presents under a Christmas tree.

One present was larger than the rest. Even in darkness, it held a special magic.

Then morning light and laughter. Music played and there was the smell of something sweet baking. She was opening that large box, with a man and a woman smiling down—her parents—and an older woman, too, with white hair, whose kind eyes seemed to follow her every movement. Wooden legs were revealed. A straight back. An easel!

She sat before it. The woman with white hair held her hand gently. Her mother stood behind, watching. Three generations of women traced a shape together. The sense of shared joy, of love and belonging, hung in the air.

And even as Eko experienced that feeling of deep and unshakable family security, she was aware of total chaos and hysteria in a faraway place, as an alarm sounded . . .

Smoke swirled in the air. Desperate shouts rang out.

A village was under attack by the Dark Army! P.J. heard those alarms and smelled the smoke from Eko's childhood as the young ninja warrior plunged into the thick of the fighting, whirling a laser saber, defending women and children who fled for their lives.

Right in front of her, a little boy was decapitated by a swipe of a razor-sharp claw. His blood pumped out and sprayed the battlefield like a scarlet geyser.

She turned on the fiend who had struck the blow, dodged a deadly strike, and sliced his chest apart.

Blood was all around. Piercing death cries shrilled. And tears were shed for an embattled, dying world.

P.J. saw that world the way Eko recalled it, in a series of indelible images. The lifeless, acid oceans. The parched land, drained of groundwater. The cloudless skies with a merciless sun blistering down through an ever-thinning atmosphere. It was a disaster but it was also a cause. P.J. felt the young woman latch on to that cause as a reason to live.

And even in the midst of desperation, there was one faint last hope. It could all be reversed. The Prince of Dann might yet change things. A name, repeated to Eko from girlhood. Jair. A prophecy of a shared destiny. Something to cling to as the darkness closed in.

She volunteered for a mission. Passed through the womb of time. Was reborn in a sunlit world of eagles and dolphins, of blue oceans and sweet sea breezes. So this was the Eden that had been lost, and that might be again!

And one day, Jair himself stumbled into a barn beneath her. The beacon of hope was her charge, her student, her great responsibility. Eko loved him from the first moment, even as she commenced training him for the mission ahead.

As P.J. relived Eko's loving memories of Jair, on the Outer Banks and the Amazon, she reached out her right hand and passed the yellow sphere to the woman across from her.

No words were necessary. It was a gesture of understanding and trust. Their hands brushed. Eko took the sphere in her own palm. She was right there with P.J. on the boat . . .

But she was also with P.J. beneath silent and shadowy bleachers on a wintry afternoon. She saw Jack looking at her in that moment just before a friendship blossomed into a romance. The gleam in his eye. The slow turning of his head. It was a silly thing, an innocent thing, but in its own way profound and powerful. A glance offered and held, and then a cautious first touching of lips. Promises whispered by the banks of the Hudson. Steamy petting sessions in the backseat of a car.

Eko followed the thread, to the moment it frayed.

Jack disappeared, and suddenly P.J.'s safe, secure, sheltered life came undone. How could he simply vanish?

Night after night, she waited to hear from him. It was more than she could bear. There were even thoughts of suicide, pushed away but not entirely conquered.

P.J.'s pain resonated with Eko—she understood sudden loss and wild grieving.

Eko followed the increasing misery to the moment the fraying rope snapped, and P.J. was kidnapped off a dark street and swept up into the nightmare. Flown to the Amazon. Confined alone in a dungeon till all hope seemed lost, and sanity itself was ebbing.

And then a familiar voice sounded outside her cell. It was Jack. Calling to her.

There was the miracle of liberation. The twists and turns of the Amazon. The whirl of the waterfall. The final battle in the Dark Lord's cell as Jack fought a demon for her.

Finally it was over. They were together, riding in an outboard canoe down a winding river channel.

Through P.J.'s eyes, Eko saw every turn in that river, every tree, every rock . . .

28

The hovercraft moved slowly.

Inside the cabin, the two women still faced each other. The radiance of the yellow sphere flickered over them. Sometimes it seemed as fickle as firelight, at other times it was fixed and purposeful, as it projected on the wall of the boat the changing contours of a wondrous map.

The map flowed and ebbed. No, not such a wide bend. A narrower one. Oh yes, two tall trees.

Eko bored into the moment when the dog and boy split off and P.J. and Jack were alone together—the smell of the river channel, the plumage of the birds that flew over them, and the leaves of the shrubs on the banks.

The powerful outboard motor ate up the miles. P.J. reclined in

Jair's arms—in Jack's arms. The sky began to lighten in the east.

New and even more helpful details became visible in the dawn light. The pattern of treetops against the sky. A mountain looming in the distance.

The golden map on the wall of the hovercraft transformed constantly with the new information.

The hovercraft whisked them upriver.

"It's over for me," Jack said and kissed her.

P.J. kissed him back. Asked him what would happen if they didn't let him go. "You were born into their struggle. You're of their time."

He stared down at his father's watch. The blue hands glinted on the white background.

He took the watch off.

The sky was lighter behind Jack now. The crags of the nearby mountain caught the morning light.

The hovercraft followed this scent of memory faster and faster, weaving through a labyrinth of streams.

Three tall trees with interlacing vines.

Jack flung the watch far out over the dark river. It gleamed when it touched the surface.

The golden map shrank in upon itself. Many rivers. One channel. A single long stretch of that channel.

"What did you do that for?" P.J. asked. "Didn't that come from your father?"

"Yup. But I'm no longer operating on his time." The feel of his tight embrace. "My connection to them and their time is sinking to the bottom of this river. Right now all I want is to live my life, my own insignificant Jack Danielson life, with you."

"Bozo," she responded, "you got yourself a deal."

A blue light flashed on the golden map.

The hovercraft floated to a feathery stop.

Eko and P.J. broke apart at the same moment.

P.J. blinked and looked around.

They were on a narrow river, near three tall palms with interlacing vines. Somehow it looked very familiar.

Then she glanced at Eko who was staring back at her. There was a bond between them now that did not need to be discussed.

"Thank you," Eko whispered, stepped out of the cabin of the hovercraft, and dove over the side.

P.J. followed her out through the door and stood there, looking down.

The thick, throat-clogging smell of the Amazon came back to P.J. in an instant, the heat of the sun on her arms and shoulders, and the constant buzz of the millions of birds and insects.

Dark water. Thick mud. But there was a blue glint deep beneath it.

That blue point of light began to move. The palm trees suddenly appeared bluish, then the rocks on the bank, and the birds in the air, till even the flickering light from the yellow sphere yielded to the blue tide.

Hands broke the surface. Eko held the watch, a treasure retrieved!

29

Slowly and painstakingly, Eko took the watch apart on the deck of the hovercraft. With each tiny screw that was removed and every layer of crystal and casing that was stripped off, the blue glow increased till the steamy river channel was infused with a mysterious boreal presence.

P.J. felt as if the great steam bath of the Amazon had suddenly been chilled by a cold breath of arctic air-conditioning. The sun still beat down, but the temperature dropped in seconds by at least fifty degrees. In the febrile dank of the river channel, thrumming with sound and life, a zone of frozen calm took hold.

Songbirds quieted. Insects stopped humming. Even the foliage ceased shaking in the morning wind. Leaves flattened and stalks stiffened, as if frozen into stillness by the polar majesty of the Blue Star of Dann.

Eko removed the backing and the transparent crystal top, and then separated the movement plate from the back plate. Gleaming brilliantly from inside a tangle of miniature gears and dials was a blue jewel, fragile as a teardrop. It was so small that it fit snugly into this tiny niche, but as Eko lifted it up with two fingers, it began to change shape and size.

The tiny blue teardrop swelled into a perfect shimmering pearl, and the pearl darkened and ripened into a walnut-size blue diamond with a thousand shimmering faces.

Eko lifted it up with two fingers, closed her eyes, and her fingers trembled. A look of surpassing sadness flashed across her exquisite features.

And then a truly freakish thing occurred. It began to snow. Dime-size white flakes sifted down out of the cloudless sky and dusted the leaves and dimpled the river.

Eko opened her eyes and looked across at P.J. "I could never have found it without you," she whispered. "Do you want to hold it for a second?"

P.J. held out her palm. She had thought of the Blue Star as a lifeless mineral—a very precious stone, yes, but as inanimate as a lump of coal. It was only when it touched her skin that P.J. realized it was alive, albeit in a way she didn't understand.

As she held the gem, and snow fell on her face and hair, she seemed to cross a monstrous chasm into a white world of stark beauty and howling pain. There was water, but not the mud-brown streams and green-banked rivers of the Amazon. These were churning arctic seas at the top of the world, with iceberg islands lashed by frozen gales.

P.J. felt primordial anger flowing through the blue gem—pent-up sound and fury at centuries of defilement. Icebergs cracked with deep-throated roars of rage as vast avalanches tumbled into surging surf. A mother whale and her calf were harpooned side by side, calling out to each other in their final agonies. Polar bears swam endlessly in search of floes, stubbornly clinging to life but weakening and finally sinking beneath the iceless oceans.

Then there was a time when all the glaciers and ice sheets had melted, all the whales and polar bears were gone, and the noble heart of the polar regions beat on alone in a stiff, mournful cadence. The world was dying even at the equators, those hubs of life; but the top and bottom of the earth were lifeless and empty, wiped clear of what had once been so magnificent.

P.J. opened her eyes and found herself back in the Amazon river channel in bright daylight. The snow had stopped falling, a breeze rustled through the leaves on the near bank, and everything was as it had been, yet P.J. knew that nothing would be quite the same for her ever again.

Eko seemed to understand this as she lifted the blue jewel out of P.J.'s hand and whispered, "So now you know."

P.J. looked back at her and nodded. "Can it still be saved?"

"Maybe," Eko responded, walking over to the yellow sphere. "This is the last and only chance."

Holding the Blue Star with her right hand, she touched the yellow globe with her left, and it began to pulse. She lowered the Star of Dann into the throbbing golden light, and the flickering nimbus seemed to reach up and enfold the blue gem. Then the jewel slipped from Eko's fingers and dropped slowly inside the yellow sphere, as a pebble might sink into a fish tank.

The Blue Star floated for a moment atop the throbbing current of golden light, and then there was a tremendous flash, and a thunderclap that came not from the sky above but from another place and time entirely. P.J. shut her eyes at the bright light as the booming sound knocked her to her knees. Then all was still and silent, and she opened her eyes again.

The yellow sphere sat on the deck of the hovercraft, empty as a bowl of broth. The Blue Star of Dann had vanished, leaving not so much as a snowball in its wake in the long trail through time.

"Where did it go?" P.J. asked.

"To Jack," Eko told her. "And now we've done all that we can do to help. I can take you back to New York. You can resume your life there."

P.J. hesitated a long beat and then shook her head. "Thanks, but I don't think that's possible."

"It's very possible," Eko told her. "This is not your fight. You were drawn into something beyond you and outside of you, which can only cause you pain. I know who you are now. Here is my advice. Let it go and move on."

"How can I, after having seen what I've seen and felt what I've just felt?"

"If the future is ultimately saved or the earth dies—it is of no consequence to you," Eko told her. "During your lifetime, you will still have enough food to eat, enough fresh water to drink, and the seasons will change. The sun will shine, birds will fly, and fish will swim. Go home and enjoy it, and let the rest go."

"You mean let Jack go?" P.J. whispered.

"He's a thousand years in the future. Out of your reach in so many ways. I know that you're strong enough to forget him. You must do so."

For a long moment the teenager from Hadley-by-Hudson looked back into the eyes of the Priestess of Dann, and neither spoke. Then P.J. whispered, "He's coming back, isn't he? That's why you're staying here, in this time, instead of bringing the Star to the future world yourself. You have to prepare for the final battle. Right?"

Eko hesitated and then nodded. "That's very clever of you, and you're right. If Jack can use the Blue Star to save his father, then the final showdown will be in this day and age. It will be a terrible fight, on the fringes of the earth, with light and dark hanging in the balance. I say it one more time, because I like you and respect you. Let this go. It's not your cause, your problem, or your fate."

P.J. stood and a strange calmness came over her as she made an enormous decision in a heartbeat. "I love him," she told Eko, "and I can never forget what I felt when I held that blue gem. I'm making his cause my cause. You don't completely understand fate and my role in how this will all unfold. You can't send me away, because I helped Jack this time and I may be able to help him again, in some way that you can't foresee. Wherever we have to go, whatever we have to do, I'm ready to help Jack and try to save his world."

"Okay," Eko murmured back. "We may never be friends, but we're not enemies. Welcome to the cause."

She held out her hand and P.J. took it.

✸

PART THREE

30

The cavern is pitch-dark and numbingly cold, but by far the worst of it is the quakes. They seem to come most frequently at night, when I lie with my eyes closed and try to sleep. It's a total farce because anything resembling sleep is impossible under these conditions, at least for me. I'm trapped in a waking nightmare and I'm pretty sure the only way out is death, which is now knocking on the door, or at least thumping furiously on the walls.

Boom, boom, boom, the cave chamber shakes. Dust and ice filter down over my back.

My mother, who is lying next to me, shifts in her sleep. I know she's a warrior queen, but I don't get how she can nod off and snore away when we may be frozen solid or buried by a cave-in at any second.

On my other side lies a ninja priest, who is apparently my second cousin, also sleeping. He's been a faithful bodyguard during our trip, but when the cavern walls come down around us, he'll be as helpless as I will. The remnants of the noble house of Dann will all be entombed together, except for my father who is scheduled to be executed in twelve hours.

Then it will really be over.

There's a lull in the seismic rumblings and I doze off into the restless half sleep that has become very familiar. I'm neither awake nor asleep, neither consciously thinking nor freely dreaming.

Fearful memories from our four-day journey to this cavern recur in the darkness, often with such vividness that I find my fingers gripping the handle of my scimitar.

My mother and I are flying over a dry oasis bed on a speeding sand sled when a faint buzz swells to an earsplitting roar and locusts darken the sky. We manage to outrun them, but some members of our group aren't so lucky. Two ninja priests scrape a dune and tumble off their sled. Before they can get back on, the dark swarm engulfs them.

We are camped beneath the stars and my mother begins telling me how she met my father. We're both so engrossed in the moment of family bonding that neither of us notices the giant lizard that emerges from a sand dune.

A sentry shouts a last-second alarm as the lizard leaps at us!

I somersault out of the way of its snapping jaws, and then fight side by side with my mother, hacking with my scimitar at the garbage-truck-size reptile that swings its spiked tail back and forth like an angry stegosaurus.

We are climbing into hills that provide no shelter, only new horrors. Freshly hatched flying snakes greet us, hungry for their first good meal. They are both venomous and constrictors, and can flatten their bodies to glide on air currents. We watch helplessly as a bodyguard gets tangled up in an airborne scaly knot, and is squeezed and fanged into a red and bony pulp.

Ice storms pelt us. Ping-pong-ball-size hail is bad enough, but they soon become icy baseballs, fired down by a vicious fastballer in the clouds.

The dark entrance to a cavern looms ahead. We dive in to escape the hail. As we start to trudge downhill I can hear the *bam-bam* of what sounds like frozen basketballs pounding the rocky roof above our heads.

Then come the quakes and the bitter cold of the deep caves.

Horrific images pinwheel around me as I lie there half-awake—giant lizards and famished locusts, flying snakes and ice storms.

Worst of all, it was all for nothing. We're now huddled in the dark near a cave opening, a mere twenty miles from the Fortress of Aighar. But if we so much as stick one toe out of this cavern, Dark Army drones will annihilate us.

My father is probably eating his last meal of wurfle egesta or beginning his final torture session, or whatever the deathwatch custom is in Dark Army headquarters. And we're no more able to help him than we were four days ago. We risked our lives for nothing. We will freeze to death here, pinned down inside the cave by the Dark Army drones that crisscross the skies outside.

I must have slipped off to sleep because I am now surely dreaming. It begins snowing in our cave! These aren't random chunks of ice that have been dislodged from the rocky ceiling by quakes. These are soft, wet flakes, falling thick and fast. I turn my face upward, and I can feel them float down onto my cheeks and forehead.

In fact, I can see them! In this strange dream I'm having, our cave is no longer pitch-dark. It's starting to shimmer around the edges with a sapphire luminescence that flickers off rock walls. But the bluish flames don't warm things up—in fact, it's getting much colder.

As I watch, the blue radiance stops flickering and grows more substantial, till it coalesces into one unblinking solid azure eye that watches me.

I get to my knees, then stand, drawn by its glow.

The rocky chamber has become so cold that I can barely bend my knees to walk forward.

I take one step, and then another, staring back into the cold blue eye. For a moment I see P.J.! She's framed against a lush green background. Can those be palm trees? I can tell that she's far away, but she somehow also feels very close.

She reaches out to me.

I hold out my hands to her.

"Jack?" she calls.

"I'm here, P.J.!" I shout back, and reach toward the blue eye, trying to poke through it to another world.

My fingers touch it and break some kind of barrier. It feels like reaching beneath the surface of a freezing lake. Then there's a thunderous roar that nearly knocks me off my feet. I duck down and cover my ears. It must be a cave-in! I'll be buried alive in seconds.

But no rocks fall on me.

"Jair?" It's my mother's voice.

I look up at her. She's standing, and so are the ninja priests. They're staring at my right hand, which is in a fist, still clamped tight to my ear. I lower it and slowly open my fingers. In the center of my palm is what looks like a pulsing blue teardrop.

The ninja priests drop to their knees, while my mother steps forward. "Well done, Eko," she whispers.

31

My mother and I stand together, waiting for a miracle. The Star of Dann is now resting in an ornate little chalice that sits between us on the cave floor. It's projecting a dark blue luminescence that covers the two of us like a sorcerer's cloak.

The ninja priests who accompanied us on our mission stand a little way off, watching and also waiting for something amazing to occur.

The dark blue light makes my arms and neck tingle, but that hardly qualifies as a miracle. Ten minutes pass and the suspense starts to wear off. Finally I walk outside the sheet of blue radiance, head over to a nearby rock, and sit down. "Are you sure this is going to work?" I ask. "Whatever that blue thingamajig is supposed to do, it's sure taking a long time to get going."

An odd thing happens. The ninja priests don't seem to hear my question. None of them even throw me a glance. Their eyes remain riveted on the Star of Dann.

A few seconds later, my mom also steps outside the mantle of blue light, and I notice that they don't react to her movement, either. "They can't see us," she answers my questioning gaze. "And they can't hear us or smell us."

"Why not?" I ask. "I can see you clearly."

"And I can see you and hear you, Jair." She nods.

"Jack," I remind her.

"But to everyone outside the protection of the Star of Dann, we have become ghosts," she tells me.

That's a little hard to swallow. I don't feel like a phantom. I'm still one hundred and seventy-five pounds of Jack Danielson, unshaven, hungry, and slightly frostbitten from my long night in the cave. I walk over to the ninja priests and wave my arms at them. They don't even give me a glance.

One of them has been a hard-ass toward me the whole trip. He's a sour-faced little man who was always telling me what to do or ordering me to keep quiet. I throw a punch at him, and stop my fist an inch before his nose. He looks at me and right through me. I step right in front of him and jab my finger at his eyeball. He doesn't even blink.

"Are you done yet?" my mother asks.

"Not quite yet," I tell her. I crouch down in front of the curmudgeonly ninja and say, "Yo, lemon-face. I think you've got cave lice. And you need a bath."

He scratches his nose and goes on staring at the Star of Dann in the silver cup.

"We don't have time to joke around," my mother reminds me. "We've got to get your father out of the fortress."

"That should be a lot easier to do now that we're invisible," I point out. "Are our weapons invisible, too?"

"Clothes, weapons, and whatever you were carrying when the Blue Star touched you."

"Then let's go get Dad," I say, gripping the handle of my scimitar. "But are you sure this cloak of invisibility will work at long range?"

"I don't know," she confesses. "That's why you're going to bring the Blue Star with us." She walks over to the chalice.

"Don't you mean *we're* bringing it with us?"

"You must carry it. You are the Prince of Dann."

"You're the Queen of Dann," I point out. To be honest, I'm a little afraid that the Star of Dann may be pissed off at me for dumping it in an Amazon backwater.

"I married into the royal family, but you are your father's son, of the direct blood lineage of Dann himself. He found the Star and you must carry it with you to light our way."

She picks up the chalice and tips the Star of Dann out into a tiny silver locket that dangles on a thin chain. "Wear it around your neck."

As she pours the star from chalice to locket, the ninja priests look startled.

I try to imagine it from their point of view. If my mom's right, and they can't see us, then it must look to them like the Blue Star just floated up from the silver cup, and is levitating three feet above the cave floor.

I reach out and take the chain from her, and gently snap the locket shut. The Blue Star dwindles to a spark, as if settling comfortably into its new home.

The ninja priests freak out. "It's gone!" one of them shouts, jumping up and grasping his sword.

"They're gone, too!" a second one observes. "The Queen and the beacon of hope! They must have taken it!"

"Or it's taken them! What do we do now, Donnerell?" they ask their leader.

"Stay and wait," he answers softly. "It's all up to them now."

32

We emerge from black cave into dark night. Clouds blot out the moon and stars so thoroughly that it's easy to imagine we're still deep inside the cavern. But a numbing night wind blasts my face, so we must indeed be aboveground, out in the open, heading for the dreaded Fortress of Aighar.

Eko taught me to pick my footing through blackness, but traversing what feels like the Himalayas without a flashlight is tricky. A single misstep on one of the ice patches and I'll plummet down a fissure, taking the Star of Dann and all hope for the future with me.

My mom walks ahead of me, picking the best path, and I'm pretty sure that a mountain goat couldn't do a better job. We don't exchange a word, even telepathically. She's completely focused on the mission ahead, and I guess that's understandable. She's not only trying to save her husband, but she's also attempting to turn the tide of a centuries-old war that is all but lost.

I remind myself that she's been fighting since she was a little girl. If we don't succeed today, everything she's loved and striven for will be lost. In the darkness, I listen to her footsteps, steady, confident, and determined.

We're wearing goggles to ward off the glare, which even in darkness radiates up from the mountainside. The hoods of our coats have bands that stretch over our mouths like scarves and act as air enhancers. We're at a pretty high altitude, in a world with a damaged atmosphere, and even with help it's hard to get a good breath.

The first light of dawn glazes the high peaks, and I glimpse a bleak and lifeless landscape. It's a mountain wasteland, an alpine desert, with not a tree or a hut or even a stray wildflower to soften the desolation.

Drones buzz overhead, but they don't slow down to give us so much as a look or a sniff. They can scan for shapes and movement, for body heat, and even for telepathic thought, but they can't spot ghosts.

I walk next to my mother and match her silence and moodiness. My own emotions are strong and complicated. I'm about to try to save the man who abandoned me as a child. I don't want him to die, but I also don't know how I'll react when I see him.

The sun is higher now—its unfiltered radiation does a slow burn through the layers of my protective coat.

We round a craggy precipice and I see a thin ribbon up ahead, snaking through the peaks and valleys. It's a road, but it's not yellow brick and filled with dancing Munchkins. It's as black as pitch, and I'm pretty sure that instead of leading us to the Emerald City of Oz it will take us straight to hell.

Still, a road is a road, and my mother heads right for it. Soon we're jogging side by side on a six-foot-wide pathway of crushed black stones. It's hard to run this way in high altitude, but we have no choice. My father is set to die at noon, and the sun has already separated from the jagged horizon.

My mother runs in a steady rhythm, barely breathing harder as we climb steep slopes or changing her running motion as we speed down into cleft valleys. She would have definitely challenged the leaders in the New York Marathon.

For a moment I flash back to Central Park, and my run around the reservoir on the night that launched me on this adventure. It's a good thing I was in training. I'm more than twenty years younger than my mom, and I can barely keep up with her.

Our narrow pathway joins another thoroughfare, and then merges with a third one. We are soon on a wider roadway, and we spot other travelers.

They're wrapped up to protect themselves from the extremes of temperature and the radiation. Even so, I can see that none of them are fully human. It's a Via Appia full of Frankensteins of nature—chimeras and cyborgs with jumbled DNA and skulls full of microcircuits.

I glimpse hideous features beneath hoods and fur hats— viperlike fangs flash behind red lips, and machine-cold eyes gleam from otherwise human faces. They're all either traveling on foot or riding nematodes—none are flying with antigravity jackets or zipping around on levitation sleds. I guess the Dark Army likes to control its airspace, and the drones will shoot down anything airborne.

A forbidding mountain looms in the distance. As we jog closer I recognize it, though it's hard to believe that such a thing could be man-made, or rather Dark Army–made. This was the terrifying image the computer wiz showed us in the Dannites' subterranean desert hideout. In real life it's even more menacing— the biggest, baddest castle of the Dark Ages, rendered creepier by futuristic science.

At its base, licking up with a thousand poisonous tongues, is the river of acid. The metal walls rise above it to such heights that they dwarf the surrounding mountains. At the top I glimpse the battlements that can slide to chomp on unwanted airborne visitors.

The road we're following is the only way in. "Let's join these cyborgs," my mother says to me, and falls in behind three tall, black-cloaked figures. "When the gate opens for them, we'll slip in."

"Sounds good," I tell her. "What do we do when we get inside? Do you think there's an escalator to the roof?"

She doesn't look amused. I guess using humor to take the edge off a scary situation isn't appreciated by the royal family of Dann. "Careful," she warns. "Here come the guards. They can't see you, hear you, or smell you, but their senses are acute. If you so much as kick a tiny pebble, they'll devour us."

33

Two large shapes bound toward us on four legs. As they draw closer, I shiver. They're beautiful and horrible at the same time. Powerful legs drive their large, low-slung torsos forward, tufted tails lash the air, and their ferocious yet noble faces are framed by flowing red-brown manes. Lions!

The three cyborgs stop walking, and don't move so much as a biomechanical finger. My mother also stands stock-still, and I freeze-tag myself.

"Are they real?" I ask her, watching their flowing manes and flashing teeth as they gallop toward us and growl deep-throated warnings.

"Of course not," she answers. "The last real lions went extinct in the middle of the twenty-first century, with all the other big cats. These are clones made from stored DNA, engineered to follow commands and report back to overseers inside the fortress."

Her answer saddens me, and also makes me feel personally responsible. So the King of the Beasts died out in my own century. Some of the cubs I saw in zoos on family trips must have ended up among the last members of their species.

I read somewhere that 10,000 years ago the two large land

mammals most widely spread on earth were lions and humans. Lions were in Africa, Asia, India, and all through the Middle East. How strange that man should have taken over and destroyed the earth, while the lions—far stronger in every way—were hunted down, herded onto game reserves and into zoos, and driven out of existence.

The lion guards reach us. They have handsome, leonine faces with red eyes that glow unnaturally, lit from inside. As they stand sniffing and growling, their bloodred eyes flash over the cyborg travelers, scanning them.

My mother and I wait motionless a few paces back. The lions are enormous—they must each weigh five hundred pounds. But they're also keenly sensitive—I can see their noses and ears twitching. Something tells me that they would not hesitate to charge an invisible foe, and that being pinned down by those enormous paws and torn apart by those jaws would not be a pleasant way to die.

I guess the three travelers check out okay, because the lion sentries bound away as quickly as they came, and we all proceed down the road toward the castle.

As we draw close to it, I inhale an acrid smell that creeps inside my throat and nostrils and makes me cough and gag.

"That's the acid in the moat," my mother cautions me, hearing me struggle for breath. "Be very careful."

"What am I supposed to do about it?" I try to ask, but I can't get the words out. The acid is setting fire to my lungs! The air enhancers we're using don't seem able to filter out the noxious stench. Mom, help! I shout out to her telepathically. I can't breathe!

Try to hold your breath! she suggests. *We just have to make it across the bridge.*

It's hard to hold your breath when you don't have much breath to hold. I lock my lips together, clamp my nostrils shut with my fingers, and follow the three cyborgs out onto the bridge.

They don't seem affected by the fumes—I guess their lungs are more robotic than human.

The bridge is wide and dark—a great iron plank. As we start across, I have the strange feeling that the river of acid beneath is alive and aware of us. It bubbles up higher and hisses suspiciously.

The moat can't be more than fifty feet wide, but the trek across the bridge seems endless. I can't keep my mouth shut any longer, so I rip a bead off the necklace that Eko gave me long ago when we went diving on the Outer Banks, and open my mouth to swallow it. As soon as my lips part, the acid fumes force their way in.

One whiff of the bubbling brew nearly knocks me off my feet. I cough and feel faint but just before I topple over, the condensed oxygen from Eko's bead kicks in and I'm suddenly okay again.

I glance at my mother. The Queen of Dann is too proud to complain, but she looks like she's about to asphyxiate. I offer her a bead. Mom, this will help you breathe.

She swallows the bead and nods gratefully. And then she sends me an urgent message: *Don't let the vapors touch you!*

Up ahead, I see that the crimson and black tongues licking upward from the acid river have geysered high above the bridge and completely encircled the cyborgs. It looks like they're captive inside a living, probing mist. The miasma shifts and billows, and its grasping tentacle-like edges come within inches of me. I jerk away, but there's not much room to dodge.

What's happening? I ask my mother.

They're being checked one last time before being granted admission to the fortress.

Checked how?

Validated as Dark Army down to the cellular level. When they were created, I.D. markers were planted in their DNA. If the vapors brush you, all is lost.

Easy advice to give, but nearly impossible to follow, as bright tongues from the river flick around us.

My mother and I bob and weave, duck and jump, like two shadowboxers in the fight of our lives. Somehow we keep from being touched.

The vapors finally recede back into the moat, and the cyborgs walk forward again. The bridge appears to lead smack into the metal wall of the castle, but as we get close a spider crack appears on the metallic facade. I see that it's the outline of a semicircular door.

The cyborgs are now five feet from the metal wall, and we're right behind them. The spider crack thickens and darkens, and suddenly the portal slides open. The cyborgs hurry inside, and my mother and I dash forward and just make it in before the doorway seals back up.

We're in a small, dark transitional space—not inside the fortress yet but no longer outside. A strong wind blows so hard that it almost knocks me over. Then I realize it's not blowing but rather air is being sucked out with such force that I feel my skin stretching off my face and my hair is yanked straight up. What's going on? I ask my mom as an orange light flashes across the tiny chamber.

Re-oxygenation and sterilization. They're just making sure no unwanted pathogens get in.

The wind blows again, more gently, as new air is pumped in, and then the other side of the air lock opens and we step out into the Fortress of Aighar.

34

It's a crowded, cavernous space that reminds me of an Escher drawing with stairways leading to other stairways and hallways that seem to bend in upon themselves. The three cyborgs hurriedly walk off and my mother and I stay by the door, taking it in.

If there's safety in being lost in a throng then we should be more secure in this bustling chaos, but to me it feels more threatening. For the first time I see the population that intends to take over what's left of the earth, and I start to understand what fate my parents spent all these years fighting against.

Dark Army life-forms are all around us, designed for survival under the increasingly harsh conditions of a deteriorating world. They've shed their coats and hats because the temperature inside the fortress is regulated, and I see them clearly as they pass.

Some of them might almost be human if one or two features hadn't been augmented with the DNA of another species. They are the saddest to me, because something inside me wants to reach out to them and call them brother. Then I see their mechanical eyes or taloned hands and know that there's no kinship possible.

Others appear to have crawled straight out of a medieval bestiary—nightmarish creatures that are too freakish to be characterized as human, animal, or cyborg, let alone mammal, reptile, or amphibian. Their genetic reshufflings may have given them a better chance in the survival of the fittest, but a steep price was paid for that. I peer into their eyes as they pass and it's very clear they are not of nature—they all appear soulless. Their creators, in appropriating God's power to fashion new life-forms, seem to have lost the spark of the divine.

I shiver, and my mother puts her hand on my shoulder.

"Let's go," she says softly, and we randomly choose a corridor and start down it.

We are soon in a labyrinth of endlessly corkscrewing tunnels. "So how do we find our way upstairs to Dad?" I ask. "Do you have a map of this place?"

"No, we'll have to ask directions," Mom replies.

I look around at the Dark Army life-forms walking and crawling and slithering past. "I don't think they'll be helpful. Do you think there's an information booth?"

"We'll ask one of those guys in black with the stars on their shoulder," she says. "They're Fortress Enforcers—special guards. They probably know all the secret passages that are closed to normal travelers."

She nods toward an eight-foot-tall guard standing a short way off. He's got six mechanical eyes spread out on all sides of his head so that as he walks he's able to see in all directions at once. The outfit that he's wearing is black from head to foot. A single gray "Eye" insignia glistens on his shoulder.

"I don't think he's going to want to help us, either," I tell my mom.

"Probably not," she agrees. "But we're not going to give him a choice."

35

We trail the Enforcer through the maze of tunnels, waiting for our chance. His job seems to be to move around constantly and watch everyone. It's a bit ironic that this six-eyed surveillance freak doesn't realize that he himself is being followed.

Finally he enters a gloomy and relatively deserted corridor. Up ahead, an even darker side passage appears.

"Now's our chance," my mother says. "Let's grab him and drag him in there."

"Won't he immediately send out a telepathic SOS to every guard in the fortress?" I ask.

"Yes," she agrees, and pulls what looks like a purple felt pad from a pocket. It's encased in some kind of transparent wrapper, and I notice that she handles it with great care. The purple blob flattens and elongates itself, trying to escape. "This is a thought leech. Once I get it on him, it will suck up every telepathic message he sends out."

"But even if we do get him in our power, why would he help us?" I ask. "He's a cyborg. I'm sure he'd rather die than betray his creators."

"No doubt," she agrees. "Come on, Jair. Let's go!"

We creep closer to the Enforcer. His mechanical eyes, coupled with the fact that his head can rotate completely around, make him appear very robotic, but as we trail him I start to glimpse his human side. He swings his arms jauntily as he walks, and as he tromps deeper into the gloomy corridor he starts to make a strange noise that rises and falls. I listen and begin to suspect that it's the cyborg equivalent of whistling or humming a happy tune.

"Get ready, Jair. I'll hit him high and you grab him low," Mom says. "We've got to drag him off into the darkness before anyone else sees."

The dim tunnel is momentarily deserted and the dark side passage is now a few paces away.

"One," my mother says, inching near him. "Two."

I move up with her, so that we're both just a step behind the Enforcer.

She fumbles with the wrapper that holds the thought leech. "Three!" she announces, leaping up like a basketball player pulling down a tough rebound, and grabbing the Enforcer from behind in a choke hold.

The cyborg is jerked backward, and for a split second he's too startled to react. My mother yanks his head back and clamps the purple leech onto his forehead. The leech almost instantly begins to engorge, sucking up alarms.

The cyborg tries to fight his way out of the choke hold, but it's tough to break free when the Queen of Dann herself is holding you from behind. He rocks back and forth, but I take out both his knees with a diving tackle. He's strong as hell and fighting desperately, but he has no idea what hit him and he can't see any targets to punch or kick.

We drag him into the shadowy side passage and force him to the stone floor.

The thought leech on his forehead has swelled to the size of a softball. Old six-eyes must be trying to send out SOS calls on all hailing frequencies.

"Hold him down," Mom orders me, and I tie him up with one of Eko's most reliable jujitsu holds. He's tremendously strong, and strains and bucks wildly to get loose. I can't hold him this way for long, but luckily I don't have to.

Mom releases her choke hold and spins away. In a second, she's kneeling on the Enforcer's chest. Her right hand dips into a pocket and re-emerges holding a small mechanical device. It has a tiny monitor screen connected to two long sharp prongs that look a bit like curved knitting needles.

She takes a prong in either hand, snakes her body up the cyborg's torso so that her knees are pressing down on his shoulders, and with all her strength she jams the prongs deep into his ears.

The Enforcer goes into agonized contortions as the mechanical device switches on and makes a shrill whirring sound, like a food processor.

"What's it doing to him?" I ask her.

"Draining his brain."

"You mean downloading it?"

"No," she says. "Draining it of everything. Human thoughts and memories and mechanical commands and memory chips."

"Will it kill him?"

"Of course," she says. "He will be an empty shell in less than five seconds. There, it's over."

The Enforcer writhes one final time and then lies still.

My mother disconnects the mechanical device, leaving the prongs embedded in his ears. She's careful not to touch the thought leech, which is now the size of a basketball. The moment the cyborg dies, the leech stops growing. It detaches from his forehead, drops off onto the floor, and starts squirming around.

"Careful, Jair. It's looking for a new host," Mom cautions.

We step around the bloated parasite and drag the dead cyborg farther into the shadows, till his body is hidden.

My mother manipulates her device and studies the tiny screen, scrolling quickly through what I assume are different areas of the cyborg's drained memories. "He was programmed with the full blueprint of the castle," she notes triumphantly. "There's a secret riser for guards that will shoot us right up to the roof."

"Is that like a back elevator?" I ask.

She's studying the screen with great concentration. "The problem is that in order to go up we'll have to go down first. We've got to pass through the labs." She steps over the cyborg's body and says, "Come, Jair. The execution is less than an hour away. If they move your father from his cell, we'll never find him in time."

I follow her out. As I step over the cyborg's corpse, I glance at his face, frozen in final death agony. I can't stop myself from feeling a little sorry for him. He may have been a Dark Army cyborg Enforcer, but part of him was very human. I recall the way he hummed as he walked down the dark corridor. No organism that hums in the dark deserves to have its brain drained.

36

We follow a series of sloping passageways down into the basement of the giant fortress. My mother now knows the layout of the place, and she sets a brisk pace.

The lower we descend, the more the security tightens. There are guard stations and scanning devices at every bend. None of them can detect us, but I find myself wondering what needs to be so closely guarded. "What kind of lab are we headed toward?" I ask my mother. "Is it their weapons factory? What exactly do they make there?"

"What should never be made," she answers cryptically, and then we stop before a massive closed door. It must be fifty feet high and thirty feet wide, and looks absolutely impenetrable. I remember that according to Dante, the words "Abandon hope, all ye who enter here" were inscribed on the gates of hell. This massive door has no such legend, but I get a very similar vibe.

I consider trying to hack it apart with my scimitar, or blow it apart with one of the Big Popper bombs from the Dann's arsenal, but my mother waves me back. "The bombs wouldn't even put a dent in it," she assures me. "Anyway, if you so much as brush it with your finger, they'll know we're here. Let's wait for someone to let us in."

It's hard to just stand and wait. My father has reached his final hour and the remaining seconds are ticking away fast. Finally, footsteps approach.

A doctorly-looking chimera appears, part man and part rodent. He's wearing a mask over his rat's face, and his knee-length robe could almost be a lab coat. He stops before the door and stares up at the ceiling. A spinning circular yellow hologram descends over his head. It whirls around him for a few seconds, no doubt authenticating his iris patterns or brainwaves for one final identity verification. Then the gate to hell slides soundlessly open.

Dr. Rat heads inside, and we hurry in on his heels.

It's a netherworld of shimmering darkness that not even Dante could have imagined. Vials and beakers glimmer, their phosphorescence set off by what I assume are ultraviolet lights. The black lights are beyond the spectrum visible to the human eye, but the photoluminescence of the lab equipment creates an eerie, spectral glow.

In what might almost be the strobe light of a disco, I glimpse computers and long robotic arms with dozens of tendril-like fingers that manipulate infinitely delicate machinery. Here and there lab workers pad about, but most of the work in this place is clearly done by machine.

We walk through the lab, which is bigger than five football fields, and frightening sounds ring out around us. There are soft animal yelps and plaintive wolf-like howls, and the whimpers of what sounds like human babies crying for their mothers. Inside test tubes and vials I glimpse glowing eyes and tiny, grasping hands, and I start to realize what is being cooked up in this vast test kitchen.

It's a maternity ward without mothers, a hatchery and neonatal facility and assembly line for the soulless world to come. Machines are creating new and hardier life-forms, cloning cells and nurturing them on gels, combining species and machines to create ever funkier variations.

I can't bear to look but I also can't possibly look away, because if I trip on something or knock over a beaker, our presence will be revealed. So my unwilling eyes have to take in the whole freak show exhibit by exhibit, cyclopean embryos, hybrid fetuses and half-mechanical hatchlings, wailing webbed newborns that look like they were created by taking something from column A and something completely different from column B.

And yet they're still babies—that's what's most terrible about it! They still cry and suck milk from artificial teats and stare at the world inquisitively through glowing, technology-enhanced eyes.

As the horror show swirls around me, I momentarily flash back to Eko sitting on the roof of a beach house on the Outer Banks and telling me for the first time that I was living during the Turning Point. The world I grew up in, the beautiful earth I romped around in as a child, was at a critical crossroads, she said. She looked very sad as she sat there, and I knew that she was comparing the natural beauty all around us to some nightmarish future.

Now, walking through the Dark Army laboratory, I can't help wondering if this could really have been averted. Was there a road not taken one thousand years ago, a last chance not grasped by my generation? Or was the downward spiral preordained—were we as a species simply not smart enough or wise enough to be entrusted with the stewardship of our beautiful planet?

"Come," my mother whispers, taking my hand and leading me through the maze. "We're near the riser to the roof."

"Good," I tell her. "I've had enough. Let's get out of here."

Beyond the labs I see what looks like a black glass column rising from the floor into the high ceiling. It's as thick as a sequoia, and guarded by three Enforcers.

"Let's go find your father," my mom whispers, and steps toward an opening at the base of the glass pillar.

37

We pick our way between the three Enforcers and reach the opening in the black column. My mother steps inside and vanishes, like a letter into a mail chute. I hesitate a second and then follow her in.

The upward thrust is staggering. It's like blasting off in a rocket, except that there's no spacecraft around me. I'm not sure what's propelling me upward, but at this rate I'll smash right through the roof.

A heartbeat later I pop out into darkness. "Mom?"

"This way, Jair."

I follow the sound of her voice. A wall slides open and we find ourselves stepping out into bright daylight.

The view is dizzying. We're on the very top of the fortress, looking down at the mountains. The razor-toothed battlements are all around us, and I can see the windowless cell tower with its guardian gargoyle.

The demon is perched atop that windowless cell, squatting and immobile, like the grotesque figures on Notre Dame. But I sense that this gargoyle wasn't put here to spout off unwanted water or to ward off evil. He's intended as a last line of defense, and his glowing scarlet eyes tell me he's fierce and ever vigilant.

"We're just in time," my mother tells me. "Here they come for your father."

A door opens in a minaret a few hundred yards from us and four dark figures set out toward the windowless cell. Two incredibly powerful-looking Enforcers lead the way, holding double-headed laser axes. Their arms and legs are as thick as tree trunks and they walk hunched over, as if they are part picked palace guard and part lowland gorilla.

A short, wizened figure in a black coat and hood trails them, swinging a censer that emits thick black smoke. He reminds me of the Mysterious Kidah—the great wizard of the future who I met in the Amazon. This is not only a world of cyborgs and chimeras, but also of spells and prophecy, when science and magic have merged. I've seen Kidah in action, and I can only guess what dark spells this Dark Army warlock has at his command.

The enormous, simian guards and the micro Merlin are bad enough, but it is the final figure that makes me shudder. Even from a distance, his graceful and cocky walk, his broad shoulders and handsome, middle-aged features remind me of an older version of Dargon or a younger Dark Lord. I know at a glance that he is a member of that same bloody royal family, come to extract final vengeance on the King of Dann.

The four dark figures head straight for the cell. My mother is right—I can tell from their purposeful demeanor that they've come to take my father to his execution.

We hurry over and join the grim procession. They can't see us, hear us, or smell us, but I have the feeling they sense that something is amiss. The two Enforcers look fidgety, the tall cowled figure swings his censer in ever widening arcs so that the smoke billows ominously, and the broad-shouldered scion of the Dark Army's royal family turns to throw several backward glances right at us and through us.

I look into his swirling, anthracite-black eyes and recall Dargon on the lip of the volcano, and the Dark Lord in his candirú chamber. Dargon had raptorlike eyes and the strength of a bull, and the Dark Lord was part man and part tarantula. Their middle-aged relative who I now encounter atop the fortress is also clearly a chimera.

His handsome, chiseled features could have made him a soap opera star a thousand years ago, but when he opens his mouth I see a pink forked tongue. While his face and neck have human skin, his hands are plated with green scales. He's got plenty of reptile in him, and something tells me he's more cobra or Gila monster than garden snake or friendly gecko.

As the procession nears the cell, they slow and let the hooded sorcerer take the lead. He looks up at the roof of the cell, staring right at its guardian demon.

Now that we're close, I can see the gargoyle clearly. It's more than twice the height of a human, with pointed ears and a face like a feral cat. Corded muscles stand out on its long, sleek body. It's sitting on its haunches, staring down suspiciously. It can't possibly know that my mother and I have joined the queue, but as we approach it rises from its sitting position and edges forward. It draws back its lips to bare its teeth and emits a guttural growl that would frighten a tiger.

The procession instantly stops. Even the two lowland gorilla Enforcers aren't stupid enough to take on this hell troll.

The warlock hands his censer to one of the Enforcers, steps forward, and draws back his hood. I see his face, or what's left of it. Mostly it's just blood and bone—he's a walking skeleton! The zombie conjurer waves one hand and barks a curt command, as if ordering a dog to heel.

The gargoyle growls and refuses to back off. But the warlock shows no fear and repeats his command, and this time the gargoyle reluctantly uncurls its lips over its teeth and settles back into angry silence.

The four dark figures move forward again and reach the narrow door to the windowless cell. It appears to be made of solid gold, and its gleaming panels are engraved like the entrance to a cathedral. To me they look like visions of hell, but perhaps they're imagined renditions of what the world will be like under Dark Army control.

One of the gorilla Enforcers reaches out to open the golden door and then jerks back his arm and emits a howl of agony. I see that his hand and half his arm have been burned off. He falls onto his back and rolls around, wailing and clutching the still smoking stump.

The other members of the group seem to think this is hilarious. For a moment the tension is broken as they share a chuckle. Then the zombie sorcerer steps forward again.

He unbuttons the top of his robe and draws it apart. His body is a moldering mess of flesh and bone, blood and pus, festering mold and crawling maggots, as if he's been dead for months. Suddenly something flashes brilliantly from deep inside him. For a moment, his ribs and inner organs are lit from within. The flash originates on the left side of his chest, where his heart should be. Instead of a heart, I believe it's some sort of key to this cell's door.

There's a corresponding flash from the ornate gold door, which then begins to slowly open.

The dark figures pass through the narrow doorway one by one and my mother follows them. I hesitate, feeling dizzy at the enormity of the moment: everything that has happened since I fled from Hadley-by-Hudson more than a year ago has brought me here—to this slit of a doorway leading into a dark cell. I sense that my father is inside—a man who I don't know at all, but already love and hate. In many ways it was easier for me to swim to the bottom of the Atlantic or canoe to the lost regions of the Amazon than to cross this threshold.

I take a breath and force myself to walk in.

38

An old man with white hair lies on a platform in the center of the cell. His arms and legs are bound with golden ropes, so that he lies flat on his back looking up at us. He doesn't react in any way to his visitors, and his face seems frozen in a death scowl of defiant agony. I fear we're too late.

Then he very slowly turns his head to peer at the dark figures who have crowded into his cell, and his mouth opens. "Food," he rasps in a dry voice. "Water."

The reptilian Prince of the Dark Army's royal family steps forward to look down at my dad, and his hatred makes him almost drip snake venom. "No, Simeon, I haven't come to ease your suffering. Exactly the opposite."

My father looks back up at him, and licks his parched lips. "Then let us go into the sunlight," he whispers.

"We will go soon," the Dark Prince assures him. "Thousands are waiting to watch. But don't be in a rush. What we have prepared for you will take hours from start to finish. So let's savor every moment of it."

If these words scare my father, he doesn't show it. "When you are ready, I am also," he whispers. "We will go out into the blessed sunlight."

He turns his head toward the doorway and blinks at the bright sunlight. I've visualized him in several out-of-body experiences during my adventures. Seeing him now in person is a very different thing.

As if sensing my presence, he looks right at me and I see his face more clearly. He's got my features—my nose, my cleft chin, and my blue eyes. Or, I suppose more accurately, I have his. Our eyes meet and I suddenly feel such a deep kinship with this help-less stranger that all feelings of anger are swept away. I want to run up and touch his face and speak to him, and relieve his suf-fering.

I take a step forward, and my mother puts out a warning hand. "Wait, Jair. Don't do anything till they untie him, or we'll never get him out."

When she speaks to me, my father looks right at us, as if he can see us, and he gives a tiny smile. His parched lips twist up-ward, and his blue eyes sparkle.

He's not as old as I initially thought—not really an old man. But his hair and beard have turned as white as snow and his deeply lined face has endured so much for so long that it is a bat-tlefield of suffering.

"Take your time," he whispers to the Dark Prince. "Why should we be in a rush on such a magnificent day?"

"He's lost his mind, my lord," the Enforcer observes almost apologetically. "A shame."

"I guarantee you he has enough mind left to feel what I've prepared for him," the Dark Prince replies. "For hundreds of years these dogs of Dann have nipped at our heels. Today the last one will die nerve by nerve. When he utters his final cry for mercy, the long battle will be over and the future will be ours." He smiles down at my father. "Do you understand that, my dear cousin?"

"I understand everything," my father replies softly. "There's a rat that crawls into this cell at night through a tiny hole. I can hear him and smell him and sometimes I even talk to him. He's a smart rat, and he only comes for conversation because there's nothing here for a rat to eat." For a moment my dad's mad old eyes flash contemptuously as he stares up at the Dark Prince. "I can hear you and smell you and there's nothing left here for you to consume, either. So you must be just another sad rat that has crawled in for the conversation."

"And I can smell you, you reeking old cur!" the Dark Prince fires back, and kicks my father in the side of the jaw with the toe of his boot.

It's a vicious blow, which resounds in the small room like a pistol shot. My father's head jerks sideways.

I can't bear to watch this. Again I start forward, and my mother tries to stop me. But this time she's a second too late. I kick a pebble across the floor.

The Dark Prince wheels around. His reflexes are lightning fast. "What was that?"

"What, my lord?" the Enforcer asks, raising his two-headed ax. "I heard nothing."

"Analam, what was it?" the Dark Prince asks the zombie warlock. "Are we alone here?"

"Alone and not alone," the living skeleton hisses back. "Perhaps the spirits of Dann have come to escort their King to the other side. Let us see." He swings his censer and mutters an incantation. The dark smoke curls around us and seems to stick to us.

I feel a tingling similar to what I felt when the Star of Dann turned us invisible. But this time it has the opposite reaction. Looking down I can see faint lines where my limbs are, as if someone is sketching me as a stick figure, and slowly shading it darker and darker.

The Dark Prince draws his sword. "Whatever they are," he bellows, "kill them!"

39

Jair," my mother commands, "strike now!" As she says it, she ducks out of the way of the simian Enforcer's ax blow and draws her laser saber.

I pull out the haft of my scimitar and telepathically switch on its ten-foot sapphire blade. I'm hoping that the Dark Prince can't see the weapon yet, but when I swing it at him he must glimpse its outline because he leaps out of the way with a speed I've only seen twice before. He's not only a blood relative of Dargon and the Dark Lord, but he also apparently trained in the same Dark Army martial arts academy.

He probes the air delicately with the point of his sword, as if searching the ether for me. I circle, and see out the corner of one eye that my mother has sliced the Enforcer in two and turned to face the zombie sorcerer.

The Dark Prince slashes at me with a lightning stroke that I barely manage to parry. The force of his blow knocks the scimitar spinning out of my hands.

I dive to get it, but the clattering sound it makes when it hits the floor tells the Dark Prince exactly where I'm headed. He anticipates my dive, leaps toward the spot, and aims what would surely be a deathblow at me.

But his leap takes him over my father's tied-down body. Somehow my dad is able to raise his head several inches and grab the Dark Prince's right boot in his teeth. The Prince pulls his foot loose as he flies through the air, but Dad's bite tugs him momentarily off balance and disturbs the downward arc of his sword swing.

I twist my body to avoid his death stroke and, at the same time, grab my scimitar and plant it upward. His sword misses me and then the Dark Prince stumbles a half step as he lands awkwardly and impales himself on the point of my scimitar. I thrust upward, and the sapphire blade cuts right through his chest and pokes out through his back. His forked tongue flicks out one final time as he makes a gurgling noise that rises to a shrill, high-pitched scream.

No, I realize, the scream didn't come from him but rather from my mother. The zombie warlock has cast some spell on her that is forcing her backward, inch by inch, against her will. She is soon backed up against the cell's wall and she stands there helplessly, battling to be free but unable to move.

The sorcerer draws a long, ceremonial black dagger from a sheath and steps forward, raising it as if to sacrifice her.

I'm too far away to grab his arm so I hurl my scimitar end over end. He senses that it's coming and turns, just as the curved blade bites into his neck and decapitates him. The zombie's surprised shriek is cut short as his head falls to the floor and rolls into a corner. His body stays upright for several seconds as his bony arms thrash. Then his torso totters and falls.

As he dies, whatever invisible force is pinning my mom to the wall melts away. She quickly runs to my father and bends to examine him. He's tied to the platform by what appear to be thin golden cords that glisten like the ornate door to the cell. The cords are mere strands—they look so thin I'm positive I can snap them with my fingers. But when I grab them and yank, they hold tight. I try to saw through them with my scimitar, and I see my mother trying with her saber, but the golden cords don't even fray.

Meanwhile, an alarm is sounding from outside. I can hear it rise and fall, and I also hear a furious snarl.

Turning toward the doorway, I see the gargoyle peering in at us. He's too big to squeeze through the narrow doorway, but he's clearly enraged at what's going on inside.

"There's no way to cut him loose, Jair," my mother says.

"Go," my dad commands, and I see that he's far more in command of his senses than he let on to the Dark Prince. "You've done all you can. They'll be here in seconds. Save yourselves!"

"We're not going anywhere," I tell the King of Dann. Then I turn to my mother. "The ropes he's tied with look like they're made from the same material as the door."

She looks back at me. "How can that help us?"

I take the black dagger out of the hands of the dead zombie wizard and slice deeply into his chest. I cut through skin and bone, pus and maggots, and soon I've gutted him open, like a fish. The odor from his decaying corpse is nauseating, but I pry the two sides of his chest apart, and see something gleam on the left side where his heart should be. I stick my hand into that foul cavity, and pull out what looks almost like a mirror.

I hold it up toward the platform my father is tied to, and it gleams. The golden ropes flash in an answering gleam and fall away.

My father climbs slowly to his feet. He sways for a second, and I run over to brace him.

But the King of Dann recovers quickly. He picks up the sword that the Dark Prince dropped when he died. "Let's go," he says, and starts for the door.

It's not exactly a warm father-son reunion moment. Oh well—I suppose now's not the time to catch up. I grab my scimitar and follow him and my mom toward the door.

I can hear the gargoyle growling and snarling eagerly just outside, waiting for us.

40

The gargoyle is waiting for us right outside the only door, so we're going to have to exit another way.

I take out one of the Big Popper bombs that the armorer of Dann gave me and switch it on telepathically. I count in my mind—five, four, three, two . . . and then hurl it and we all lie flat. The explosion in the confined space is deafening, but when the dust clears I see that a hole has been blown in the far wall of the cell.

We squeeze out through the smoking hole and the gargoyle crawls toward us, fangs and claws slicing the air. Lumbering behind it I see the Enforcer who burned his arm off and was left behind by his fellows. He's holding his ax in his remaining hand, and swinging it back and forth with a vengeance.

"Split up!" my dad commands as the gargoyle gets close to us, and we separate as if we've practiced this tactic a hundred times.

The gargoyle knows who the most valuable prey is here. It launches itself in a soaring leap so that for a second it seems to take wing, and then it swoops straight down like a hawk toward my dad. Its jaws are gaping wide open and its talons gleam like a set of knives.

I'm sure it will shred my father. But before the hobgoblin can pounce on him, Dad goes airborne himself. I saw Eko execute high leaps on the Outer Banks, and she taught me that the secret was a kind of mental discipline. But I never saw Eko try anything remotely like what my dad does to meet the challenge of the flying gargoyle.

He pitches forward and rolls, and uses the momentum to

launch himself skyward. He times his leap so that he's rising just as the gargoyle is falling, and his flight path takes him behind the hell-troll.

Somehow the gargoyle manages to twist its body in midair just as my dad's sword falls on it. The blade bites into the heavily muscled shoulder of the hobgoblin, who lets out an earsplitting yowl of surprise and pain as it falls to earth.

The gash in its shoulder instantly heals itself. When the gargoyle turns to confront my mother and father again, it's just as strong as before and twice as angry.

I would like to watch round two, but I hear my mother shout, "Jair, watch out!" just as a double-headed ax swipes at my head.

I duck under it, and circle to my left, attacking the simian Enforcer from the side where he lost his arm. He pivots to protect his weak side, but he's a heartbeat too slow. My scimitar bites through his ribs, and he goes down screaming and shouting curses at me.

I wheel around to see how my mom and dad are faring with the gargoyle. They're swift and skilled fighters, but they don't have a chance. No matter how seriously they wound the creature, it immediately heals and comes after them again. They're tiring from the furious struggle, and the gargoyle's claws and teeth are getting closer and closer to ripping them apart.

I run to try to help them, wondering how we can possibly kill a creature that can regenerate itself.

As I sprint across the roof of the fortress, I recall reading about Hercules and the Hydra back in Hadley Elementary School. Every time Hercules cut off one of the serpent's many heads, two grew back in its place. He finally slew the monster by figuring out that if he cut off a head and scorched the neck with a flaming torch, that would keep replacement heads from growing back.

I don't have any torches on the roof of this fortress. But I do have a source of extreme cold. I open the silver locket that dangles from the chain around my neck.

I point it at the gargoyle, and try to switch it on. Come on, Star of Dann. Do your thing.

Nothing happens.

Meanwhile, I see the gargoyle catch my mother with a blow that knocks her fifteen feet, end over end. She gets up very slowly. I can tell that she's hurt.

I open myself up and try to apologize to the Star. Look, I'm really sorry I threw you away. It was extremely unappreciative of me to toss you into an Amazon stream, given the many times you'd saved my life. I just didn't understand what you were. Forgive me. You've been loyal to the House of Dann for generations. The King and Queen need you now. Help them!

At first nothing happens. Then the blue flame from the locket shimmers out. And the temperature on the rooftop dips noticeably.

The gargoyle has cornered my mother with her back to a wall of the cell. She is not in good shape, and my dad runs over to make his last stand with her.

The gargoyle swipes at them and Dad beats him to the blow and severs one of the clawed forelegs.

Before the limb can grow back, blue flame flashes out of the locket and singes the wound. The gargoyle yowls and carries on the fight with three legs. Mom chops at its shoulder, and blue flame keeps that wound from suturing itself. Sizzling yellow gargoyle blood seeps out.

I join the fight and try to hack off the beast's head from behind. It senses my presence and evades the blow so that my scimitar hacks off one of the pointed, twitching ears. Again, the wound is instantly cauterized by cold blue flame. We're digging chunks out of this cat-faced griffin, but it's still clawing and snapping and fighting.

Then the King of Dann seizes his moment and flashes forward, moving at incredible speed. Dad darts in under the gargoyle's claws and buries his sword deep in the center of the troll's chest.

A plume of cold blue flame jets out of the locket and encases the beast in a glowing cocoon. The gargoyle screams, writhes, and spits out a geyser of yellow blood. When the blue flame subsides, the creature is dead.

My father helps my mother up, and the three of us come together on the roof of the fortress. A light wind blows my father's bushy beard and stirs his white hair. We all look at each other. "Well done, Jair," my dad whispers.

I look back at him. "That's it? Not 'Thanks for saving me' or 'I'm sorry I sent you away as a baby, never arranged for you to learn the truth, and screwed up your whole life'?"

He glances at my mother. "He is much like you."

"No," she says, "he gets that from you, Simeon."

I look from one of them to the other. "I don't get anything from either of you," I say. "I wasn't around you so I couldn't have learned anything from you. But now I'm right here on this roof so instead of talking about me, why don't you try talking to me! And one more thing—for the hundredth time, my name isn't Jair. It's Jack!"

My father smiles slightly, and this time it isn't a pained smile. "Thanks for saving me, Jack. I'm sorry I had to send you away as a baby. We're in a bit of a bind here, so can I please have my Star?"

"What bind?" I ask. "We killed the monster."

Dad nods behind me and I wheel around. Dozens of heavily armed Dark Army fighters are pouring out the minaret doorway a few hundred yards away. They immediately spot us, and make a beeline in our direction. The zombie wizard's censer smoke must have finished making us visible.

This is clearly not the time for a father-son argument. I take off the locket and hand it to the King of Dann. "Here, take it."

He places the chain around his neck and the Star gleams. "Thank you, Jack," he says.

"You're welcome," I tell him. I'm watching the Dark Army warriors run at us. There must be two hundred of them, and they're moving fast. "Even with the Star of Dann, how can we possibly fight all of them?" I ask.

"We can't," my father whispers back. "We'll have to jump."

41

We run to the edge of the fortress roof and look down. The ground below is distant, and the prospect of leaping off is dizzying. This is what it must be like to seriously contemplate hurling oneself from the Matterhorn.

"Where are the antigravity suits?" I ask my mother.

"There are none," she says.

"Put your arm around me, Jack," Dad suggests. "And grab hold of your mom. We'll make this jump as a family."

I look back at him. "Excuse me. Don't take this as teenage rebellion. But are you nuts?"

He looks at my mother quizzically. "I believe it's a colloquial expression," she tells him. "Jair is asking if you're out of your mind."

"Oh," he says. "No, I'm quite sane. Come, grab hold. We don't have time to waste."

That's a bit of an understatement. The Dark Army fighters are less than a hundred yards away. They have weapons out and I'm sure they could fry us with their lasers from this distance, so they must want us alive.

"I'm open to the idea of family reconciliation," I tell my father, "but a nice group hug followed by joint suicide doesn't do much for me."

"Trust me," he says.

I glance down over at the ground far below and then look back into his eyes. "Why should I?"

"Because I'm your father."

"You've never been a father to me. Try again."

"If we stand here another three seconds, the Dark Army will capture us," he points out softly. "Take a chance on me now, son, or we'll all be tortured to death."

As I look back at him I can hear the approaching footsteps of the thundering horde of Dark Army warriors.

"Okay," I mutter. "I can't argue with that one."

I step to my parents and put my arms around them. My right arm goes behind my mother's back, and my left arm loops around my dad. Each of them puts an arm around me. We pull each other tight. "And off we go!" Dad shouts.

We jump off the roof. Actually, they jump and pull me off with them.

I can't say this ushers in a nice moment of family togetherness. We immediately plummet toward the poisonous moat below. I hear myself shouting, "DO SOMETHING!" Then: "YOU SAID YOU WEREN'T CRAZY!" And finally I just find myself screaming, "HHEEEELLLLPPP!" as I wonder whether the impact will kill us, or if we have a chance of surviving the high dive to be eaten alive by the bubbling acid.

Usually when I panic I feel a rush of blood to my brain and start to get hot, but this long leap to my death leaves me cold. In fact, it's freezing. No, wait a minute. It's not the plummet that's numbing. It's the snow that has begun sifting down out of a cloudless sky.

Flakes as big as hubcaps collect around us in a milky white cloud. They stick to each other, forming ever larger and more complex white starbursts. And then they start sticking to us!

We are falling more slowly. Somehow the Star of Dann has made us part of this blizzard! We are drifting down on the softest of natural parachutes, three human snowflakes, wafted by mountain winds.

My father is on one side of me. My mom's on the other. The snow is all around us, falling so thickly that I can barely glimpse the land below.

For a moment I am transported by the power of the gem. The snow whirls around me, and blinds me. When I blink and open my eyes I'm atop a glacier, a vast and mighty ice field that stretches as far as the eye can see. Snow geese fly over it, and foxes dart across it.

Then that glacier begins to melt, drop by drop. I see it dwindle before my eyes, as if through stop-motion photography over hundreds of years.

Soon it covers a square mile. Then an acre. Finally that great ice sheet has diminished to a last snow patch.

A gray bear comes shuffling into view. No, he's a man, in a heavy coat, and he looks a bit like my father, and also like me. But he's bigger than we are, taller and with wider shoulders even than my dad. Also, this guy in the gray coat looks like he's suffered as much as it is possible for a man to suffer without completely giving way to madness. My dad's been tortured by the Dark Army, but I sense that this haggard polar explorer has been doing it to himself.

His eyes glow with sadness. He's been alone for a long time. Wandering and witnessing. Tromping the earth. Like a monk in an isolation cell, except that his cell is the top of the world. And his meanderings and meditations have brought him to this last pathetic glacial remnant.

He reaches the snow and ice and stands before it, arms folded, as if suddenly overcome with the horror of what he's discovered.

He bends and touches the ice, and then straightens up and lets out an agonized wail of self-loathing. It's a wordless scream, but the sentiment is clear: "What have we done?!"

And then he falls to his knees.

A few feet from him, something gleams.

At first he doesn't see it, but then he does.

It's not a cheerful radiance—not a Christmas light gleam or a wedding candle sparkle. The sudden flash of blue light seems to acknowledge and reconfigure the howl the big man just gave. His wordless question: "What have we done?" is somehow echoed by the pale blue luminescence: "What has been done to me?"

The tall man crawls across the ice, and the blue light washes over him. His tousled hair, his sunburned forehead, his cracked lips, and even his sad eyes begin to glow.

He glimpses something beneath and reaches for it. His hand and his wrist disappear into snow and ice. His fingers close around it and he stiffens, as if hit by an electric current. Inch by inch he pulls the Star of Dann up, and holds it wonderingly in front of his eyes.

And somehow in the blink of an eye, as I fall through the air outside the Dark Army's fortress, I share that moment hundreds of years ago in the warming Arctic. The rage of a man who understands the suicidal folly of his species. The agony of a very special region of the earth, as the last of its beauty and majesty is stripped away. And I feel the common cause they make together— the desperate, lingering hope that maybe if they join forces the damage can be reversed, and the healing may begin.

The ground is rising up toward us. No, we are floating down to it. We've been blown away from the fortress, perhaps a half mile beyond the moat. Fifty feet till we hit the ground. Thirty, and I can see snowcapped rocks. "Roll when you hit," my father says.

Thump, the impact is much harder than I thought, but as soon as my feet touch I somersault forward the way Eko taught me.

I sustain a few cuts, but I would have to call it a good landing. Dad and Mom also make it safely. We get up and smile at each other.

"Well done, Jack," my father says.

"Thanks," I tell him. "Let's not try that again for a while."

"Suits me," he says with a grin. And then his smile fades. "What's that?"

I look around. The snow is still falling all around us. It's hard to see or hear anything.

"What?" I ask.

My mother closes her eyes and listens intently. "Five," she announces, gripping her saber. I see that she's bleeding badly from the shoulder. The gargoyle's strike did serious damage. "Whatever they are, they're large, Simeon. And coming fast, on four legs."

"Some kind of wild beast chimera," my dad speculates grimly, raising his sword. "Elephants? Or rhinos?"

I can see their outlines through the curtain of white snow. Lions. A pride of the enormous cyborg beasts! Racing toward us. They spot us and let out ferocious growls, preparing to rip us to shreds.

✳

42

Form a triangle, facing outward," Dad commands. "We'll make our last stand here. My darling, how are you?"

"Ready to keep fighting," my mother answers weakly, and takes her place next to him.

"What good will a triangle do?" I ask them both. "We're being attacked by half a dozen cyborg lions, and I'm sure reinforcements and killer drones are on the way. Do some other trick with the Star of Dann to save us."

"I'm out of tricks, son," my father confesses. "There comes a time when one must accept one's fate bravely. Stand with us."

"Yes, Jair," my mother echoes. "Come over here and join us. Let us be a family this last time."

"No," I tell them, as the snarls from the approaching beasts get noticeably louder. I catch glimpses of their flashing teeth and billowing manes through the snow. *"No, I won't join you,"* I repeat, more forcefully. "We've never been a family, so why start now?"

My father observes sadly, "What terrible hardness is in your heart, my son."

"The hardness that you put there," I tell him. "You made all the choices. You led me here."

"But don't you understand that people carry burdens that dictate their lives and choices? And that the burden a king carries is sometimes hard to bear?"

"No, I don't understand that," I reply, switching on my blue scimitar. "You make your last stand with my mom. I'll die as I lived, alone."

"I forgive you your anger, Jack," Dad whispers.

"Well, I'll never forgive you," I tell him.

Forgive me for throwing my two cents in, Your Majesty. A familiar telepathic voice suddenly shoehorns into our father-son squabble. *He's a fine young man and I'm quite fond of him, but he's always been like this. He carries grudges the way a sheepdog carries fleas.*

I peer through the falling snow but all I see are the approaching lions. Gisco?

I believe it comes from not spending enough time around noble role models in his formative years, Your Highness. By noble I of course mean yourself and my beloved Queen, although I would also humbly include that most loyal and selfless of animal species—the canine.

Gisco, where the hell are you? I demand. Stop spouting drivel and get us out of this mess.

Hello, Jack. Welcome to the world that is, but doesn't have to be. Kidah also sends his regards.

I notice that one of the lions is closer to us than the others, and is in fact galloping at us from a completely different direction. As I squint through the curtain of white, I can see that he doesn't have a tufted tail, a flowing mane, or a sleek, muscled feline body. In fact, he has a tail like an old whisk broom, a shaggy coat like an alpaca, and his rotund body more closely resembles a stampeding water buffalo than a charging lion.

I'm glad Kidah is well, I respond telepathically, but we're about to be devoured by a pride of cyborg lions. This isn't exactly the moment to exchange small talk about old friends.

There is always time for civil discourse, our one-dog rescue party declares, drawing near.

True, faithful servant, my father agrees, joining the telepathic exchange. *But there is also a time to act expeditiously. Along with his salutations, did Kidah send anything potentially useful?*

As a matter of fact he did, Your Highness, Gisco announces. *Here, catch.*

The mongrel carried something in his jowls while he ran, and he now flips it to my father.

Dad catches it neatly. It's a small red disc—the size and shape of a checker piece. He touches the edges of the checker with his index fingers and slowly draws them apart. The red disc stretches out in all directions. It enlarges till it looks like one of those cherry-colored plastic saucers that kids sled down hills on. In a few more seconds its circumference is equal to Dad's full arm span. And then it's expanded to a bright red ten-foot circular one-dimensional lifeboat.

"Get on," Dad orders.

I hesitate for a second.

The nearest lion is twenty-five feet away and coming fast. I can see the snow fringing his magnificent mane. He opens his mouth and roars at us.

I hop onto the red disc with my parents and Gisco. Maybe this is the time for a family reunion after all.

The large disc starts to slide across the snow. It *is* a sled! But not much snow had a chance to collect from the storm, and our red sled drags over dirt and rocks.

The lion leaps at us.

Dad fends it off with a whistling sword swipe. The beast dodges, recovers its footing, and jumps at us again. Two more lions charge at us from different directions, as if cutting off the angle on a fleeing gazelle.

But we're gathering speed. The drag of the rocky ground has somehow released. Then I see that we're several inches in the air! We zigzag around the lions as they futilely wave claws at us. They're fast but we're much faster. They snarl and try to knock us off the sled with their paws, but they might as well be waving goodbye.

I hear a whining sound high above and look up. A giant steel mosquito appears in the distance—a Dark Army drone! It streaks toward us as we accelerate in the other direction. We're soon moving at such a clip that I have to lie flat. I find a handhold and grab on tight.

Ouch, that's my tail. Let go!

Sorry, Gisco. I was falling off the sled. It's every man for himself.

And every dog for himself, he responds. *I'm also falling off,* and he locks his jaws around my ankle.

The drone comes right after us, anticipating our twists and turns. It fires energy bolts that streak down and incinerate massive boulders.

I steal peeks over the edge of the sled and see the mountainous terrain beneath us whirl by in a blur. We are taking evasive action at an incredible rate. We flit around massive crags and flash through deep gorges.

The drone matches us turn for turn. It hasn't hit us yet with one of its lightning bolts, but it's steadily gaining on us and we can't seem to shake it. A lucky shot will soon end the chase.

We dive into a particularly deep and narrow valley, and the drone swoops down from above, sealing us in. As soon as we try to climb above the sheer walls the drone will have a clear shot and take us out.

But we don't climb. We streak through the valley, which gradually narrows into a bottleneck and then comes to a dead end. We're flying right at a cliff! At this speed, we'll smash ourselves to skin and bone fragments in about three seconds. Our only chance is to soar upward and take our chances with the drone, but instead we descend even farther. We're speeding straight for the base of a cliff!

"Dad, take us up! We're going to crash!"

I'm not sure how he's steering this thing, but he looks determined. "This is the only way," he says through gritted teeth. "Trust me, Jack. Hold on."

"I don't trust you. The only way is no way—" I start to shout.

We fly straight into the cliff, and I throw my hands up in front of my face.

43

The dense shrubbery around the base of the cliff whips at my arms, and I steel myself for the final collision with solid rock, but the next thing I know we're flying through empty blackness.

There was a cave opening at the base of the cliff, and we're now rocketing through subterranean chambers.

The Star of Dann lights our way. Either my dad is a master navigator or the cherry-colored sled has its own built-in steering system. Despite the fact that we're slaloming through the caverns at great speed, we never so much as brush a stalactite or nick a stalagmite.

Finally we slow, and soon come to a stop in a large cave chamber. The ninja priests who accompanied my mother and me on our journey are waiting there, and they don't look surprised to see us arrive. My father or Gisco must have contacted them telepathically.

"Your Majesty, we are overjoyed—" the leader of the priests begins his speech of welcome, but my father cuts him off.

"Help me with the Queen," he commands, and in seconds Mom is lifted off the red sled and gently helped to the ground.

I'm alarmed at how weak she seems, and how much blood she appears to have lost. I recall my angry words to my parents when the lions attacked, and I suddenly feel very guilty. She could be dying.

One of the ninja priests who doubles as a doctor bends over her and does a quick triage. "She'll have to stay here, Your Majesty," he says. "There's no way she can travel for a few days."

"Yes," my father agrees with great sadness, "and we must leave immediately."

This is news to me. "Where are we going? We just got away from the fortress. Can't we catch our breath before we take off for the next hideout?"

"We're done with hiding," he tells me.

"Then what's our plan?"

"The time has come for a final showdown. We will take them on directly—the might of Dann against all the power of the Dark Army."

"I'm not sure that's such a good idea," I tell him. "Don't forget the drones. They may not be able to find us down here, but the minute we stick our noses out of a cave opening, they'll blast us."

"We're not going out through a cave opening, Jack," he tells me.

"Then where are we going?"

"You're going home, Jair," my mother whispers from the cave floor.

"Home?" I repeat, as if it's the strangest word in the world.

"To the world you grew up in," Dad fills in. "Back to the Turning Point, where all the forces of good and evil will soon be arrayed against one another to turn the future to light or darkness. And I'm coming with you."

Count me in, too, Gisco chimes in. *The food was much better a thousand years ago. And Kidah is waiting for us.*

I'm having a little trouble processing this. "If we're going back through time, why do we have to leave right now? Why can't we wait here, and make sure Mom is okay? Whether we leave now or a few days from now, it won't make any difference because we'll be heading back to the same date a thousand years ago."

"True," my father says, "but the Dark Army will guess what we are planning and create as much interference as they can with the time portals. I sense that they have already started. The longer we delay leaving, the more perilous the journey becomes."

"Yes," my mother says, "you must go right now, Simeon. I will stay and continue the resistance till you return."

My father bends to her. "Mira, my love. Fate has been very cruel to us."

She looks up into his eyes and strokes his white beard. "Don't cut this till I see you again."

"Not a hair of it," he promises.

Watching them, I realize just how heavy their burden is. They obviously love each other deeply. They've been separated for years while he languished in prison, and now, at the moment when he's been liberated and they're finally back together, he must leave and they may never see each other again.

She tugs gently on his beard, bringing his face down to hers. "One kiss."

My dad whispers that he loves her and kisses her softly on the lips.

"Enough," she whispers, breaking away. "More than this I can't bear."

He straightens up, looking sadder than he did when we first found him tied up in the Dark Army's torture cell.

"Jair," she gasps, and then corrects herself. "Jack."

I step over to her. "You finally got my name right."

She smiles back at me. "Can you forget your anger long enough to accept a mother's blessing?"

"Under the circumstances, I guess so."

Her arms come behind my head and draw me down, and she kisses me softly on the center of the forehead. "Even if you can't forgive, try to understand," she whispers.

"I will," I hear myself promise her. "And you try to get better. I've already lost one mother."

She looks up at me and nods, and then she releases me.

My right hand is wet with her blood. The sight of my mother's blood makes me stagger back, onto the red sled, which is now resting on the cave's floor. The room seems like it's swirling around. My father puts a hand on my back, bracing me. Gisco is on the sled, too.

No, wait, the sight of Mom's blood didn't make me faint. The cave chamber really is swirling!

Or perhaps we're the ones spinning, as the red sled revolves faster and faster.

I see images in the cave chamber. The faces of the ninja priests.

My mother's eyes watching me.

Trying to hold on to me as long as they can.

And then her eyes release me and the images from the gloomy cave chamber are overwhelmed as I am propelled at incredible speed through a tunnel of blinding light.

✳

PART FOUR

44

The trip back through time is as painful as when I came hurtling forward a thousand years, except that on this return voyage I sort of know what to expect.

I am sucked into the black hole of the event horizon, and feel myself being torn apart. But if I can stand it a minute more, just a few seconds more, I will be through it . . .

I scream, and I have a sense that Gisco and my father are near me and are also screaming. No one could endure this level of agony and keep any self-control. It feels like I'm being scrambled alive in a giant eggbeater.

And then I'm bursting past a golden membrane into a cottony haze. And the good news is that this time I'm pretty sure I won't find myself alone, in a sandstorm, in an unknown future world.

This time I'll rematerialize on my safe old earth with Kidah and Gisco and my father.

Particles. A quanta snowstorm. The dandruff of space-time. I'm sailing through it, head over heels.

This isn't the scorching, salty sand that I landed in when I journeyed into the far future.

It's cool and soft. Like sinking back onto a giant bed in an air-conditioned hotel room.

I lie there for a few minutes, recovering my senses.

It's more than cool. It's cold. Freezing!

And the bed isn't soft. It's a rock-hard slab. Also, I sense that it's moving!

Floating!

I turn my head to where the white slab ends and see glistening blue water.

I get to my knees and see that I'm on a vast ice floe, surrounded by a polar sea. There's no sign of any other pieces of drift ice, and no solid land.

I turn back to the iceberg and look around.

My father lies on his back about twenty feet away, unmoving. I crawl in his direction.

Beyond him, I see a rotund shape stirring—it looks like a beach ball that someone left outside for the winter. A great head and snout are slowly raised above the ice, and they rotate in my direction. *So we made it, old friend.*

Yes, I tell Gisco, but my dad's not moving.

The dog struggles to his feet and hurries over to my father, and I do the same. We stand together for a second, looking down at that prematurely old, pain-lined face.

I feel a stab of guilt, just as I did when my mom was bleeding in the cave. Suppose he died during the trip through time, and my last words to him were in anger.

My father groans and clutches his chest. He opens one eye and looks up at us. His lips move. "Where's Kidah?" he gasps weakly.

"I don't know," I tell him. "There must have been a screwup. We're all by ourselves, on an ice floe."

"Dark Army interference," Dad gasps, trying to sit up and then sinking back down. "Must have knocked us off our trajectory. Kidah will locate us soon." He lets out a sigh and his eyes close again.

Rest, Your Highness. We'll be perfectly safe here till he finds us, Gisco contributes optimistically. *Would you like me to get some water to wet your lips? Ice floes are an excellent source of fresh water.* The learned hound waits for a reaction from my father, and explains: *The salt is filtered naturally by brine rejection and leaches out the bottom, so the meltwater on top is drinkable . . .*

My dad's eyes flutter, and he looks like he's going to sleep. But he opens his mouth and whispers weakly, "We're not as safe as you think."

Uh-oh. I've learned not to underestimate my father. I look around but don't see anyone or anything dangerous.

Gisco has a superb nose for sniffing out danger. He inhales deeply and also comes up empty. *What threatens us, Your Highness?* he asks warily.

My father raises one hand above the ice and points.

The ice gleams in the sunlight, so it's hard to see. Gisco and I squint in the direction of his finger. The floe we're on must be five miles wide, but in the far distance I can just make out a small white dot moving toward us. Whatever it is, it matches its surroundings so perfectly that it looks like a tiny snowball has broken off the ice floe and is rolling in our direction.

No, not rolling, bounding. Gisco, I ask, what is it?

The big dog sniffs again and does not look happy. *It's a peculiar and not particularly appetizing scent that I've never smelled before, but if I had to take a wild guess I'd say it's a large specimen of male polar bear.*

How large? I ask. It looks tiny.

That's because it matches its surroundings so perfectly. Gisco is looking around to see if there's anywhere to retreat, but we're at the edge of the ice floe. *They're the biggest land predators in the world—twice the size of Siberian tigers.*

This is not good news. I glance at my father to see if he will be able to help us. He's lying flat on his back, eyes closed, barely breathing. We're going to have to fight this battle ourselves. Do they eat humans? I ask the knowledgeable mutt.

Polar bears are apex predators—they eat anything they can kill, Gisco informs me haplessly. *Seals, fish, musk ox, walruses—and, of course, dogs and humans. They're especially dangerous when they've been marooned on drift ice with little food.*

What do you suggest we do? I ask him.

Kill it before it eats us, Gisco advises, his eyes on the bear which has bounded close enough to us so that I can see its hulking shoulders, its flowing cream-colored coat, and its tree-trunk-thick legs capped with enormous paws.

I telepathically switch on the blade of my sapphire scimitar. I also dip a hand into my pocket and take out my last remaining Big Popper bomb.

Gisco drags my father behind me. *Good, Jack. Chop it down or blow it up. I would fight with you, but it's my sacred duty to keep watch over the King. So go to it! That albino bruin is no match for the beacon of hope!*

The bear stops twenty feet from us and sniffs the air, as if enjoying the aroma of its first good meal in weeks.

I step forward to meet it, moving in the circling sidestep that Eko taught me on the Outer Banks. I'm scared, but at the same time it's kind of thrilling to be walking out like David against Goliath, a lone warrior carrying all the hopes of his people, versus a giant.

The bear rears up on its hind legs. It must weigh more than a thousand pounds and when it stands upright it's more than twelve feet tall. It has a much longer neck than I would have imagined, which it extends to give it an even more towering presence. When it waves its forelegs at me I can see long, razor-sharp claws poking out of its snowshoe-size paws. Eager to display all its weapons, it growls and shows me a mouthful of long, sharp teeth.

I stop circling forward and back up a step. It's truly a colossal beast, fighting in its own element. One swipe of a giant, clawed paw will kill me. Perhaps I should give up on my samurai ambitions and just blow this beast to smithereens.

I telepathically switch on the Big Popper bomb and draw back my hand to hurl it. It will explode in five seconds. I take careful aim. Four. Three . . .

Suddenly, my right hand is seized from behind in an iron grip. My fingers are pried open and the bomb is ripped out. Two seconds left . . .

I spin around and see my father, on his knees, holding my bomb.

There's one second remaining!

✴

45

Dad hurls the bomb out over the water. It explodes with a tremendous BANG, creating a small tsunami that washes over the iceberg, wetting us to our ankles.

The bear stops advancing, puzzled by the loud noise.

"Why did you do that?" I ask my father. "That was my last bomb. Now I'll have to fight it with the scimitar."

He looks back at me and shakes his head. "No."

"Why not?"

"Because we don't have the right to kill it."

"Doesn't the fact that it wants to eat us give us that right?" I ask.

"Not in the least," he says, and struggles to his feet.

But, Sire, Gisco chimes in respectfully, *while I couldn't agree with you more that our lives are valueless in and of themselves when weighed against the pristine beauty of nature and its marvelous predators . . .* Gisco pauses to cast a fearful glance at the bear. *Surely since we carry all the hopes of Dann and the future world with us, we have a moral imperative to survive at all costs, even if it means in this one tragic instance slaying this boreal eating machine before it ingests us.*

"Absolutely not, faithful servant," my father tells Gisco, taking a step toward the bear. "That is the self-serving logic that led mankind and the earth to ruin. Behold the wisdom of Dann: We are part of a magnificent web of life greater than ourselves. We do not have the right to unravel a single thread of that fabric, or we greatly risk destroying the entire magical tapestry."

My father and the bear are now only ten feet apart. I grip the handle of my scimitar and step out a few paces behind my dad. I'm willing to trust the wisdom of Dann to a point, but if eat-or-be-eaten time comes, I'm planning to fall back on Darwin and survival-of-the-fittest logic.

The bear rears up again and snarls at us. Seen this close, it looks like a white Godzilla of thick fur and prodigious muscles, with scythe-like claws and more than forty gleaming teeth.

Dad takes another step and marvels softly: "What beauty! I have waited my whole life to see such a thing!"

The bear takes a leisurely swipe at him. Dad stumbles back, barely avoiding the blow.

My father stops retreating and stands still, looking up at the bear. He raises his arms, as if reaching out to the enormous beast, and peers directly up into the bear's black eyes.

The bear looks down at him and growls again, but it's a different sort of growl—less ferocious and more inquisitive. Then it slowly lowers itself to four legs and sits, watching us carefully.

My father steps even closer to it.

I've seen Eko communicate with animals and fish, so I know it can be done. But she mostly seemed to pal around with friendly pink dolphins and wise old sea turtles. This ferocious bear is a hungry apex carnivore, and I could tell it intended to kill us. It's pretty impressive to watch my dad walk toward it, step by fearless step, until he's right in front of it.

"It's hungry and confused," my father explains. "It was hunting seals, and tried to swim from one piece of drift ice to another. But the ice is melting because of rising water temperatures and there was no place to pull itself up and rest."

Dad reaches out and touches the bear's white fur. The bear puts a big paw on his shoulder. For a moment, the King of Dann and this lone bear look at each other. "It swam for three days and nights," my father continues. "When it was about to drown, it found this iceberg. And it's been marooned here, wondering whether it should try to swim again, but fearing it would drown in the open ocean."

I try to imagine what it would be like to be as strong as this bear, able to swim hour after hour in freezing seas, but slowly weakening.

Suddenly the great bear rears up and snarls, and for a minute I think it's going to bite my father. But its head swivels around on its long neck, as it senses danger from another direction.

It wheels around quickly and faces the waves.

I follow its gaze and see a very strange-looking boat drawing near, with the Mysterious Kidah standing in the stern, waving at us.

46

The boat looks like it is made from driftwood that was lashed together and covered with stretched seal or walrus skins. A dozen short men—six to a side—paddle with long-loomed oars. They don't seem to be stroking very hard, but the boat shoots through the water. I recall that on our trip upriver from the rain forest's sacred valley, Kidah used his wizardry to still the current and speed us on our journey. Something tells me he's using his unique powers to help these Eskimos propel this primitive craft over the choppy polar sea.

By a combination of paddling skill and magic, the boat glides very near the edge of the ice floe. "Come on," Kidah shouts, waving for us to jump. Gisco leads the way, running over the ice and building up speed till he leaps like a ski jumper and comes down safely inside the boat. Not a bad jump for a rotund, stumpy-legged canine.

I go next. It's hard to build up speed slipping and sliding on the ice, but a breeze stirs up out of nowhere and blows at my back. I reach the edge of the iceberg and leap, and for a long moment I hang in the air, certain I'm going to come down in the freezing waves. Then I grasp the side of the boat, and a dozen strong hands help me in.

"Welcome home, Jack," Kidah says and gives me a big hug. "So how did the big father-son reunion go?"

"Swell," I say. "Mission accomplished. He's here."

The wizard reads my face. "Sheesh, you gotta cut your old man a break. He was locked up longer than you've been shaving." He studies my eyes a second more and then shrugs. "Anyway, you guys made it back just in the nick of time."

"In time for what?" I ask.

For a moment Kidah's usual optimism and good cheer slip. "Things are not good," he mutters. "In fact they flat-out stink." Then he regains his enthusiasm. "So we've got to start fighting back and find a way to turn things around. First, let's get your dad on board."

"He'll never be able to make the jump," I caution the old sorcerer. "The trip back through time was hard for him. He can barely stand."

"He's stronger than you know," Kidah assures me. Then he breaks into a big smile. "Anyway, it looks like he's found a friend."

I see that the polar bear is lying flat on the edge of the ice floe, and my father is climbing onto its back. The Eskimos gasp as the bear slides into the water and swims straight for our boat with my dad along for the ride.

Two Eskimo men near me pick up rifles and take careful aim. If they shoot the bear, my dad will sink into the icy sea.

Kidah whispers to the Eskimos in a chant-like language and they grudgingly put their guns back down. They don't look pleased at the prospect of having an apex predator on board, but the old wizard seems to have won their trust, much as he immediately assumed a position of leadership with the lost tribe of the Amazon.

Instead of shooting the bear, the Eskimos lower a fishing net. We all grab hold and brace ourselves as the bear clambers up the netting. He looks at Kidah and the Eskimos and growls, but it's not an "I'm going to attack you" growl—it's a "We're all in this together" growl. He finds a spot in the bow of the craft, sits down, and curls up.

I notice that Kidah doesn't call my father Your Highness or Sire or bow and scrape to him as many other Dannites do. Instead, he grins and hurries forward, shouting, "Simeon, you creaking bag of bones."

"Kidah," my father calls back, "by the whiskers of Dann, you wrinkled sea horse!" and for a moment all threats to present and future worlds are forgotten as they embrace like long-separated boyhood friends.

They finally pull apart, and Kidah gives my father a worried look. "What have you done to yourself?"

"It's nothing," my father assures him. "Just travel fatigue. You've met my son?"

"Of course," Kidah says. "He got you out of that tower, I gather."

"On the day I was to be executed," Dad says proudly. "It was a fine thing."

"Happy to be of service when needed," I mutter.

My father glances at me, and then his eyes move on to Gisco. "And you know this resourceful and faithful servant of Dann?"

"We fought a battle together in the Amazon," Kidah says, smiling at Gisco. "And of course I knew his father well. That rascal used to steal my lunch!"

My father was not a thief, Gisco huffs telepathically. *It was a mat-*

ter of family philosophy. I don't acknowledge ownership when it comes to food, and I'm sure my father didn't, either. A good meal is the property of no man or beast. It belongs to the universal empty stomach. And since we're on the subject, unless my nose is playing tricks on me there's some dried fish and seal meat on this boat that would make a very welcome snack.

A few minutes later I'm digging into a salmon steak while Gisco is munching on seal meat and the polar bear is ripping apart an entire reindeer leg. I notice that my dad doesn't partake of the feast—something tells me the King of Dann is a strict vegetarian. He stands in the bow of the boat, talking to Kidah. I'm not sure what they're discussing, but they both look worried.

We seem to have picked up speed even though the Eskimos have stopped paddling to eat. Whatever spell Kidah is using, our driftwood boat is racing through the choppy sea. In the far distance, I see a thin black streak and resist the temptation to yell "Land ho!" Instead, I finish my salmon and walk forward to join the discussion.

"Looks like you enjoyed lunch," Kidah says.

I wipe a piece of salmon off my chin. "Time travel gives me an appetite."

My dad doesn't look pleased. I sense that he's trying to restrain himself, but then he says, "Jack, you're a Prince of Dann. How can you eat your fellow creatures?"

I shrug. "I dunno, Dad. I guess that was how I was brought up. If you were there, maybe you would have raised me another way. But you were busy at the time."

Kidah raises an eyebrow, but doesn't intercede.

"Where did you get the Eskimos?" I ask the wizard.

"They're Inuit," he corrects me. "One of the very last groups that remember the old customs. They shop in a grocery and they have aluminum boats, but they still hunt and fish in traditional ways. And they remember how to build an umiak."

"That would be this funky boat?"

"Yes. The kayak was the 'man's boat,' and the much larger

umiak was the 'female boat,' used to transport many people over the water to new hunting grounds. Which is exactly what we're going to use it for."

"We're going hunting?" I ask.

He nods. "As soon as we drop off our friends. They've been most hospitable, and since we don't need them for the hunt it wouldn't be fair to risk their lives. Especially since the odds of our surviving are not particularly good, and I speak as a well-known optimist."

I don't see what possible good a dog could do hunting from a boat, Gisco pipes up telepathically. *Much as I would love to accompany you on this vital and heroic mission, I would hate to get in the way. Perhaps you should drop me off at the nearest Inuit village.*

Kidah gives him a smile. "If I didn't know you better, stout friend, I would think that you were serious. But your fearlessness is well documented."

Gisco looks back at him and nods a bit ruefully. *Yes, it's true. I fear nothing. I laugh in the face of death. But just for the record, exactly how low did you say the odds of us surviving are?*

"Unfortunately, quite low," the wizard responds and shades his eyes. "There's the village. We'll make straight for land, drop them off, and then we can begin the hunt!"

As if hearing his words, the umiak darts across the water toward the distant spit of land.

47

The polar bear doesn't wait for us to find a place to dock. When we get close to land he stands, gives my father a last comradely growl, and then jumps off the umiak and swims to shore. He clambers up on some rocks and trots inland, and the Inuit seem happy to see him go.

We sail around the spit of land into a spectacular fjord, and I soon spot the Inuit village on a mountainside. I was expecting igloos and kayaks, but I see several dozen wooden houses and aluminum boats tied to a wooden pier.

Our umiak runs aground on a gravel beach, and the Inuit say goodbye to Kidah and then hop off and wade ashore. I notice they take almost everything useful with them—food, rifles, and even the fishing net. Kidah waves goodbye to them and the same mysterious current that beached us yanks us back out.

I stand with Kidah, my father, and Gisco and watch the village recede as we slowly glide out of the fjord, back around the point, and head for open water.

It's a sunny day, and the sky and the water both look pristine. I savor the fresh taste of the breeze, but something keeps bothering me. Finally I admit it: this beautiful world doesn't feel like home to me anymore.

Not that I miss glagour or giant scorpions. But something deep inside of me connected to the far future earth, damaged though it was. Ever since I came back through time, I've had the strange feeling of being a visitor—an interloper in the world I grew up in.

A breeze blows at our backs and the current pulling us out to sea grows stronger. I'm sure we could go even faster, not to mention more safely, with a modern boat and an engine.

"Wouldn't it be easier to hunt if we borrowed an aluminum boat?" I ask the wizard.

"No," he tells me, "I had them build this umiak especially for us. It was blessed by their angakok . . ."

"Their what?"

"Their shaman," he tells me. "He said some old spells over it, and I added a few of my own. There's not much you can do to tinker with an aluminum boat, but this umiak will do just what we need it to."

We are now speeding out into open ocean. Gisco watches us pull away from land with a wistful look, as if he doubts he'll ever get a hot meal on terra firma again.

I share his doubts. We're in a handcrafted wooden boat, heading out into open sea to do battle with God only knows what dangers.

"What are we going to hunt with?" I ask Kidah. "They took all the guns and nets."

He passes me a paddle, and hands one to my father. They look handmade, with long handles and narrow blades.

"I don't think we need to paddle," I tell him. "This current is pulling us out pretty fast now."

"It's not for paddling. This is what you're going to hunt with," Kidah tells me.

I look at him in disbelief. "Should I use it to try to bash the Dark Lord over the head?"

"That's not a bad idea," the wizard answers with a grim smile.

"If and when we find him, I'll take care of him," my father promises in a low voice. I see fury in his eyes, and recall that my dad was tortured for years at the Dark Lord's command. In addition to all our greater goals, my father's clearly out for personal revenge, and from the look on his face he means business.

"So we're hunting for the Dark Lord?" I ask. "He's out there somewhere on a boat?"

Kidah is silent for a minute. The current is speeding us along at such a pace now that we're already out of sight of land. "No, Jack," he answers. "He's not on a boat."

"Then where is he?"

The wizard looks out at the glittering water as if he's pondering my question and somehow giving me an answer. "Destroying this world," he whispers. "And our world a thousand years from now. Heartbreaking, isn't it?"

My dad is also staring out at the blue ocean. "Yes," he says. "I can feel it. Truly terrible."

"What's terrible?" I ask. "What's he doing? And where the heck is he if he isn't out here on the ocean?"

Gisco finally helps me out. *The point is, old fellow, we shouldn't be able to do what we're doing right now. That's the key.*

"The key to what?" I ask. "Don't talk in riddles. What shouldn't we be able to do? We're just sailing across a polar sea on an umiak. I thought that's what they were made for. What's the big deal?"

The big deal is that this is the Arctic Ocean, Gisco informs me. *If I'm not mistaken, we're heading straight for the North Pole.*

Yes, Kidah agrees. *We're about three hundred miles from the pole. It's time to go down.*

"Down where?" I ask.

But Kidah doesn't appear to hear me. The old wizard has closed his eyes and begun whispering. And the strange thing is that someone or something is answering him.

48

I hear faint chanting. At first all I can make out are muffled voices rising and falling in a beautiful but spooky chorus, like waves crashing into a distant shore. The wizard smiles and makes a circular motion with his hand, as if summoning the spirits to come closer. The chanting gets louder, till I can tell that it's the same singsong language I heard when Kidah talked to the Inuit.

Gisco, do you hear that singing? I ask.

I wouldn't exactly call it singing, my four-legged traveling companion responds uneasily.

What would you call it?

The hound's sensitive ears twitch. *A powerful angakok calling upon his tribe from a deep trance.*

A shaman? I ask. What's he saying?

Who knows? It's an old tongue. The dog listens to the chanting for a few seconds, and his expressive eyes grow sad. *The Inuit shamans believe in an underlying animating force called Sila that unites man and nature, and brings life or death,* the learned hound informs me. *It controls the weather and the waves, and is the spiritual breath of this harsh but beautiful environment. The shaman can intercede with it for mankind's benefit . . .*

I can't understand a word of the rising and falling chant, but as I listen to Gisco's explanation I get a picture in my mind of several dozen Inuit standing around a fire on a frozen coastline as snow falls. An old man, toothless and wind-scoured, stands in the center of the circle, backlit by the flames.

I see that he is standing near what looks like the carcass of a beached whale. The old shaman's face is painted, and he's wearing a feather headdress. He raises his arm and shakes a rattle, and begins chanting faster and faster, caught up in a wild ecstasy.

The men in the circle repeat the song back to him, and the chant accelerates as the winds quicken and the snow falls more heavily. Soon the shaman's incantation swirls and gusts in tandem with the howling blizzard. I see the old man's striking, weather-chiseled face twist in a sudden paroxysm of suffering. It looks like he's plugged into some great spiritual force, but instead of channeling its majesty he's sharing its desolation.

He raises his left hand and hurls some powder into the fire, and flames rocket skyward. In the explosion of firelight I see that he wasn't standing over the carcass of a whale, but rather over a long wooden hull. He was blessing an umiak!

I blink and I'm back on the boat with my father, Kidah, and Gisco, but something has changed. Perhaps it was the angakok's chant, or maybe Kidah's spells, but the umiak we're riding in is no longer an open craft, with driftwood and sealskins beneath and sky above. It's sealing itself up with a thin, glittering membrane that will soon encase us in a football-shaped transparent shell. The yellow dinghy Gisco and I sailed up the Hudson in a year ago did a similar thing, but that craft used futuristic technology to seal and submerge. What I'm seeing now is pure magic.

There's no computer here, no buttons to push or operating system to manipulate. Our wooden umiak is the most primitive craft imaginable, and the glittering shell that is encircling us looks as thin and fragile as a soap bubble. It quivers as two- and three-foot waves slap against it, and I think to myself that it can't possibly shield us from water pressure.

Down we go, into the Arctic Ocean. The blue water closes over our heads, and the white-capped waves recede as we drop straight down. Our bubble-topped bathysphere descends silently and at great speed. The sunlight soon dwindles to one last tiny candle flame, and then is completely extinguished as we are immersed in inky blackness.

I try not to think about the tons of freezing water pressing on the frail-looking bubble from all directions. Surely my dad and the greatest wizard of the future wouldn't have brought us down here if our craft couldn't handle it. But even as I try to reassure myself, I shiver with cold and fear. We're sinking endlessly into an icy ocean near the North Pole. It seems impossible that we'll ever see daylight again.

Hey, Gisco, I reach out telepathically. I'm feeling a little nervous and claustrophobic. Any cheerful words?

I should have stayed with the Inuit, Gisco responds miserably.

Caribou steaks. Campfires. I'm not exactly a sled-pulling husky, but it's a culture that respects dogs.

You're pretty husky in your own way, I assure him, trying desperately to lighten the mood.

Or I could have stayed with Mudinho in his village. His parents were so happy when I brought him back, they threw a three-day fiesta! Chicken and roast pork, cakes and cookies! They feted me and pampered me. When Kidah's call to duty came, I should have announced my retirement. I would still be in their rustic little casa, *dozing by the fire, instead of sinking into the Makarov Basin like a dying walrus waiting to be flash-frozen or devoured by some bug-eyed bottom-feeding cold-water crustacean!*

You're not exactly raising my spirits, Gisco.

We're doomed! Doomed, do you hear me? In fact, we may already be dead. This is the darkness of the watery grave that has no bottom and no roof. O Great Dog God, rescue your humble acolyte from everlasting cryonic entombment. Draw me up from these abysmal depths with your glorious paws, and I shall forgo the roast pig and abstain from the fatty goose. Give me one chance. Give me light!

I know just what he means. The blackness is so oppressive and enveloping that I feel dizzy, and sink to my knees. "Give me light," I shout out desperately.

As if in answer to our pleas, a spark kindles. It's the Star of Dann, shimmering to life from the chain around my dad's neck. I see my dad's concerned, careworn face as he turns to me. "Are you okay, Jack?"

"I've been better."

"Such moments are tests. Have faith."

"In what?" I ask him.

"Destiny."

"I've never had any faith in destiny," I respond, struggling to stand up. "Fate seems cruel and fickle. The best people die horrible deaths for no reason. If this boat were to implode, and we were to drown, what would be the point? We wouldn't have changed anything."

"Sometimes fate is unfair," Dad admits. "All we can do is the very best we can, and then maybe a tiny bit more. But you're wrong to say that those who die trying to accomplish their dreams have failed. Always remember this—the measure of a man is not the extent of his success but the quality of his struggle."

I am tempted to dismiss his words as mere platitudes. But I recall his bravery when we first found him awaiting his own execution in the fortress's dark tower. If he's right, and the measure of a man is the quality of his struggle, then several men I've encountered during my adventures who met terrible fates were heroes rather than failures.

I recall the governor general of the Amazon being machine-gunned to death near the falls. He never accomplished his dream, but he battled with everything he had. And the man who raised me in Hadley-by-Hudson also measured up well. When his moment came, he blew off his own foot to force me to leave, and then turned to make his last stand alone against the Dark Army assassins.

My father shifts his attention to Gisco. The Star of Dann has grown brighter, and the dog's terrified features are clearly visible. "And how are you, stout four-legged warrior? A little religion is not a bad thing in times of peril."

Gisco looks back at the King, and appears embarrassed. It's clear that my dad heard his frightened appeals to the Great Dog God. Now, Gisco draws himself up to his full height and responds, *As Your Highness well knows, the measure of a dog is not in his bark but in the strength of his bite.*

"Quite so," my father agrees. "And you have never failed us when the time comes to act." Dad looks past him, to the front of the boat. The old wizard stands vigilantly at the helm, as if somehow probing the black waters all around us. "Kidah?"

The time-traveling seer half turns. "We are deep enough, Simeon. It's time to go hunting."

My father nods and takes off the chain with the locket. He

wordlessly passes it to Kidah, who hangs the Star of Dann from a notch on the driftwood prow. Its radiance warms the inside of the boat, while its sapphire light flashes in front of us and pierces the inky depths. We stop descending, and our umiak with its bubble top begins to move forward.

49

Our umiak speeds silently through the depths, and we gather at the front. When you're beneath the Arctic Ocean hunting an arch-fiend, it's comforting to stand near a wizard. The Star of Dann illuminates our path, but nothing is visible in the cone of blue light except endless water and an occasional floating crustacean.

"We're nearing the polar ice cap," Kidah tells my father. Then he corrects himself, "Or maybe I should say the polar ice cube."

My dad nods sadly. "So it's irreversible?"

"I wouldn't say that," Kidah responds. "We're at the edge of the edge. The last tick of the Turning Point."

"What's almost irreversible?" I ask. "What's happening to the Arctic ice cap?"

It's disappearing, Gisco informs me. *And the Greenland Ice Sheet along with it. They've been melting at an accelerating rate for the past few decades. The Arctic is the most sensitive of earth's biomes to global warming—it heats up twice as fast as the rest of the planet. Even if the Dark Lord hadn't decided to lend a hand, the Arctic Ocean would have been completely free of ice in a few decades.*

I picture a globe in my mind, with a white cap sitting on top of it. I imagine that white cap getting smaller and smaller till it totally disappears, and the top of the globe gleams bright blue. "And why would that be so bad?" I ask. "I know polar bears hunt from the sea ice, and I'm sure it wouldn't be much fun for the seals, either. But people I know don't use Arctic ice. How would it hurt New Yorkers or Parisians or Tokyo-ites, now or in the future?"

"You're right about the polar bears," my father says, and I can tell he's thinking about the enormous beast he befriended on the floe. "They'll be the first to go. And mother seals won't be able to climb up onto the ice and will have to give birth at sea, where their babies will immediately drown. But the rest of us will follow soon enough. We're all on the same earth, Jack."

Arctic ice is the earth's air conditioner, Gisco tells me. *It reflects the sun's rays. When it's gone, the land and sea will absorb much more light and heat. Global warming will speed up and the ice sheet will melt. As the seas rise, coastlines will be swallowed up, and wars will break out over food and water. The ocean currents will shift, creating extreme weather conditions . . .* The dog stops and shrugs. *Basically, if you want to screw up the planet, melt all the polar ice and just stand back and wait.*

"And that's what the Dark Lord's doing?" I ask. "How is he melting it?"

"LOOK!" Kidah shouts, and extends an arm to point dramatically out at the distant depths. "There!"

I peer in the indicated direction, but see nothing. "What is it?" I ask, dreading to hear the answer. "Is the Dark Lord coming to get us?"

Before Kidah can answer, a bizarre shape pierces the farthest shadows—a gigantic spear, hurtling at us! Then I see that the spear has a massive cylindrical body behind it, pushing it forward. We've been targeted by a colossal sword-tipped torpedo! Another missile breaks out of the murk, and yet another. There must be dozens of them, bearing down on our fragile, bubble-topped boat.

"What are they?" I ask. "I've never seen anything like them."

Gisco watches the wizard worriedly.

My father is staring at the oncoming torpedoes, and it's hard to read the expression on his face. "I don't think anyone's ever seen anything like this," he whispers.

Kidah's mouth opens and he licks his lips, and then his wizened face breaks into a slight smile, and he claps his hands delightedly. "You're right about that, Simeon," he says. "Not in such numbers. They're unicorns!"

I look from my father to the wizard and try to figure out if this is one of their inside jokes. "There's no such thing as unicorns," I point out. "They're just mythic creatures. Anyway, they're supposed to be land animals."

"These are the unicorns of the deep," Kidah tells me.

The unicorns of the deep have swum much closer. They have blue skin with pale white blotches. I can now gauge their immense size—the biggest must be nearly thirty feet long, and their lance-like noses add an additional ten feet. "Are they going to pierce our bubble with their swords?" I ask.

Gisco looks a bit calmer, as if he's figured out a mystery. *Not swords*, he explains to me, *tusks. Or more properly, teeth.* The dog turns to the old sorcerer for confirmation. *They're narwhals, aren't they?*

"You bet your tail they are," Kidah agrees, smiling in childlike wonderment. "Pods and pods of them!"

I turn to Gisco. "Narwhals? Help me out."

The mysterious whales of the northernmost Arctic, the oceanographically erudite hound explains to me. *They went extinct soon after the Turning Point from a combination of warming water and whalers with high-powered rifles and harpoon guns. These must be a good percentage of the last narwhals left on earth.*

"Yes, they've come to welcome us," Kidah explains, now smiling broadly. "And to guide us." He gives them a big wave.

The lead narwhals reach our umiak and swim around it. I can see them clearly through the bubble top. They don't try to pierce the bubble, but they do rub their tusks back and forth across it, like violinists drawing their bows over strings. The tusks project outward from the left side of their upper jaws in a helix pattern.

"What do they chew with teeth like that?" I ask.

Nobody knows for sure, Gisco tells me. *Some experts think they use their tusks to spear fish, or to break sea ice, or even to sword-fight rivals during mating season.*

"Nonsense," Kidah interrupts. "You're not even close." The wizard lowers his voice and gives me a wink. "They're magic wands, Jack."

I watch a narwhal swim right up to the umiak, peer in at me, and slowly draw its tusk over the bubble. "What kind of magic are we talking about?"

"The kind we could use right now," the wizard answers and his eyes gleam. "Those tusks are really supersensitive antennae, with thousands of tiny tubes that connect to their central nervous systems. They pick up temperature and salinity changes at tremendous distances."

I ponder Kidah's explanation as I watch the narwhals circle our boat. "So that's how they can help us?" I guess. "The Dark Lord is down here somewhere, speeding up global warming. And the narwhals are going to lead us to him?"

"It's the only way," Kidah agrees. "This is a big ocean. And time is running out for us. But they'll pinpoint him for us with their tusks." He turns to the bubble and raises his arms dramatically, and I hear him sending out a telepathic call to arms: *Wave your magic wands, my long-toothed friends, and sing your ancient songs. Search out the fiends for us, and let the final battle begin!*

50

A few of the narwhals stay with our umiak. The rest of them swim off in different directions.

"Narwhals are the most social and vocal of whales," Kidah observes. "Listen to them gossip and chitchat! Have you ever heard anything like it in your life?"

Gisco and my father smile. Kidah's gaze falls on me, and I shrug. "I don't hear anything. I've never been able to communicate with wild animals."

My dad is standing at the front of the umiak, watching the narwhals split off in pods of four or five. "Come over here, Jack," he says.

I walk next to him. "What's up?"

He puts an arm around me. I pull back—I wasn't expecting an undersea display of paternal affection.

His powerful arm tightens around me, and draws me closer. "What's going on?" I ask.

"Come," he repeats. I stop protesting and let him pull me right next to him. Now that I'm by his side I see that he must be at least two inches taller than I am. He's also strong—I can feel the rock-hard muscles in his arm and shoulder. He leans against me and we're cheek to cheek, facing out at the narwhals.

It's strange to be this close to my father. I feel the warmth of his skin, and the softness of his white beard. "What are we looking for . . . ?"

"Shhhh," he hisses. "Silence."

So I stay quiet and wait for something to happen.

Seconds pass, and nothing very dramatic occurs. It's like my dad and I are standing at the bottom of a goldfish bowl, watching the fish circle the tank above us.

Then I find myself wondering who switched on the music. It sounds like the percussion section from a haunted orchestra pit— dozens of rising and falling groans as if someone is opening and shutting rusty doors in such a way that they start to harmonize and answer each other. The weird thing is that none of the sounds are particularly pleasant by themselves, but taken together they have an otherworldly beauty that leaves me breathless.

"Hear them now?" Dad whispers.

"It's lovely." I nod.

"Can you understand them?"

"I don't speak Narwhal."

"Close your eyes and give me your hand," he commands.

I shut my eyes and extend my right hand, and he lifts it to his face. He presses my palm tightly to the side of his cheek. "Now," he whispers, "*listen.*"

I listen very hard, and suddenly I'm in two places at once, standing next to my father and also floating inside his head, hearing what he hears. I can clearly understand the meaning of the narwhals' songs. They're calling out to each other as they rise to the surface for air and then dive back down. Family members shout playful greetings, old friends exchange narwhal small talk, and lovers tease and flirt. And all of this is going on constantly in hundreds of simultaneous conversations, as if they're plugged into the same cetacean social networking site.

But most of all what I hear is their determination to locate the source of the heating. And they're already zeroing in on it! "Do you feel that?" "Yes, this way." "I feel it, too." "Deeper." "Over here it's stronger." "Come. We're on the trail for sure. Bring the King!"

The narwhals who have stayed with us obediently swim off in the chosen direction, and we follow them. When members of our escort have to dart up to the surface for a fresh breath of air, new ones swim down to take their places. Narwhals may be big and odd-looking, but they're graceful and fast in the water. Our umiak is soon booking along at high speed, but they keep throwing impatient looks back at us, as if to say, "Come on, King of Dann, get your boat in gear!"

All of the narwhals seem acutely aware of my dad's presence, and they pay him respect and a kind of reverence. They sense he has a special connection with them, and that he's championing their cause. I suppose this unique link he has with animals explains how he got the polar bear to give him the piggyback ride to the umiak. As I stand there with my hand on his grizzled cheek, I can't help feeling proud of him. He's part Dr. Doolittle, part Tarzan, and he cares about whales and bears just as much as they revere him. So this is what it means to be a King of Dann!

The only time I've felt anything close to this was when Kidah gave me his torch during our night march in the Amazon, and I suddenly plugged into the entire living web of the rain forest. But that was a magical moment, created by a wizard on a special night. I can tell that this is the way my father thinks and feels all the time. As I stand next to him, I contemplate what agonies he must have gone through in the far future, to live on such close terms with the natural world and to feel it dying all around him.

"We're getting close," Kidah says, and lifts the Star of Dann off the spar where it was hanging. Its radiance changes color, growing darker, and my connection with my father—and through him to the narwhals—is broken. "Time to arm ourselves," the wizard announces grimly.

The narwhals break off to either side and head back the way they came. "What's happening to our escort?" I ask.

"The water is getting too hot for them," Kidah tells me. "They've done their work, and pointed us in the right direction. Now we have to finish the job. Hold up your weapons."

Feeling a little foolish, I hold up my umiak paddle. Kidah swings the Star of Dann from side to side like a pendulum. It has

darkened to a purplish color. As the gem swings close to my paddle it pulses, and I feel an electric shock zap my palm and fingers.
I almost drop the paddle, but manage to hang on. It's now glowing from handle to blade with dark flames that dance and sizzle
but do not consume the wood.

Kidah swings the Star again, and my father's paddle ignites.
"Now," Dad says grimly, "we're ready for them."

Gisco is holding a small paddle in his jaws. In a second it is
also glowing dark purple, but the flames don't seem to burn the
dog's mouth. They do flicker over his large eyes, which glint with
fierce determination. *Yes, my lord,* Gisco pledges telepathically, *we
are ready to spray ice on the fire. Enough damage has been done. It's time
to put a stop to it in the name of all that's holy.*

I know what he means. I can feel the long-contained rage of
the Star of Dann coursing up and down the handle of the paddle.
This Arctic region of ice and snow, this austere and majestic home
of brave and hardy fish and animals, has suffered blow upon blow
till its very existence is imperiled as it warms degree by degree and
melts drop by drop.

Now, through us, it finally has a chance to strike back.

I raise my paddle to my shoulder like a gun, and gaze out
through the bubble top of our umiak.

51

It's tense and silent as we hold our fiery paddles at the ready and
gaze out at the murky depths. One last brave narwhal still swims
ahead of us, enduring the warming water to keep us on course.

My father stands next to me, scanning with his eyes from side to side, as if expecting to spot his nemesis at any second. I follow the sweep of his gaze, peering out into the purplish cone of light. My paddle is raised and ready.

"Jack," my father says softly, "I'm sorry for all the pain I caused you. It was not my choice, but it was my doing. I wish we had more time together now, but fate has not been kind to us. Whatever happens, I see the man you've become, and I'm very proud of you."

My throat tightens and tears well in my eyes. I answer him telepathically because I'm too choked up to speak. *When I put my hand on your face and heard the narwhals, I was also getting to know you,* I tell him. *I hope we get the time to become real friends.*

The last intrepid narwhal turns and swims back the way he came. The water must have gotten too hot for him. I can feel it now inside our enclosed umiak.

At first the extra warmth is pleasant—it's nice to float beneath the Arctic sea in a toasty warm little egg. But from toasty warm it soon becomes uncomfortable, and in a few more seconds it's almost unendurable.

I peel off my coat, then my shirt, and soon I've stripped down to my underwear. Gisco pants next to me—he looks like he's about to faint from canine heatstroke.

"Can't we air-condition this umiak?" I ask Kidah.

"The Star of Dann is keeping the temperature bearable," the wizard replies.

This isn't actually in the bearable range for a long-haired dog, Gisco points out.

"The water temperature outside is more than three hundred degrees," Kidah tells us. "Without the Star of Dann helping us, we'd be boiled like lobsters in a pot."

There is no good way to cook a dog, Gisco responds miserably, *but better flash-boiled than slowly sautéed.*

Sweat runs through my hair, down into my eyes. "So this is

how the Dark Lord is destroying the Arctic ice cap?" I ask. "He's down here slowly cranking up the heat?"

"No, this is a big and very cold ocean, and that would take too much time," Kidah tells me. "They're being far more strategic. Arctic ice varies greatly in thickness, from three meters to more than twenty meters. The Omega Box is capable of creating a concentrated beam of tremendous heat and aiming it at the thinnest and most fragile targets. They're slicing and dicing the polar ice cap along its fault lines into smaller and smaller pieces. The more it's segmented, the faster it melts."

And it is melting fast, Gisco adds, looking like he himself is also slowly liquefying. *Even without the Dark Lord's help, global warming caused by greenhouse gases was shrinking the ice cap nearly ten percent every year. With the Dark Lord and the Omega Box strategically slicing up the ice cap from below, the damage is accelerating exponentially. As the sea ice disappears and the water heats up, the Greenland Ice Sheet melts much faster.*

"We need to stop them now, today," my dad cuts in grimly. Suddenly his voice becomes very tense. "Kidah, I feel them!"

"Yes," the old wizard agrees, raising the Star of Dann high over his head. "Their heat beam is right up ahead. If it so much as grazes us, we're finished. Hold on, everyone, it's time to take evasive action."

The umiak begins zigzagging at tremendous speed. I grab the wooden rail to steady myself.

"THERE!" the wizard shouts. "Off to starboard!" His voice rises, and his tone becomes urgent: "Shoot, Simeon! Fire, Jair! Let fly, Gisco! Don't wait! They've seen us!"

52

I see their laser beam first, a pulsing orange-red Roman candle exploding continuously upward. Shielding my eyes against its glare, I trace the beam down to its source. The Dark Lord and the Omega Box are not in anything as cool and mysterious as our bubble-topped umiak. The red beam is blasting up out of the roof of what looks like a small Soviet submarine from the nineteen-eighties. It has been painted bloodred and retrofitted with a few futuristic touches, apparently including a heat-resistant outer skin.

Before I have time to take aim at the sub, my father "fires" and a purple comet of frothing polar energy surges from his flaming paddle. It bursts out through the transparent membrane covering our umiak—which instantly re-forms so that no puncture hole is created—and whizzes toward the mini-submarine.

The Dark Lord must have seen the projectile coming because the mini-sub dive-rolls out of the way at the last possible second. As the sub twirls, its bolt of scorching heat—which had been focused upward at the ice cap—rakes the ocean all around us like a machine gun firing wild bursts at random.

Our umiak whirls upside down to avoid being hit, and I am hurled off my feet. My forehead thuds against the bubble ceiling, which has now become the floor. The impact stuns me, but searing heat revives me and I find myself screaming in pain. The energy blast passed close enough to the bubble top of our umiak to make it scorching hot! Kidah is right—if an Omega Box's ray so much as touches us, we'll melt like a marshmallow in a campfire.

Our umiak keeps spinning to avoid being hit, and then flips end over end. I slide back and forth the length of the deck, and drop my paddle as I scrabble desperately for a handhold. The Inuit built this boat out of irregularly shaped pieces of driftwood and there are protruding boards and spars, but it's hard to grab on to them. I scrape both knees and knock out a tooth, and when I try to brace myself with my right hand it feels like I fracture my wrist.

In the topsy-turvy bedlam, my father manages to squeeze off a second shot. The pulse of his firing lights the inside of our craft for a second, and I spot Gisco wedging himself into a narrow nook between two slats. The intrepid canine turns toward the bubble top, his paddle clenched between his jaws. *Every dog has his day*, my old comrade trumpets ferociously, and then his paddle spits two bursts of purple ice energy at the mini-sub.

The Dark Lord is as good a navigator as he is a martial-arts master. He jockeys the mini-sub between my father's shot and Gisco's twin blasts, so that one icy comet passes high and the other two miss low. Then he steers the submarine into a sudden dive, and our target vanishes beneath our umiak's wooden deck. For several heartbeats, they're completely out of our sight.

Kidah tries to turn us, but there isn't time. I know what's coming next, but when the red bolt strikes from beneath, it feels like we've been thrown into a giant furnace! I scream, and I hear Gisco howling near me. Please, death, come quickly to end this pain!

But just as the red starburst of heat and energy engulfs us, I see Kidah standing tall and holding the Star of Dann high over his head. He shouts out a few desperate words, and the blue gem comes to life and swells larger and larger. I have a momentary vision of a great blue wave washing over a roaring fire and dousing it.

I blink and the wave vision is gone. The inside of the umiak feels like an oven, but I realize that I'm alive. Gisco and my father also survived the laser strike, but I notice that their umiak paddles are no longer flaming. Perhaps they only had two shots each, or maybe the polar energy from the Star of Dann needs time to recharge.

We roll upside down and I spot my own umiak paddle, which I lost hold of while we were rolling around. It slowly slides out into the center of the transparent bubble, which, since we are inverted, has again become our temporary floor.

I let go of the spar I'm clinging to, tumble down onto the bubble top, and shriek as my hands and knees start to singe. The transparent shell of our umiak retains far more heat than the driftwood hull, and I feel like I've just jumped down onto the curved surface of a sizzling hot Chinese wok and am being stir-fried. But I need that paddle! The only way to prevent another deadly laser blast from the mini-sub is to put an end to this underwater shoot-out. And my paddle seems to be the only one left with any firepower.

I smell the sickening stench of smoldering skin from my hands and knees as I force myself to crawl forward across the bubble. Each move is a separate agony, a test of my will and ability to endure pain. I'm wailing and crying like a baby, but somehow I make it to the paddle, and grasp the long handle. I notice Kidah following my progress. And just as I grab the paddle, he throws our umiak into a half spin so the scarlet mini-submarine appears right beneath us.

I don't even really think about aiming or pulling the trigger. For one thing, I don't have the slightest clue how to fire an umiak paddle at a Dark Lord and an Omega Box. It's just a wooden oar—there's no sighting mechanism and no trigger. I look at the red mini-sub and lock my concentration onto it, and will the paddle to fire the same way I willed the blade of my scimitar to appear.

I feel the paddle surging with energy, and then a little blue bolt of polar energy breaks off and zips out, heading right for the sub. My shot penetrates the bubble and flares through the water, but during the split second it takes for my shot to travel, the Dark Lord hits the gas. The submarine speeds up and easily outruns my blast.

I have one shot left—perhaps the last shot any of us will be able to take. This time I try to aim just in front of the mini-sub, leading the target, in case he tries to speed up again. But just as I start willing the paddle to fire, I feel a telepathic presence probing my intention and already starting to react to it. It's been a long time since I last crossed swords with the Dark Lord in the Amazon, but I know it's him.

In the final microsecond before firing, I radically change my aim and swing the paddle so that it points behind the submarine instead of ahead of it.

The red mini-sub stops and reverses direction as the Dark Lord anticipates my original intention to fire ahead of it. And then he seems to realize that I've changed my plan, and that by reversing direction he's heading just the way I'm now shooting. But he's a heartbeat too late.

I squeeze off my last shot. The icy comet streaks away from my paddle, bursts out through the bubble top of our umiak, and scores a direct hit on the side of the red mini-sub!

There's a loud roar and a blinding blue flash. The submarine lights up like a Christmas decoration, and keeps growing brighter and brighter. I can't be sure, but I think I glimpse something detaching from the top of the mini-sub and speeding up toward the surface. And then the sub explodes, sending out shock waves that hurl our umiak away through the depths.

We finally stabilize, and the four of us gather at the prow. I see that we've all taken our share of bumps, knocks, and burns. *Well done, Beacon of Hope,* Gisco congratulates me. *Ding, dong, the Dark Lord is dead! You blasted them into crab niblets!*

"Not quite," Kidah cautions. "They still live."

Impossible, the celebrating dog declares. *I saw their sub go up in flames. I mean down in flames.*

"Kidah's right," my father says. "They made it out just in time, and rose to the surface in some sort of lifeboat pod. But they're wounded. We have to go up and finish them once and for all."

"Then let's go before they get away," I say.

Kidah smiles at me. "That's the stuff, kid." The wizard turns to Simeon. "Your boy fires a pretty mean umiak paddle."

Dad pats me on the shoulder. "Nice shooting, Jack," he grunts. "I'm glad you're on my team."

53

We ascend through the dark water for long minutes, till finally a ray of light shimmers through the depths from far above. I can't tell you how welcome and uplifting that first hint of sunlight is. "Gisco, we'll be out of this umiak soon enough."

Thank God, the dog responds, watching the light grow brighter with eager eyes. *The next time I go on a cruise, it will be with buffets and a swimming pool.*

Our bubble top soon breaks the surface. The dome of blue sky that opens above us feels vast and freeing after our tense hours in a claustrophobic umiak far beneath the polar sea. Unfortunately, there's little time to celebrate because we didn't exactly pop up in a good spot.

Waves lash against the side of our craft, and enormous floating icebergs press in on us from all sides. Our bubble top retracts and I hear a constant angry fizzing sound, as if the islands of floating ice are alive and resent our presence. The buzzing reminds me of the swarm of locusts in the far future world.

"What's that sound?" I ask nervously, as Kidah negotiates our umiak through narrow gleaming ice channels that wind like serpentine alleyways in a frozen bazaar.

It's called bergie seltzer, Gisco tells me. *It's made when icebergs melt and compressed air bubbles suddenly pop.*

"These melting icebergs have calved recently," Kidah notes. "We must be near the ice sheet."

Sure enough, we emerge from between two huge icebergs that look like they would each be capable of sinking the *Titanic,* and see an amazing sight. Ahead of us is what looks like a continent of ice, with outlet glaciers flowing away from the ice sheet, down the sloping coast to the waves. The seaward faces of those glaciers toss off pieces that break away with thunderous rending sounds and splash down into the water as newly calved icebergs.

Near us, another glacier runs out beneath the water, so when icebergs "calve" or break off from it, they announce themselves by floating up to the surface and exploding suddenly into view.

The spectacular splashdowns and sudden pop-ups create all shapes and sizes of calves, from drifting blue baby bergs as small as our umiak to massive floating mountain ranges of ice, miles wide and as tall as Manhattan skyscrapers. The cracking and rending sounds are constant and deafening, and they seem to come from all around us and also from above, as if someone is sawing away at the sky.

"I've never seen anything like it," I say. "So this is how icebergs are born?"

The nursery is pretty full these days, Gisco remarks, sweeping his head around at the thousands of newly calved icebergs. *The Greenland Ice Sheet is melting faster and faster. Of course, there's a lot of it to melt.*

Just how big is it, Professor? I ask the dog with all the answers.

Fourteen times as large as England, he replies without missing a beat. Then he adds sadly, *But in a few years it will be gone. When it melts, the seas will rise and swallow coastlines and whole islands. So it's beautiful to see, but the way it's melting is sad and dangerous for hundreds of millions of people.*

I gaze at the seaward tongues of the outlet glaciers and follow them back with my eyes to the gleaming foothills of the ice sheet that point upward to great white mountains even farther inland. "That's where the Dark Lord and the Omega Box are heading?"

"There are plenty of hideouts for them up there, in hidden ice valleys and deep caves," Kidah tells us, steering our umiak toward a spot where the ground rock touches the water so that we can land without fear of hitting a newly calved iceberg.

There's their lifeboat! Gisco waggles his snout at what looks like a giant crimson packing box that has been torn open and now bobs in the surf near the shore.

Instantly I'm on my guard, fingering the handle of my sapphire scimitar. "Are they in it?"

"No, they've made it to shore," Kidah says. "But they're close."

"Very close," my dad agrees. "I can feel them there," and he nods toward the mountain ranges of ice that tower skyward in the distance. "We've got to find them and finish this now, while they're still licking their wounds. If we give them a chance to recover they'll slip away and we'll have to hunt them down all over again." He pauses, as if catching a new scent. "And I see that someone has come to help us."

"How about that for good timing, eh, Simeon?" Kidah says enthusiastically. "Not that we couldn't handle this ourselves, but reinforcements are most welcome."

"Who is it?" I ask. "Some warriors you've brought from the future to help with the final battle?"

"Fierce warriors indeed," my dad says and grins. "Wouldn't you say, Kidah?"

"No doubt about it." The wizard smiles back, and his black eyes flash merrily as the two old warriors share a light moment. "You'll be very happy to see them, Jack. Although I must warn

you, our fight with the Dark Army may not be the only battle set-
tled on this ice sheet."

"What are you talking about?" I demand. "Who is it? What's
going on?"

Kidah steers the umiak into a sheltered cove behind the spit of
ground rock. He shades his eyes and points. "There they are!"

It's hard to see anything because of the glare reflecting off the
ice. But as I blink, I can just make out two shapes moving toward
us down the steep slope of the nearest glacier. As I watch, one of
them waves at us and starts running.

54

Kidah beaches our umiak, and we clamber out onto the bay
rocks that lead like giant black stepping-stones to the lip of the
glacier.

I can see the two figures more clearly now, and both of them
are moving fast. I recognize the one who is trailing behind first,
because she has such a distinctive gliding step. Watching her, I
flash for a moment to a deserted barn on the Outer Banks, where
a mysterious birdlike ninja stalked me with the shuffle steps of a
boxer and the lithe grace of a dancer. Only Eko moves that way—
she seems now to skim over the snow and ice.

But even Eko's effortless steps can't keep pace with the figure
in the lead, who has broken into what looks like a full sprint.
Twice she loses her footing and wipes out, but each time she
struggles back up to her feet.

She's wearing a light blue parka with a hood, and I still can't
see her face clearly. But I recognize her body and her stride and

there's only one person in the world who would dash straight down an icy glacier just to greet me.

I find myself running also. It's hard work sprinting uphill over snow and ice, but I barely notice my own rasping breaths.

She's calling to me, and I shout back to her: "P.J.! I'M COMING!" Our words are swallowed by the thunderous roar of an iceberg calving from a nearby ice cliff.

Her parka hood comes off, and her auburn hair flies free. Plumes of her breath steam into the frigid arctic air. I hit an ice patch and have to glance down. When I look back up she's twenty feet from me, and I can see her red cheeks and her hazel eyes.

And then she's in my arms! I wrap her up tightly and lift her into the air, and we drink each other in with a kiss that seems to go on for half an hour. When we finally separate my father, Kidah, and Gisco have joined us, and Eko has gone over to them and is bowing to my dad.

"What are you doing here?" I ask P.J., my arms still encircling her in a protective embrace.

"I came to help," she says. It's not much of an explanation, but then nothing about this makes much sense. If she asked me the same question, I'd have to answer that I just came from an underwater gunfight where I wounded the Dark Lord with a polar energy blast from my umiak paddle.

"You shouldn't have come," I tell her.

Her bright eyes search my face. "You don't want me here?"

"Of course I do. But it's too dangerous."

"I know what's going on," P.J. says. "She told me everything," and she nods toward Eko, who is watching us.

"You shouldn't have brought her here," I tell Eko. "You had no right to put her in this kind of peril."

"Hello, Jack," Eko responds, and gives me one of her mysterious little smiles. "Did you enjoy seeing your world—your real world?"

"*This* is my real world," I reply. I try to sound decisive, but as

I say it my voice quivers and my arm slides off P.J.'s shoulder and drops to my side. The truth is that ever since I've come back from the far future, I've felt like a bit of an interloper on this earth.

"As for P.J.," Eko continues, "she's a strong woman and she made the choice to come here for herself."

"That's true, it was my choice," P.J. says. "I think everyone here should make their own choices from now on. Wouldn't you agree, Eko?"

"In a perfect world, absolutely," Eko replies. "But this is not a perfect world, and the one Jack just visited is far worse. In such circumstances, personal choice becomes a meaningless concept. Duty and fate must take precedence. Jack understands that now."

P.J. looks back at Eko for a long second, and then turns to me. "Did your trip to the future really change you, Jack? You look the same to me."

My father and Kidah are standing together, watching me try to deal with these two women and not lifting a paternal or wizardly finger to help. In fact, both of them seem to be suppressing grins.

I've got to do something fast to change the subject. "P.J.," I say, "let me introduce you to my dad."

This sounds a little strange coming out of my mouth because P.J. has known me since we were in kindergarten together, and she was always very close to the man who raised me as my father. She once painted a portrait of him, and I also remember her knitting him a purple scarf for his fortieth birthday.

Now, I lead her over to a total stranger, but she doesn't seem at all intimidated in the presence of the King of Dann. She looks up at his broad shoulders and handsome, careworn face, and I know she must be thinking that he looks a great deal like me. "I'm Peggy Jane Peters," she says, extending a hand. "Everyone calls me P.J."

My father looks down at her for a moment, and then he

smiles and his enormous hand closes gently around her palm. "My friends call me Simeon. I hope you will, too."

P.J. slowly withdraws her hand. "To tell you the truth, I'm not quite sure how to feel about you," she tells him. "You see, I knew Jack's father—the man who raised him and spent time with him— and he was a very good man. He really loved and cared for Jack."

My father looks a little surprised by this. She's speaking to the King of Dann with the same disarming, forthright honesty that she always used to call me to account back in Hadley.

"You, on the other hand," she continues, "sent Jack back in time when he was a baby, without arranging for him to find out who he really was. I know you had your reasons, but I don't think that was fair to him." Her voice hardens a bit as she finishes: "You hurt him and other people, too, in more ways than you can know."

My father considers her words, and when he speaks his voice is soft but strong. "I see that you care a great deal for my son, and I'm grateful he had your friendship. I did have my reasons, but you're right that it wasn't fair to him. Now we have work to do, and your presence gives us a problem. I assume you flew here in a small plane?"

"Yes," P.J. tells him. "It's over there, on the edge of that glacier."

"We can't fly after the men we're chasing," Dad says. "They'd shoot us out of the air in a second. The only way to go after them is on foot. Across the ice sheet." He pauses as if he's just given P.J. a way out, and he's waiting for her to take it.

"Then we'd better start walking," P.J. replies, returning his steady gaze.

"Crossing the ice sheet isn't easy under the best of circumstances," Eko warns her.

"I didn't expect it would be."

"Listen, honey," Kidah cuts in gently, "what Simeon is trying to say is that if you come you'll be risking your life. We would hate for anything to happen to you."

She turns to the wizard and nods. "Isn't that the point? It's *my* life. Not yours, or his, or hers," and P.J.'s eyes flick to Eko, "or the future's, or the People of Dann's. It belongs to me. I'm making my choice entirely for myself, which is more than I can say for the rest of you. So let's go before it gets any colder."

P.J. turns and leads the way up the glacier toward the ice cap. One by one we all follow.

As we tromp after her, my father takes my arm and whispers to me, "I like her, Jack! She reminds me of your mother, twenty years ago."

"She shouldn't have come," I mutter.

"I am the King of Dann, and you are the beacon of hope," he tells me. "And walking just ahead of us is the mightiest wizard of the far future. Between us we have great powers. But there are some things on this earth no man can control, and I think that girlfriend of yours may be one of them!"

55

We climb through a beautiful, silent, and pristine wilderness of snow and ice. The shapes and colors, contours and wind patterns seem endless, and it would be a magical uphill hike with all my nearest and dearest if it weren't so cold and dangerous.

Gisco claims that his saliva is freezing inside his mouth, and even though the hound is given to hyperbole, I'm not sure he's exaggerating. Eko warns us to watch out for crevasses and moulins—hidden shafts in the ice where water drains out. It's hard to enjoy winter scenery and a reunion of old friends when you're tracking the Dark Lord and the Omega Box across a frozen ice sheet that may open and swallow you at any moment.

Kidah and my dad are certain that we're hot on the Dark Lord's trail, or maybe I should say cold on his trail, since a frozen wind has begun to whip around us. It makes walking even harder, and when it gusts, snow sprays up into our faces and we get twenty-second bursts of whirling whiteout. I'm still wearing my protective coat from the far future, but even so the cold is numbing. P.J. shivers beneath her parka and when she stumbles I take her hand and offer to trade coats.

"Eko gave me five layers and they're keeping me pretty warm," she tells me. But I notice that she keeps hold of my hand. "Jack, we don't get much time together," she says. "Talk to me for a minute. Where exactly did you go when you vanished from New York without saying goodbye?"

"You can't blame me for that," I tell her, noticing how the rest of our group has moved a short distance ahead, perhaps to give us a little room to catch up. Eko hangs back near us for a few seconds, and then, almost reluctantly, joins the leaders. "I ducked into a florist on Broadway to buy you flowers," I tell P.J. "Then some goons from the future drugged me and—"

"Hold on a minute," P.J. interrupts, sounding dubious. "You never brought me flowers in your life. Not even on Valentine's Day."

"I was buying you a dozen red roses. I was a construction worker and you were an elusive college girl, but I was trying my best."

P.J. flashes me a smile from under her parka hood. "Really? Red roses."

"Look what it got me," I continue. "They put me in some kind of cellular whip-o-matic and I re-formed a thousand years in the future in the middle of a burning-hot sandstorm."

"What's the future like?" P.J. asks. "Is it as bad as Eko says?"

I watch the snow swirling across the ice sheet, and I remember the sandstorms and the glagour and the barren kill zone where the Garden of Eden once bloomed. "Yeah. As bad as it could be."

We trudge along in silence for a few moments, and then P.J. asks, "Did you meet your mom?"

"Yes. We went on a weeklong journey together."

"Meeting her for the first time must have been a little strange."

"Luckily I was only half-conscious. She came into my hospital room and took my hand and sang to me, and we both started weeping. Later, we talked and she tried to explain why they sent me away. I was angry with her, but I started to understand . . ." I break off for a second.

P.J. nods to show that she understands, and then she asks softly, "Did you tell your mom about me?"

"There wasn't much time to talk. We were on a mission, fighting for our lives."

She's watching me closely. "I thought you went on a weeklong trip together?"

"Sure, battling giant lizards and ducking flying snakes."

"So you didn't tell her about me?"

I stop walking and look at her. "No," I admit. "It feels like I have two different lives. She's part of one. You're part of the other. It's easiest if I keep them separate."

"Easier for who?" P.J. asks. "Aren't your two lives converging? They have been ever since that man looked at you in the Hadley diner the night after the football game. Now we're all here together, your dad, your girlfriend from the future, and me, on the same ice sheet. Which is your real life?" she asks. "Which is the real Jack Danielson?"

I look into her hazel eyes and whisper back, "This feels real to me. Walking next to you. Holding your hand. In Hadley or on an ice sheet in Greenland. But there's also something I have to do. I was born to do it and I can't run away from it. That's all I know, P.J." I bend and give her a kiss on the cheek. "If it's not good enough for you, you should go back to New York and try to forget me, and hang out with that lacrosse player."

She shivers, and for some reason I don't think it's just from the cold. "I'm with the guy I want to be with," she whispers. "I helped Eko find the Star of Dann. I held it in my hand. I saw. I understood. And I want to help, too. Now, let's catch up with the others."

But as we hike on in silence, her questions keep pulling at me. Why *didn't* I tell my mom about her? Which is my real life? Why do I feel like I belong in a world a thousand years from now that I barely know, and that this epoch I grew up in is just a visiting place for me, a temporary stop before my true life's work begins?

Kidah, Gisco, my father, and Eko are waiting for us by the side of a gleaming blue lake. As P.J. and I join them, Eko watches us carefully with her glittering eyes.

I look back at her for a moment. We shared a great deal together, and I can't hide the fact that I have strong feelings for her. She gives me a little smile of understanding. I smile back. We're both in difficult positions, now that P.J. has joined our mission. I can see that Eko is trying to balance her feelings for me with her duties to the group.

Be careful, she advises me telepathically.

I'm doing the best I can, I answer her. It's an awkward situation for everyone. You know how much I care about you.

She means be careful of moulins, Jack, Gisco warns me, and I remember that I'm surrounded by telepaths. *This lake was made from melting snow,* the dog explains, *and it's draining out now.*

How far does it drain? I ask him.

All the way to the ground rock, which is twelve thousand feet beneath us. We're walking over one hundred thousand winters of accumulated snow and ice. But it's melting now, faster and faster.

I look over to warn P.J., but just as I do, she lets out a scream as the ice shelf opens beneath her and she slips into a hole. I keep tight hold of her hand, and am yanked in after her!

56

The moulin is dark and very steep, a pitch-black bobsled course. I hear P.J. screaming as we pick up speed, and I get one arm around her and pull her close. Eko taught me on the Outer Banks how to avoid unseen obstacles in darkness, and I use that training now to visualize the tunnel ahead and guide us around bumps and ridges. But if this chute drains to the bottom of the ice sheet, we're about to fall thousands of feet and land on solid rock.

I claw and kick to find a handhold or foothold that will at least slow us down, but the walls are too slippery. Suddenly the echoing thunder of what sounds like Niagara Falls roars up ahead. Our moulin is about to join a larger drainage chute, filled with surging, freezing water!

I have to find a way to stop us. I reach my free hand into my coat pocket and take out the handle of my scimitar. It's made of a futuristic metallic alloy, and tapers to a point. The laser blade won't do me any good in this ice tunnel, but I grasp the metallic handle and jab the pointed end as deep as I can into the icy wall of the moulin.

The sharp end of the scimitar handle bites in, and P.J. and I jerk to a stop. The torque almost pulls my arm out of its socket, but I don't let go.

"HOLD ME!" I shout to P.J. above the roar of the nearby torrent, and as she clings to me, I take my left hand and feel around for the slightest ridges or cracks that we can use to try to climb higher. The ice walls around us are as smooth as glass. All we can do is hang here and wait until my strength gives out, or until the ice melts from our body heat and my scimitar handle slips free.

"We can't last here much longer," P.J. gasps.

"There's no place to go," I tell her. "The walls are impossible to climb."

Beneath us in the darkness, the waterfall roars like a hungry beast demanding its dinner.

"I'm sorry," P.J. whispers.

"For what?"

"Falling into that hole."

"It was pretty well concealed," I tell her, and my lips graze her ear. "Anyway, they aren't holes. They're called moulins."

"You never could pronounce French," she whispers back, and I hear her voice tremble.

I kiss her on the neck. "I love you," I say softly.

"I love you, too, Jack," she whispers. "I always did and I always will. I guess this is goodbye."

Why do you humans persist in being so damn heroic in moments of extreme peril? a familiar canine telepathic voice inquires. *Find an escape. Pray to your gods. Play a long shot. But don't just exchange noble, poignant sentiments and wait for the grim reaper.*

I look around the moulin. Gisco? Are you coming to save us, or are you just going to insult us at long range?

Dogs can't climb, and I suffer from a touch of claustrophobia. It's a family malady. My great-grandfather was once trapped in a chicken coop for three days and he nearly went mad. Well, it was his own fault. He was hungry and there is a family weakness for poultry . . .

Gisco, we're about to fall to our deaths!

Hold on and fear not. Help is on the way.

I can feel the scimitar handle loosening. Gisco, help better get here very soon or we're finished.

Just a few more seconds, Jack, my father advises me telepathically. *Don't give up.*

P.J. sobs, and I can feel her grip slipping. "Hold on," I tell her. "They're sending someone to rescue us."

"How do you know?" she asks.

"Gisco told me telepathically. And my dad."

"Tell them to hurry."

"I did."

"Jack, let me go. My weight is pulling us down. You're the one they need."

"No," I say.

"I can't hold on any longer." She loses her grip and starts to fall, but as she slides away I grab for her with my left hand and snag her parka hood.

"Let go," she pleads. "Save yourself."

"They're coming. We can make it."

"They'll never reach us in time."

"They already have," I tell her.

A faint blue light illuminates the ice tunnel from above. A shadow descends toward us, sliding swiftly and gracefully down an ethereal blue rope. It's Eko! She appears to be at the end of the rope, but as she continues to descend, the rope lengthens. As she nears us, she calls out: "Jack, are you okay?"

"Yes," I answer, "but we can't hold on much longer."

Eko sees the precarious way we're dangling, and she realizes how dire our situation is. She quickly rappels down to us and says, "Grab my rope."

P.J. grabs it and I do, too. Just as my fingers close around it, my scimitar handle slips free from the ice wall. I catch it and tuck it back into my pocket.

Now the three of us are hanging from the same thin blue rope. "I can't climb up," P.J. tells her. "I don't have the strength."

"We're not going to climb up," Eko replies. "There's a much faster and easier way."

She clings to the rope with one hand and uses the other to take a small blue disc out of her coat pocket. It's the size of a CD, and reminds me of the red disc my dad stretched into a flying sled to get us away from the lion cyborgs. Eko fastens it to the end of the rope, just beneath us, and moves her fingers outward. The disc begins to widen out. It increases to the size of a dinner plate, then a car tire, and soon it has the same diameter as the ice tunnel. "Sit on it," she instructs us. "Keep your balance centered in the middle."

We sit there, on top of the stretched-out blue disc, waiting for something to happen. "How are we going to get out of here, if we're not going to climb?" P.J. asks.

"Propulsion," Eko answers.

"Who or what is going to push us up?" I ask.

Eko smiles, and then I hear a roaring sound. The torrent beneath us suddenly sounds much closer. I can hear waves slapping against ice walls. Water is being drawn up the moulin, toward us!

"KEEP YOUR WEIGHT IN THE MIDDLE!" Eko shouts above the roar. A second later, I feel a gentle nudge as the first waves graze the bottom of our blue saucer. The water pressure builds steadily beneath us, and we start rising, faster and faster. Soon we're flying upward through the chute. I feel like a champagne cork flying out of the bottleneck.

A circle of sunlight shines down from far above like a halo. We speed toward it, and burst out onto the ice. Water geysers above us for a few seconds, and then recedes back into the hole as Kidah slices his arm through the air in what looks like a karate chop. The thin blue rope vanishes back into the Star of Dann.

"Are you guys okay?" Kidah asks.

"Never better," I tell him. "Thanks for getting us out of that tight spot."

"I just put some water to good use," he says. "You should thank the gal who climbed down to you."

I turn to Eko, but P.J. has beaten me to it. "That's the second time you saved me," she says, her hand on Eko's arm. "I'm sorry I made you risk your life."

"It might turn out to be a good thing after all," Eko tells her.

P.J. looks back at her. "How could it be a good thing?"

"Because we're very close to the ice fortress where the Dark Lord and the Omega Box have holed up," my father explains. "Our best chance against them is a surprise attack."

And you and Jack just showed us a very original way to go in through the back door, Gisco adds telepathically.

I look at his face, and then I turn to my father and the wizard. "You're not going to try to slide into their ice fortress through moulins? It's too dangerous. Believe me, I've been in one."

Kidah gives me a grin. "Oh, I believe you. That's exactly why we think it might work."

57

We press on across the ice sheet and snow begins to fall. At first the soft flakes are welcome, but it's soon snowing so hard that we can barely see. The wind picks up, too, and blasts the fallen snow back up into our eyes, so that every step becomes a slippery adventure. We walk in each other's footsteps, five people and a dog sharing their fates like mountain climbers tethered together.

I don't think that even Kidah would be able to stay on the Dark Lord's trail through this storm if he didn't have help. Arctic foxes trot ahead of us, and I see white owls with great wingspans diving in and out of the billowing blizzard. We reach the top of a ridge just in time for me to spot a polar bear rear up on its hind legs and then duck out of sight and vanish in a puff of new-fallen powder.

P.J. sees the huge bear, too, and reacts.

"He's on our side," I tell her. "There's a much narrower web of life here than in the Amazon, but we've got friendly eyes and ears on every glacier."

Kidah stretches out his arms to stop us. "They're very close," he announces. "The good news is that our journey will soon be over!"

"And the bad news?" I ask him.

The wizard gives me a mischievous smile, and his eyes glint. "I'm afraid the weather is about to take a turn for the worse." He holds the Star of Dann high in one hand while he moves his other arm in slow circles, as if stirring water in a cauldron.

The sky darkens, and wind blasts down at us in savage gusts that knock P.J. and me back several steps.

My father catches us, and for a moment P.J. and I share his safe, fatherly embrace. "Stay low," he counsels.

"We are staying low," I tell him. "Trying to walk in this storm is crazy."

"It's as hard for them as it is for us," he says. "We need to pin them down and blind them." He releases us back to the winds.

You're staying low, but you're not low enough, Gisco advises. I notice the savvy hound is now practically slithering along on his belly. *Unless I'm mistaken, this is a katabatic wind.*

A what? I ask as P.J. and I stagger forward, holding on to each other and crouching down.

A rare and dangerous weather pattern. It's a powerful drainage wind that blows off a mountain or glacier. Air becomes denser as its temperature drops, and it starts flowing downward, faster and faster.

Eko silently takes my other arm. It feels very strange for me to walk with these two women who I've shared so much with on either side of me. But there's no other way to move forward—we might all get sucked off the ice at any moment and blow away to Oz.

How strong can one of these katabatic winds get? I ask Gisco.

There's something called a Piteraq, he tells me. *It's a hurricane-force katabatic wind that can form over the Greenland Ice Sheet when conditions are just right. A Piteraq can blow right off the scale.*

Great, I say. I take it that they're just right?

Yes. I believe we're smack in the middle of a Piteraq.

How do we get out of it?

Find shelter immediately or die! the dog replies without hesitation. *And my mother didn't go through the pains of birthing a litter just to have her favorite son glaciate on this ice sheet. Follow me!* And he bravely crawls out in front of our slow-moving column.

My father and Kidah link arms and fall in behind Gisco. I watch them stagger along ahead of us—even the wizard and the King of Dann struggle to take each forward step.

Suddenly, we see snow rising off the ice sheet in an endless column reaching to the dark sky. A cyclonic wind is heading toward us, and we can hear the shrill howl as it spins closer and closer.

P.J., Eko, and I stop walking. There's nothing to do and nowhere to run. We just stand there, holding each other and waiting for it to hit.

The mesocyclone slams into Gisco first, since he's out in front. He dives flat and tries to hug the face of the ice sheet, but the wind lifts the hunkered-down hound off his stomach and blows him back at my father and Kidah like a canine bowling ball. *Whoa!* he howls telepathically. *Somebody catch meeeeeeee!*

My father and Kidah crouch low to absorb the impact, but Gisco slams into them with all the force of the raging Piteraq. Gisco, Kidah, and my dad are swept back toward us. I see flailing limbs and white hair and a wagging tail flying at us like a giant living snowball in an avalanche.

I get into my best tackling stance and try to hit them low and at least slow them down, but the impact combined with the ripping wind is impossible to resist. Eko and P.J. are thrown over along with me, and we're all blown backward together, totally at the mercy of the gale.

We spin and scrape and slide at terrific speed, six out-of-control windsurfers with no way to steer or apply the brakes. I fear we'll be blown clear across the ice sheet, but after two or three minutes we thunk into something large and hard that stops us cold.

I slowly get to my feet and look for P.J. and Eko. They're both dazed, but when I call their names they rise to their knees.

A hulking shape looms above us like a giant gravestone. I look out and see another such shape, and a third. They're ice formations, as large and mysterious as Stonehenge.

Kidah and my dad crawl over and we all huddle on the lee side of one of the ice formations. "Well, we're here, right on schedule," the wizard announces cheerfully, shaking some snow out of his white hair.

"You planned that, didn't you?" P.J. accuses him.

"Well, it's not the most comfortable way to travel," Kidah admits, "but we weren't doing very well by walking."

"WE'VE LOST GISCO!" I shout, alarmed that the dog might have blown far away across the ice sheet.

It's impossible to lose a loyal dog, a telepathic voice assures me, and a second later his snout pokes out of a nearby drift. He hobbles over to us on shaky legs.

"Okay, we're all here," I say to Kidah. "What do we do now?"

"We arm ourselves for the final battle," he says.

My father adds softly, "And then we go finish this."

58

In the shelter of the ice formation, we make our final preparations.

Kidah passes the Star of Dann to my father. "Keep this, Simeon. Your ancestor found it, so it's fitting that you wear it into battle."

Dad takes the glowing Star and hangs it by its silver chain around his neck. "When Dann found this, all the ice had already melted," my father says softly. "Let's see if we can prevent that." The gem pulses, and a long blue sword suddenly flames to life in his hands.

Kidah turns to me. "Do you have a weapon, Jack?"

I take out my scimitar handle. It got banged up when I jabbed it into the ice wall of the moulin. I test it by willing the blade to open, and the sapphire flame springs out and burns brightly.

P.J. has never seen me holding the scimitar before. She studies me as the shadow of the curved blade flickers across my face.

"My dear," Kidah says to her, "you have shared all the dangers and you deserve a weapon of your own."

"A weapon like that won't do me any good," P.J. says. "I can't use telepathy the way all of you can."

"I'll find something else for you," Kidah promises, and folds his right hand into a fist. He waves it through the air, and when he opens his fingers he's holding a tiny seashell. He offers it to her. "Here is your weapon."

"Thanks," she replies with a little smile, "but that doesn't look very dangerous."

The wizard glances down. "Sheesh, I forgot." He blows on

the shell, and passes it to P.J. She holds it in her palm and it begins to elongate. It's soon longer than her arm, and tapers to a sharp point—a mother-of-pearl rapier! "This may come in handy," he tells her. "The Omega Box is heat sensitive, and may prove impossible to kill with a laser weapon. An old-fashioned sword thrust just might do the trick."

P.J. looks back at him. "I don't know if I can kill anyone or anything. And what is the Omega Box?"

"It's a doomsday device," I tell her, "created by this nutty cult in the future called the Jasai, who believe that humans have done so much damage to the earth that we should all be eliminated. The Omega Box was originally a machine capable of wiping out all life on earth, but it's developed a consciousness and joined forces with the Dark Army. It wants to help destroy our earth so it can rule with them in the far future."

"It's strange that you don't understand their cult's appeal, Jack, because I understand it all too well," my father says unexpectedly. "Jasai was a friend of mine, and one of the wisest and most dedicated of our priests."

My dad breaks off and coughs, and I notice that his hand goes to his chest, and clutches the area near his heart. The blue sword that flamed in his hands seems to retract into a pilot light, and his body sags, as if the weight of the world is dragging him down. In a weak voice, barely audible above the winds, he adds, "Now that I have been back before the Turning Point, I understand Jasai even better. We humans have been so foolish—we have done so many evil, unspeakable things for so long—it's tempting to believe the earth would be better off without us."

Then my dad shrugs his broad shoulders and straightens up, and the blue Sword of Dann flames out again. His voice grows stronger and more assured as he concludes, "But Jasai for all his brilliance was wrong. He gave up too easily. Yes, we were foolish the first time around, but we are capable of far better. We can fix things, and forge a totally different outcome." And the King of

Dann's voice rings out: "Given a second chance, humans can govern this beautiful earth as wise caretakers, and usher in a golden age!"

"Well said, Simeon." Kidah nods. "But sheesh, nobody's going to give us a second chance, or anything else on this ice block. We'll have to take it. So let's go see where they've holed up."

59

We reluctantly leave the shelter of the ice formations and creep forward, holding on to each other. Soon a jagged black line appears up ahead. As we crawl close to it, I see that it's actually a gaping crevasse that splits the ice sheet like a river valley.

We keep back from the edge, and lie almost flat so that the wind doesn't sweep us into the abyss. As I peer down through the swirling snow into that giant fissure, I glimpse a long blue snake slithering far below. It's a river of meltwater draining deep inside the crevasse, sawing away at thousands of years of accumulated ice.

"He's down there," my father announces grimly. "I can feel it."

"Yes, and the Omega Box, too," Kidah adds. "If we try to climb down, they'll see us coming, even with this snow. So we'll take a more direct route. Come this way."

We follow Kidah till he shouts out, "STOP!"

We freeze in mid-step, and the wizard claps his hands three times. At the third loud clap, the snow cover all around us shifts and two large openings become visible. It's like two manhole covers have suddenly been removed, and we're looking down into twin deep, tubular holes.

Kidah walks to the closest of them and peers down, taking the measure of it. He wrinkles his nose, as if inhaling an unpleasant odor. "Not this one," he says with a chuckle. "It's cold enough without a swim in a frozen river." He walks over to the second hole, and gives it the once-over. "Yes," he murmurs. "Very good, this will do nicely." He looks around at us. "Simeon, a last speech?"

My father nods and his eyes rest on Kidah, Eko, and Gisco as he says softly, "Some of us have come a long way, but our journey is finally over. I thank each of you for your devoted service to a noble cause." His gaze swings to me. "I know the burden was sometimes crushing, but it was necessary to bring us to this singular moment in time. It is the true turning point, when we will move the earth forward into light or let it slip into endless darkness."

He's looking right at me, and a tear glints in his eye. "I wish we had more time with each other. I'm thinking not just of my son, who I barely know, but of my wife, and I know you're all thinking of your own loved ones." His eyes flick to P.J. for a moment. I sense that she's thinking of her mother and father back in their house in Hadley-by-Hudson. Then my father's tears are gone, and he raises the blue Sword of Dann and sweeps it back and forth over us as if blessing us. "Strike hard and strike true," he says. "There are causes worth dying for, and this beautiful earth is one of them!"

"Here, here!" Kidah says. "I can't add anything to that speech, so into the rabbit hole we go!" The wizard jumps into the moulin and drops out of sight.

My father steps over to me, kisses me once on the forehead, and then follows the wizard into the abyss.

Eko goes next. She looks at me before she jumps, and her gray eyes are not hard for the coming battle but soft with memories and nostalgia. It's like she's sending me a telepathic photo album. I remember flying with her on the Outer Banks, and swimming with her and the pink dolphins in the Amazon. Many of the most exciting moments I've had in my life have been with her.

In that moment, as she looks at me, I sense how much she loves me. She doesn't express it as openly as P.J., but it's right there, shining clearly in her gray eyes. She's always believed that we'd end up together—that we're fated to be man and wife. Now, in addition to her tenderness, I see the strength of her conviction.

I nod my head very slightly. Yes, I care for her deeply, and I can't deny it. Nor can I shake the feeling that the future world is really my true home. She smiles and jumps into the moulin.

Old bean, Gisco says, *I'll be quite honest with you. There are a lot of things I'd rather do than jump into that ice pit. A good meal comes to mind, in a warm place, with amiable company. But let it never be said that when the King of Dann led the way, the only dog present even hesitated! Once more into the breach, or in this case, the abyss!* Gisco leaps forward into the gaping hole, and sinks out of sight.

I turn to P.J. "I have to follow. You don't."

She's studying my face. I'm not sure if she saw the look I exchanged with Eko. The truth is that I love both these women, in very different ways.

"It's okay," she says. "I've been down one of these moulins before. Anyway, I don't plan on staying on this ice sheet all alone. Give me your hand."

I hold it out and she takes it. We stand there for a long second, looking into each other's eyes as the snow whirls and the Piteraq howls around us.

"Just one step," she says softly. "Shall we?"

"We shall," I whisper back, and at the same second we both jump.

✹

60

Once again I'm in the pitch-black bobsled course of a moulin, holding P.J. tightly as we careen around hairpin curves and plummet down stomach-churning straightaways. I won't say it's easier the second time around, but at least we jumped into this dark tunnel, rather than falling into a hole by accident. I feel a tiny bit more in control as we slide feetfirst, clinging to each other and trying to avoid obstacles and overhangs.

Suddenly the tunnel splits, and then diverges again. I don't want to get separated from the rest of our group, but we're hurtling along almost in free fall. The twists and turns come like lightning, so there's no time to set up a telepathic conference call and try to coordinate our routes.

I make choices blindly, and when the tunnel we've ended up in evens out a bit, I call out hopefully, Dad? Kidah? Gisco? Is anyone around?

Old bean, I think I see light at the end of the tunnel, Gisco responds telepathically. *High time, too. There's a great difference between a dog and a mole.*

Lead on, old comrade, I tell him. I've got your back. The darkness of the tunnel is indeed starting to lighten.

And then P.J. and I whip around a final curve and literally encounter Gisco's broad and furry backside as the large hound tries to put on the brakes before sliding headfirst into the icy river that now glitters dead ahead. Paws kick at me and a great mop of a tail swats my face.

I register that we've popped out of the moulin into some kind of majestic ice amphitheater, but my attention is now focused on the gleaming blue ribbon that we're careening toward at break-neck speed. Gisco, if we slide into that icy water, we'll freeze to death in seconds.

Quit biting my tail and help me stop us.

I kick into the ice with my heels and grab with my fingers, but there are no handholds. I reach for the scimitar handle but I can't get it out of my pocket. I am trying to help, I tell Gisco.

Try something else! I enjoy a bracing swim as much as the next dog, but that river is liquid ice. Use those human fingers, Jack! Grab on to something!

Gisco, I can't even slow us down. You do something!

I see a drift on the bank. Steer to the right!

I hold on to P.J. and try to tilt us to the right, and a second later we burst through an enormous pillow of new-fallen snow that slows us down just enough so that we come to a stop a few feet from the frigid torrent.

P.J. gasps. "What is this place? It's beautiful."

I look around. It's like we've fallen into a subglacial coliseum. Glittering ice walls rise on all sides of us. The ice formations have different contours and textures, and sunlight filters down through the fissure and gilds those walls so that they glow in all different shades of blue and violet. I hear something and glance over, but it's just the river bubbling near us. It's splashing into waterfalls and whipsawing at the ice as it gushes through this mysterious ice river valley.

P.J. and I climb to our feet and stand side by side, looking around at the spectacular arctic scenery. "We have to find the others," I tell her. "They must have popped out of the moulin through a different exit hole, but they can't be too far."

Gisco rises from the snowdrift to stand next to us. *I can't contact them telepathically,* he informs me. *If they're close, I should be able to, but something or someone is blocking me. It could be the Omega Box. He has great powers.*

If he's blocking you, then he knows we're here, I point out to the dog. Before he pinpoints us, let's get moving. If the Dark Lord and the Omega Box find us before we locate Kidah, Eko, and my dad, we're really in trouble.

I try not to show my fears to P.J. "Let's go wizard hunting," I tell her. "Pick a direction."

She stretches out an arm. "That way!"

So we start off, slipping and sliding on the ice. The snow sifts down from above, but there are no winds deep inside this fissure. P.J.'s right—it's a silent white world, untouched by man and stunningly beautiful. If we weren't in so much danger this would be one of the most magical, secret places on earth.

Suddenly Gisco stops and sniffs.

P.J. and I see his reaction and also stop. What is it? I ask him. Is something wrong?

Old bean, I have two pieces of news, bad and worse.

Give me the bad one first, I tell him.

The ground is starting to tremble.

I don't feel anything.

My paws are very sensitive to vibrations. And it's getting stronger. I fear an earthquake, or maybe an icequake.

P.J. can't hear our telepathic conversation, but suddenly she says, "Jack, I feel something. I think the ground is shaking . . ."

I feel it, too, now. I look up at the ice walls on all sides. They no longer look quite so beautiful. If they start to come down on us, we're finished. What's the worse news? I ask. What could be worse than that?

We're not alone, he says. *Someone or something has found us.*

61

What is it?" P.J. asks, studying my face.

"Someone's coming," I tell her.

"Friend or foe?"

"Foe."

She looks back at me, nods grimly, and holds up her shell sword.

I pull my scimitar handle from my pocket and will the blade to extend. The sapphire laser arcs out, and then it suddenly flares wildly. The blue flame leaps back down the handle and scorches my hands. I drop the handle and shriek in pain. A faint blue glow continues to shimmer around my fingers, and it feels like they're still on fire.

"Jack," P.J. shouts, "touch the ice."

I drop to my knees and press my palms to the ice, and then slide them into a snowdrift up to my elbows. The burning lessens.

It's the Omega Box, Gisco warns nervously. *Only he has the power to do a thing like that.*

We look around. Snow is sifting down through the fissure, and the ice beneath our feet is trembling. Ripping sounds come from all around us—the walls of the fissure are starting to crack apart.

I glance up nervously at the shimmering sides of the crevasse. The sunlight that filters down through the top of the fissure seems to be fading, and as the amphitheater darkens, the ice formations change color, from cheerful blues and violets to ominous purples, grays, and blacks.

I wish Kidah, my father, and Eko were here. I can't help thinking that they were split off from us by design. Perhaps the

Dark Lord and the Omega Box anticipated that we were going to slide down a moulin, and rigged it so that our group was split in two. Now that we have fallen into their trap, they will try to finish off the weaker half first.

Laughter rings out. It's not the maniacal laughter of a crazed super-villain, nor is it the mechanical cackle of a machine that's come to life and is trying to simulate vocal cords. Rather, it's a hearty and very human-sounding chuckle, the belly laugh of a man who's just enjoyed a whopping good joke.

I spot a figure standing on an ice shelf, high above us. "Hands a little too hot, Prince of Dann?" he calls down in a deep, musical voice.

I rub snow on my seared fingers as I look up at him. "Why don't you come down here and see for yourself?" I shout.

"Yes, I will come down," he assures me. "But someone else wants to welcome you first. I believe he's an old friend of yours, and of your girlfriend's, too."

He steps back from the edge of the shelf and I lose sight of him.

The icy floor beneath us shakes so violently that P.J. and I are thrown off our feet, and Gisco lies flat.

I try to hold on to P.J. but she slides away from me. A web of cracks appears all around us, and suddenly a figure bursts upward, exploding through the ice with a tremendous shower of crystals. He somersaults high into the air before he lands on the shaking ice floor, as light and sure-footed as a spider.

I recognize his powerful build, his flowing white hair, and his glittering, black subhuman eyes. I can tell that P.J. recognizes him, too, from her time spent in his Amazon prison. She raises her sword and points it at him, and the point trembles.

"Hello, my dear," he says to her, stepping toward us. "Is that any way to greet an old friend?"

His left calf and thigh are heavily bandaged. I must have seriously wounded him with my blast from the umiak paddle. But the

Dark Lord is clearly a quick healer, because he barely limps as he advances toward us.

"And welcome also to you, son of Dann," he says. He turns his head slightly to look at me, and for a moment in the fading light I see a long scar down the side of his face where I stabbed him with a shard of glass. "We have some unfinished business," he tells me. "Why don't we settle accounts right now?"

"Suits me," I tell him, trying to get into a fighting stance. I can barely stand upright on the trembling ice.

The Dark Lord could probably walk across the ice, but he chooses a more direct route. He launches himself at me from twenty feet away in an impossibly fast leap. I anticipate his jump and also guess that because his left leg is injured, he'll kick with his right. Even so I'm too slow. By the time I start to raise my left arm in a block, the ball of his right foot thunks into my chest. I'm knocked spinning backward, as unable to stop myself as I was when blown by the Piteraq.

I crash into one of the crevasse's ice walls. It's as hard as granite, and the impact stuns me. When the gleaming blue world stops spinning I see that the Dark Lord has turned toward P.J. She backs away from him, her sword held at the ready. She's being very brave, but she'll never be able to hold him off! I try to run back to save her, but a vengeful canine beats me to it.

Gisco has his own score to settle with the leader of the Dark Army. When they tangled in the Amazon, the Dark Lord used his telepathic powers to scramble the dog's brains. Now, Gisco charges at him fearlessly from behind and sinks his teeth deep into the Dark Lord's injured left leg.

The spidery fiend flips over onto his back, and for a second I think Gisco has the upper hand. Once a big dog has a person pinned to the ground, it's nearly impossible to get back up. But the usual fighting rules don't apply to a human tarantula. As he falls backward he pulls Gisco close to him, and then uses the momentum of his fall to catapult Gisco into the air.

My canine friend is launched like a rocket. He flies high and far and touches down on his back with a sickening thud. The Dark Lord hurled him toward the river, and before Gisco can stop himself, he slides over the lip of the bank and disappears into the frigid blue water with a yelp and a final desperate twitch of his tail.

Then the Dark Lord turns to face me.

62

I try to control my rage as I race toward him. I saw what the Dark Lord just did to Gisco, and I'm out for blood—spider blood. But I can't just attack him with a standard kick or a punch. I know from fighting him in the past that his strength and speed are matchless, so to have any chance I have to use guile and try the unexpected.

I feint a leaping kick, but instead of jumping I fall onto my back at the very last second and slide into him low and hard. Gisco had the right idea—attack the Dark Lord's injury. I take him out at the knees and land a solid kick to his wounded left leg.

The collision knocks him over but it doesn't even slow him down. He recovers in a split second, before I can get up from my sliding tackle. He doesn't bother to stand, but instead comes scuttling at me on all fours, and it really is like being charged by a giant tarantula. His mouth is open and his fangs glint in the low light.

I kick at him wildly and put my arms up to try to keep his sharp teeth from my throat. I wrestled for years and I'm usually comfortable grappling at close quarters, but the Dark Lord's balance is extraordinary and his strength is overpowering.

He quickly gains a control position and begins pummeling away at me, picking one soft target after another. An elbow thuds into my stomach, a knee slices down at my groin, and a heavy fist finds its way around my guard and crashes into the side of my head.

I cover up and fight back with everything I have, jabbing at his eyes and throat. But when I thrust up to try to blind him, he grabs my right wrist and slowly forces my arm down to the ice, exposing me. Then he does the same with my left arm.

I try to buck him off but he head-butts me, breaking my nose. I almost black out, and blink up at him through a crimson filter of my own blood.

Both my arms are pinned and my jugular is now fully exposed. The Dark Lord lowers his head, and I feel his hot breath on my face. "Now, son of Dann, I will enjoy the meal my candirú missed out on . . ."

He senses something and breaks off, twisting his body to avoid the point of a shell sword that stabs down at him with speed and power. He winces in pain and reaches around to grab the sword before P.J. can stab him again. She tries to hold on to it, but the Dark Lord yanks it from her grasp and flings her away like a rag doll. His strength is undiminished, so I guess she missed his vital organs.

I try to use the distraction of P.J.'s attack to throw him off me, but in a heartbeat the razor point of the shell sword is pressed to my throat. I stare back up into those black eyes. They truly are subhuman, devoid of even the slightest trace of sympathy or mercy. They're the eyes of death itself—as cold and empty as a yawning grave.

His head dips toward me a second time and his fangs graze my throat as if he's searching for the exact right spot to bite down. I writhe away from him on pure instinct and try to force my right arm between us, but he pins me down. He opens his mouth to sink his fangs into my jugular, but, at the last possible second, someone else's arm slides around the Dark Lord's neck and pulls him off.

My broken nose chokes my breathing and I can barely see through the pain and the blood, but I glimpse my father choking him from behind. I try to get up to help, but I can't rise higher than my knees. So I kneel, watching the battle between the two titans of the far future.

What's the best way to kill a spider? It must be to snap off its neck. My father has the Dark Lord in a death hold. He lifts the spidery fiend off the ground and shakes him back and forth as he squeezes the life out of him. "I spent enough years in your prisons, cousin," he rasps. "Now you're my captive. I will end it for you quickly."

The Dark Lord twists and contorts his limbs, scratches with his nails and kicks backward, but he can't break the hold. Suddenly his body seems to contract in on itself and four additional limbs appear as he morphs from man to spider. He flails all eight legs wildly and hisses and spits venom, but he still can't free himself.

Then he's a man again, and his movements begin to slow. Even through my blood haze, I can see that he's dying. A final fury kindles in his glittering soulless eyes, and he makes one last, superhuman effort to free himself, spinning and arching his spine nearly in half so that for just a second my father almost loses his grip.

The Dark Lord takes advantage of that second to reach his arm behind his body and stab upward with the shell sword.

My dad gasps in pain, and then I see a matching fury in his own eyes as he conquers his agony long enough to give a tremendous final twist with his powerful arms. There's an earsplitting cracking sound as the Dark Lord's neck breaks, and he immediately stops thrashing about. My father continues twisting for several more seconds. When he finally releases his grip, the Dark Lord sinks to the ice, his head wrenched nearly completely around.

As he lies on the ice, he begins to transform. He shrinks to less than half his human size, and eight limbs hang motionless. His face, however, remains the face of a man with a grand ambition, stopped at the last possible moment, his countenance frozen forever in an expression of agonized defeat.

I struggle to my feet and stagger over to my father. "Dad, you won! He's dead! Are you okay?"

He turns toward me and gives me a tiny smile, and then I see the shell sword embedded in his chest. He opens his mouth to speak, and manages, "Yes, my son . . ."

Then he topples over onto the ice next to the corpse of his nemesis.

63

I crouch next to my father, and pull the shell sword out of his chest. I hurl it away, and it slides over the ice and disappears into the freezing river.

My father grimaces and closes his eyes for a second, and I feel that his chest is wet with blood. "Don't go," I plead. "Please."

He's fading fast, but he looks up at me and his eyes gleam. He reaches out and takes my hand. I squeeze it, and feel a slight pressure back.

I look around wildly for help. P.J. rushes up and kneels on my father's other side. "I'm so sorry," she whispers. "I couldn't stop him from taking the sword . . ."

"It wasn't your fault," I tell her. "You saved my life." I look past her and see two distant forms, hurrying toward us. Eko is running quickly over the shaking ice. But she's outpaced by the wizard, who skates along in an effortless glide, as if a secret wind is pushing him.

"Kidah is coming," I tell my dad. "He's almost here! He'll fix you up somehow. I lost one father. I don't want to lose a second one." His grip is getting weaker by the second. "Your people need you. The future earth needs you. Don't go," I plead. "The King of Dann must live!"

He moves his lips with a great effort and gasps, "The King of Dann is dead. Long live the King." He squeezes my fingers one last time and looks right up into my eyes. "Destiny, Jair," he whispers faintly. "Destiny . . . and duty."

His grip loosens, and then goes slack. I hold on to his hand for a few more seconds, and then let it fall as my head sinks to his chest.

Kidah kneels down next to me. He tenderly closes my father's eyes and whispers, "Goodbye, old friend." A tear runs down the old wizard's cheek. Then he takes the chain with the Star of Dann off my dad's neck and drapes it over my head. The blue jewel flashes as it falls to my chest. My vision clears and I'm able to breathe more easily.

Eko runs up, and then stops short. I recall that she was an orphan, and the Dannites took her in. She bows low to my father's corpse, and when she straightens back up the sorrow and loss I see in her face are not merely of a High Priestess who has lost her leader, but also of a girl who has had a revered father figure taken away.

Eko glances at the spidery carcass of the Dark Lord, lying next to my dad, and then turns to me. "Our King gave his life for the best possible cause, Jack." She reaches out and gently wipes the blood from my cheek. "You and your father have won a mighty battle."

"He won it," I tell her. "P.J. helped. I did nothing. I couldn't even stand up and fight next to him when he needed me most . . ."

"That's not true. You fought bravely," P.J. says, her eyes on Eko, who is ministering to me. "It was my fault. He was killed with my weapon."

I start to answer, and then Kidah yells, "WATCH OUT!" And he points straight up.

I follow his finger, and see that several enormous chunks of ice have broken off the walls of the crevasse and are plummeting toward us.

We dive out of the way as the ice chunks crash down all around us. It's like being targeted by a meteor shower. The fissure's floor trembles at the impact and buckles in places. Small and large cracks open. One great ice boulder falls into the nearby river, which overflows its banks and hisses up toward us. It splashes us with freezing water before quickly receding.

We stagger to our feet as a familiar laugh rings out. A voice booms from everywhere and nowhere: "I told you I would come down to you, and here I am to finish this once and for all."

64

I look around and don't see the Omega Box. Then an orange tunnel is lasered through the crevasse wall near us, and a figure strides purposefully out of the opening.

He looks like a normal man of medium height, with a pleasant, almost genial face and sandy brown hair.

"Spread out," Kidah commands. "Don't let him—"

Fire erupts from the Omega Box's eyes, and streaks toward us. It would incinerate us, but the old wizard anticipates the blast and darts forward. He circles his hands in a sweeping pattern and a disc of flowing gray energy takes shape in front of him. He tilts it like a shield just in time to intercept the Omega Box's heat beam. Some of the heat filters through the gray plasma, and Kidah begins to tremble and drip with sweat.

The Omega Box laughs. He continues to walk toward us—he's now less than fifty feet away. "Well done, you old trickster," he says, the beam of heat still flashing from his eyes. "But why prolong the inevitable?"

"The only thing that is inevitable is your failure," Kidah calls back. "It is written in the annals of Dann that you shall soon be as dead as you were before Jasai screwed you together from nuts and bolts in his workshop."

"The future appears more clearly to me than to your pathetic seers," the Omega Box answers. "I see a dead King and a foolish Prince who will soon join his father in darkness. Jasai was right—you humans all deserve to die. I will be happy to speed the process along. Then I shall return to the future, and rule the Dark Army in place of their fallen lord. They who have been built in laboratories and had their DNA stitched together will accept me as their leader." He amps up the heat beam.

Kidah grunts and almost drops the shield. He clearly doesn't have more than a few seconds left.

I find myself running. Just before Kidah raised the shield, he told us to spread out. That must be the key to fighting the Omega Box. His power seems almost unlimited, but also narrowly focused. We need to attack him from several directions at once.

Heat energy reflected by Kidah's shield nearly broils me alive as I sprint toward the Omega Box. I scream and almost go down, but somehow I keep running, and burst through a barrier of fiery pain. I remember my dad, and how he kept fighting even after he was mortally wounded. He gave his life to stop these guys, and now there's just one more battle left to win. I launch myself at the Omega Box in a desperate flying leap.

He turns his head quickly, and his heat beam swings toward me. Since I'm airborne, I have no defense.

Suddenly the Star of Dann flashes, and I see a dozen phantom versions of myself flying along on either side of me. The heat beam slices through one shadow image and then another as the Omega Box tries to pick out the real Jack Danielson. Before he can take a third guess, I'm close enough to try to kick his head off.

He raises his arm in a last-second block, and my kick thuds hard into his shoulder. It's like fighting a walking oven—as soon as my foot makes contact, the sole of my boot sizzles off. He stumbles back a few steps from the force of my kick, while I crash to the ice and skid.

The Omega Box rights himself but before he can fire a blast at me, a dark shape leaps toward him from behind. It's Eko, stabbing down at him with a black laser sword.

He senses her attack, ducks under her sword thrust, and swats her away like a pesky flea.

The only way to fight a demon from hell is to keep attacking. I get to my feet and run at him again. He wheels back toward me and opens his mouth, and crimson flame erupts. I dive underneath the tongue of fire, and punch upward at his groin.

The Omega Box's red-hot knee brands itself into my chest and the searing pain stuns me. He grabs me, and pulls me up so that we're face to face. I can feel the molten heat radiating from his body. He smiles, and then his mouth starts to open wider and I know flames are about to char-grill me. I rip the Star of Dann off my neck and shove it into his mouth, and jam it far down his throat.

He drops me and staggers in a circle, trying to claw out the Star.

Kidah runs up and waves his right hand, and what look like a hundred purple darts shoot out toward the Omega Box. Even while choking, he still has the presence of mind to aim his heat beam and irradiate the darts in mid-flight. The blast nearly immolates Kidah, who flings himself sideways across the ice to get away.

We're all taking our best shots, but this doomsday device seems unkillable. We've tried lethal kicks, laser weapons, and potent magical spells.

The Omega Box opens his mouth to an incredible circumference and with a great effort spits out the Star of Dann. He looks around at us triumphantly, and then he stares fixedly up at the sides of the crevasse. His heat beam shoots out at the glittering walls above us, and instantly the fissure begins to tremble.

Chunks of ice break off and plummet toward us. I see Kidah concentrating on them as they fall, and somehow steering them away so they just miss us. But there are more and more of them, and even Kidah has his limits. We'll soon be buried alive by these massive ice blocks.

The Omega Box is focused on bringing the walls of the crevasse down. He doesn't spot a new dark shape that charges at him from the side. I remember what Kidah told P.J. when he gave her the shell sword—it might be the only weapon that could pierce the Omega Box's defenses.

The dark shape powers in at him like a heat-seeking missile. I see four enormous paws driving a low-slung body forward, and then powerful legs thrust upward into a ferocious bound. Gisco must have fished the shell sword out of the river, and now he holds it in his jaws as he flies through the air and stabs it into the Omega Box. *Take that, microwave man!* the dog snarls telepathically.

The gleaming shell sword does what all our laser weapons couldn't. The Omega Box topples to the ground, and lies there writhing. He reaches around to try to pull the weapon out, but before he can do that Kidah sweeps his hand to the side like an orchestra conductor, and a falling ice chunk the size of a house changes direction and slams into the Omega Box, flattening him like a cockroach.

P.J. runs up, and I grab her and pull her to one side, just in time to avoid another falling ice slab. The Omega Box's heat beam has destabilized the entire fissure. The walls are shaking, and starting to crack and crumble.

"Let's scram while we still can," Kidah tells us. "We can go the way he came."

I retrieve the Star of Dann and follow the rest of them into the tunnel that the Omega Box lasered through the crevasse wall. A low rumble sounds from all around us.

"Hurry," Kidah implores, "this way!"

In the faint blue light cast by the Star of Dann, I see that the wizard has found a spot where a moulin from the surface crosses the tunnel. We climb into the moulin, and Kidah conjures a disc beneath us. A powerful gusting wind pushes us up through the drainage tunnel.

The icy walls around us shake as we fly upward through the moulin in a race against time. The rumble gets louder and the shaking more violent till it feels like we're in the middle of an earthquake.

I see daylight ahead, but the moulin is collapsing in on itself. Just as the walls of the tunnel come down, we burst outside into daylight. The disc carries us a half mile across the ice sheet before setting us down gently in a deep drift.

65

Eko, P.J., Gisco, Kidah, and I stand together on the ice sheet, looking at the gaping mouth of the fissure as it starts to close. The great plates of ice shift far beneath the surface, and in seconds the crevasse narrows and slams shut. "Well, that's that," Kidah says. "It's over."

I think of my father, lying encased in the ice for all eternity, and of the Dark Lord and the Omega Box, down there with him. "How is it over?" I ask. "First Dargon came back in time to destroy the oceans. Then the Dark Lord struck at the Amazon and the Arctic. Won't the Dark Army just send someone else back to the Turning Point, to strike at another vulnerable region?"

"You bet," Kidah agrees. "That's exactly what they'll do. But I'm going to put a stop to it once and for all."

I look back at him. "How can you do that?"

"There's only one way," he answers softly. "I have to lock time. Once I do, no one can travel back and forth. The past will feed into the future in a one-way stream, as it was meant to do. But there will be a cost."

"What cost?" I ask him warily. If I've learned anything from my adventures, it's that the costs when time-travel is involved are high and usually very personal.

"For me, it will cost my life," Kidah explains matter-of-factly. "The locking of time will drain my essence. And for you, it will mean a choice. Are you of the future or of the past?" His question hangs in the air, and I'm very conscious that P.J. is standing on one side of me, and Eko on the other.

I turn to P.J., and as I look at her I can't help remembering when my father squeezed my hand for the last time and gasped, "Destiny and duty, Jair." I have the strange feeling that my life has been building toward this decision since the moment I was born, not in Hadley-by-Hudson, as I was led to believe, but in a troubled future world a thousand years from now. My mother is still in that world, and my father, who just died before my eyes, was battling to save it. And even though I only visited that world briefly, I can feel it pulling at me, and I know that I have a crucial role to play there.

Before I can speak, P.J. reads my face. "I heard what your father said to you," she whispers, her voice shaking. "I understand now that your life is not completely your own." She stops and swallows. "Anyway, Jack, the more I've watched you with these wizards and ninjas, the more I know you're one of them. You belong with them in the future, even if part of you wants to stay here with me."

Then she looks at Kidah and tells him, with surprising strength, "You're wrong. Time can't be locked. Maybe people won't be able to travel back and forth, but nothing can stop us from remembering."

"Very true, my dear," the wizard agrees with a smile. "Everyone here will remember exactly what happened."

He turns to me. "Jack, a time traveler who makes a round-trip journey can later recall all of his experiences. If you choose the future, you will remember your entire life as Jack Danielson. We have saved the oceans, the Amazon, and now the Arctic, and the future will now heal itself. But the people who live in that future will not have made the round-trip. They will carry no memory of losing to the Dark Army or living in a wrecked world."

I look back at him and nod. "So I'll be all alone with those memories?"

No, I'll be right there with you, old bean, Gisco promises. *Sadly, I foresee a vegetarian future. When you want to reminisce about bacon cheeseburgers, I'll be ready.*

"I'm sure there will be many wonderful new things to focus on," Eko promises softly. "Shall we go, Jack?"

"In a minute," I tell her. I turn to P.J. and the rest of them step a little bit away. "This is what you want, right?" I ask her.

"No," she says. "But it's what has to be. We both know that." She tries to smile bravely, but doesn't quite pull it off. Instead, she steps forward and takes my hand, and looks into my eyes one last time. "I know it's corny but I'll think of you every day, Jack. You're a part of me, and you always will be."

"And I'll be thinking about you a thousand years from now," I promise, squeezing her hand. "Especially that first kiss you gave me, under the bleachers."

"Here it is again," she says, and kisses me long and tenderly on the lips. Finally, she steps back. "Goodbye, Jack," she whispers and turns away.

I walk back to the rest of the group and ask Kidah, in a voice husky with emotion, "How will she get home?"

"I'll take her myself," he promises. "Are you ready?"

"As much as I'll ever be."

"Good. Because they're ready for you a thousand years from now," he says. "Farewell, Prince of Dann. Travel safe." He embraces me, and maybe it's the cold wind, but when we separate I see that the wizard's eyes are tearing.

"How exactly are we supposed to get back?" I ask him.

He grins and opens his mouth to reply. I hear another "Farewell," or perhaps he says: "You can never tell," or maybe: "Listen for the bell." It does sound like a bell is tinkling, and Kidah's face starts to spin around. Or maybe I'm the one who's spinning.

Eko has taken my hand, and we're whirling together. Gisco is there, too.

For the third and last time in my life, I make the agonizing passage, and come to the dark threshold that looms like the gateway to death.

A black tongue licks me in. I'm in the large intestine of an event horizon, being digested.

And then I'm out the other side, blinking in warm sunlight and listening to a deafening buzzing sound. The good news is I didn't land in a sandstorm, or on an iceberg. The buzzing doesn't come from a swarm of locusts or sky-darkening glagour.

It's applause. I'm standing on a raised dais. There's a ceremony going on, and I'm at the center of it. A thousand people are watching and clapping.

Eko is standing next to me. And I spot Gisco on the fringes of the crowd. *Kneel and bend your head, old bean,* he tells me telepathically. *This is your big moment.*

I also spot my mother, beaming proudly. It's clear from her face that she has no memory of the horrors we encountered when we rescued my dad from the Fortress of Aighar, or how he had to leave her to go back in time.

I don't completely comprehend what's going on, but I follow Gisco's instructions and kneel and lower my head.

A dignified old man with a gray beard steps forward holding a glittering crown. "All hail the King of Dann," he says, and I feel him slip the crown onto my head.

"Thanks," I manage to mutter.

"You're welcome, Sire," he responds. "Now rise to your people."

I stand up, and the applause builds.

I wave back at the crowd, and put my right arm around Eko's waist. "Isn't it beautiful?" she whispers.

"Yes," I agree, looking out at the sun-splashed scene. But the whole thing also feels very strange. In fact, I'm a little dizzy, and I can barely take it all in.

There's the air, for one thing. I've never smelled air this pure before. It has a faintly sweet taste, as if tinged with lavender and honey.

Songbirds in nearby trees provide the musical accompaniment to the coronation ceremony. High overhead, an eagle traces majestic circles in an azure sky of crystalline clarity.

Beyond the cheering crowd, a sandy beach slopes to a wave-splashed ocean, which glitters a pristine shade of blue-green. Dolphins frolic in the surf, leaping from the water and dancing on their tails.

It's a beautiful world, an Eden-like world, but not a world I recognize.

I look out at the people clapping. They all have healthy faces, and confident, optimistic eyes. Even the oldest men and women present, with white hair and gripping canes, seem to have no sense of the horrors of the past, the vagaries of fate, or the way good can change to bad in an instant.

I whisper to myself, "It's not their fault. They just don't remember."

"Did you say something?" Eko asks, taking my hand and raising it high with her own.

"This feels very strange," I tell her.

"It's the way things are supposed to be," she replies. "You'll get used to it, and—" But the rest of her words are drowned out by the roar of the crowd.

Epilogue

P.J.

Manhattan. Ten at night. An old gentleman in a long black coat and a teenage girl in a parka step out of a cab. It's a cold October night, but compared to the Greenland Ice Sheet, it's practically mild.

The two of them stand near the Barnard campus, watching the cars speed by on Broadway. "I don't know what I'm going to tell my roommates," P.J. finally says.

"Abducted by aliens?" Kidah suggests.

"Yeah, that might work." She laughs nervously. "My parents are probably going to have me committed to an insane asylum."

"They'll be very happy to get you back," Kidah assures her. "One suggestion: if I were you I'd make a point of telling them that you're positive you won't be disappearing again. They'll believe you."

"Why do you think so?"

The old man smiles. "I am a wizard." He glances at his gold pocket watch. "I'd better be going. It was a great pleasure escorting you home, and getting to know you. You're really a swell gal."

"Too bad you couldn't be my uncle," P.J. says. "You'd make a great eccentric uncle." She looks back at him, and tries to be strong, and resist the urge to grab him, to hold on to him. Once he's gone, it will truly all be over. "Well, I guess this is goodbye," she finally whispers. "You've got to lock time, and I have to convince people I'm not totally insane. I don't know which will be harder."

Kidah grins and pulls her in for a last embrace and an avuncular kiss on the forehead. As they separate, P.J. gasps. His eyes have disappeared, and it's like she's looking into twin black holes. "I see," he growls in an unearthly voice, from far away.

Then he's Kidah again, and his eyes glint as he smiles at her. "We have many powers in the future, and the rarest of them all is prophecy. Every once in a while I have that gift. For you, my dear, I see a long and happy life." He raises his palm to her temple, as if administering a benediction. "A wonderful career as a graphic artist. A happy marriage to a gentle and caring man. Three lovely children. A boy and two girls."

P.J. looks back at him, awed and unsure. "Do you really see those things or are you just trying to make me feel better? You must know I'll never be able to forget Jack, or any of this, as long as I live."

"That's very true," Kidah acknowledges. "But time heals all wounds, my dear. And I saw one more thing you might care to know. Your firstborn will be a beautiful baby boy, and you'll name him Jack. When you nurse him, and tuck him in at night, you'll think of that other Jack and be sad. But you'll also be happy, because when we remember those we love, we keep them close to our hearts." He glances at his watch. "Now I'd really better go."

P.J. nods. She hesitates, and asks in a low voice, "Is locking time going to be very painful for you?"

"How should I know?" Kidah shrugs. "I never did it before." He flashes her a smile. "Don't worry about me. All my friends are gone, and I'm not getting any younger."

"Do you know Manhattan?" she asks. "Can I give you directions . . . ?"

"No need," Kidah tells her. "I'll find my way. Goodbye, my dear."

A downtown bus rolls to a stop, and he gets on, and waves to her once through the window.

P.J. watches the bus pull away and pick up speed down Broadway.

Then she turns and walks slowly in through the iron gate of the campus and is soon swallowed up in a small throng of other college girls.

Kidah

The Empire State Building's observation deck is almost closed when the old man enters the building through the revolving door and hurries through the lobby.

"Only twenty more minutes," the guard at the desk says, glancing up from his newspaper. He's got the sports section open to the racing page. "It's getting cold up there. You might want to come back tomorrow."

"Thanks," Kidah tells him. "Twenty minutes should do fine. Hey, not that I know anything, but if I were you I'd go with Lucky Lady in the third race, to win."

The guard gives him a curious look.

Kidah steps by him into the elevator and rides the rickety car up to the top. He gets off and pauses to watch a family hurry in, the mother shushing a crying infant, the older children's cheeks red from the cold.

Then the wizard walks to the most deserted corner of the deck. The evening has been overcast, but suddenly the clouds part and a full moon and brilliant stars shine down.

Kidah stands there with the great city spread out beneath him, and the Milky Way gleaming above. He drinks it in—two magnificent constellations, one man-made and temporary, the other eternal and infinite.

"Sheesh," he says to himself. "Sure is a beautiful night."

Then he closes his eyes, opens his arms wide, and begins to sing. It's a strange, haunting song. Sometimes its cadence recalls the pounding waves of the ocean, sometimes the wind blasting through the Amazon rain forest, and sometimes an iceberg calving off from a great Greenland glacier.

The night wind picks up and whips around him, faster and faster. Lightning stabs down out of a clear sky and strikes again and again, all around the observation deck.

Kidah's song grows urgent. His fingers begin moving, as if he's sewing stitches into the mantle of darkness.

And then his body begins to change. He stretches taller, and wider, and he also grows thinner. Soon he's twenty feet tall, then thirty, then fifty. He becomes paper-thin, and even as he transforms, his fingers continue moving through the darkness, as if making tight, careful stitches.

His essence spreads out over the night sky like smoke. He sings one final verse of his song, and ends with a smile. There's a tremendous thunderclap that goes on and on. It rattles the Manhattan skyscrapers, and the Empire State Building shivers down to its foundation.

Some in the city below are afraid that it's a terrorist bomb.

Others whisper a prayer, believing Judgment Day is at hand.

But finally the thunderclap ends, and all is calm. A gentle rain begins to patter down. It continues falling through the night and stops just before first dawn, so that early risers are greeted with a bright and cheerful sunrise.

Jair

He wakes in darkness and for a few moments has no idea where he is. Then he hears Eko's shallow breathing next to him, and remembers. A storm rages outside, and when lightning flashes he sees her beautiful profile turned toward him, her hand on the edge of his pillow as if she is reaching out to him in sleep.

Jack eases himself silently out of the bed. Eko was always a light sleeper, but now that she's pregnant, she sleeps more soundly. He manages not to wake her as he creeps across the room.

Then he is in the hall, heading for the nearest doorway. There are no guards or watchmen on duty, because there are no enemies. He slips outside, into the storm. Cold rain falls on his shoulders and runs through his hair.

He walks to the beach, strips off his clothes, and dives into the wind-churned waves. The ocean is warmer than the rain, and he swims straight out to sea in swift strokes. Half a mile out, he spots several large shapes darting toward him, and when he sees the shadowy triangles of their dorsal fins he fears they might be sharks.

But then they greet him as a friend, and he knows from their playful telepathic tone they're dolphins.

He now has the ability to communicate with wild creatures—it came to him when his father died.

He returns the dolphins' good wishes, and hitches a ride on one of their backs.

They speed along parallel to the shoreline, and in the flashes of lightning he sees the outlines of the palace and the sleeping city laid out gracefully on the hills. A school of flying fish skip over them, and in the distance he spots the enormous silhouette of a blue whale—the largest species of living thing the earth has ever seen. They had almost gone extinct at the Turning Point, but now blue whales are often seen from the palace, lumbering along like ocean liners.

He hops off the dolphin's back, and tells his fin-tailed friends that he wants to be alone. They laugh and swim off, leaving him.

The rain slackens and he floats on his back.

Yes, the memories still come to him.

Night is the worst time. They start in his dreams, and linger when he wakes. Memories of a neat colonial house in a small town on the east bank of the Hudson River. A woman weeding a vegetable garden. A gentle father throwing a football in Hadley Park. And a girl with auburn hair teasing him even as she smiles at him.

Jack looks up into the stormy night sky. Lightning flashes, and for an instant he sees a face in the dark clouds—the features of a benevolent old wizard smiling down at him as if to say, "Sheesh—nobody gets everything."

He is suddenly overcome with anger and regret, and dives deep beneath the surface, so far down that if he swam another few strokes he could never make it back up in time. But the anger passes and he changes direction at the last moment. When he kicks his way back to the surface he swims strongly for home.

As he nears the palace beach, he sees a lone shadow standing on the rocks looking out to sea. He doesn't need to see her face to know that it's Eko.

He smiles and waves at her, and climbs out of the water into her arms.